WORLD

Lines

EPICPRESS

World Lines

An Epic Press book

Copyright © 2008 O Franklin

ISBN 978-1-906557-00-3

A catalogue record of this book is available from the British Library.

Also By O Franklin

Dimension Slip
Domination: Somebody Else's War

World Lines

The alternative sequel to Dimension Slip

This story is set in the present; but it isn't real, so it isn't present...

Prologue

It was late in the evening and the old man could hear the rain starting to fall outside his window. He felt very tired this particular night and also quite cold. With a severe ache in his neck he turned slowly to gaze at the radiant heater by the fire place; it was glowing red. He sighed and reclined more deeply into his leather armchair. It too, showed all the hallmarks of great age.

The room about him was well furnished but dusty; smart but faded. It was the largest room in an apartment which also contained a small bedroom and a minute bathroom, sufficient for an old man's personal needs. He had lived here for a number of years, officially under the protection of the authorities. In recent days however, the stairs up to the fifth floor had become a challenge impossible to him - even the elevator required too much effort.

A stained patina on the wooden panelled door was matched by the grain of the cabinet on the opposite wall. Two glass panes on this cabinet were crossed with decorative rosewood fretwork. The wall paper in the room however, seemed to have come halfway from yellow to white but got lost somewhere in between. Thankfully, the elderly resident did not have much of an eye for aesthetic niceties. Also, what should have been real hardwood finishes, if the room had been up to scratch, had begun to de-laminate in some places - they were meagre veneers.

The old man was well past eighty and very tired and drawn in appearance. His face, though wizened with age, still remained determined. The pronounced forehead resembled a large domed case, and it contained, in many people's opinion, the brain of the century. But his heart was committed to peace, and that was the whole dilemma. It was 1943; World War II was raging at its height, and his expertise had necessarily grown to be highly sought after by all sides. The Americans, the Soviets and the Axis powers all desired to get inside this stubborn old mind.

He tapped the calloused knuckles of his left hand on the table beside him. Beneath his fingers there lay a small, black notebook. Unseen by a multitude of hungry eyes, many of its hundred-odd pages were labelled 'Government' in scrawled hand writing.

Deep in thought and grieved for the prospect of the world around him, the old man struggled to come to terms with the fact of his expected departure. He pondered what to do with the notebook on the table. His eye alighted on the decorative utility cabinet against the wall; it contained a locking compartment within the small sliding drawer. *Would it be safe in there?*

Among all his woes this night there was, however, one most cruel and savage. The mind that had held opposing military forces in doubt for over a decade, the mind that had proposed revolutionary ideas that, in all probability, could have altered history had failed at this last hurdle. This was now its hardest challenge of all.

Shivering slightly in the cold that was not actually there, the man grimaced as he wrestled with himself. Of all the things to test him this evening, this had to be the worst one. Incredible as it may seem, the old man could not remember... truly, he did not know who he really was... He did not even recall his own name...

Chapter 1

An Interesting Lecture

Jay lay on top of his bed with his trainers resting on the headboard. It was Saturday afternoon and he had something good planned for later this day, something that had his head filled with anticipation. The local amateur astronomy group had arranged for an eminent scientist to come and give a talk at the Town Hall, about a weird cosmological theory that Jay found just fascinating. Furthermore, he had a project to be getting on with during the holidays and he reckoned that this might give him some useful ideas.

His A-Level Physics class had been set a piece of coursework to do over the summer. They could each choose whatever subject matter they liked. The only proviso was that it had to be something innovative. A number of the students had had to look this word up in a dictionary when they'd got home on the Friday afternoon, including Jay's best friend Mike. In actual fact *he* wasn't taking Physics, but was curious to hear all about it.

The memory of this incident made Jay chuckle to himself as he lay there with the sun streaming in through the open window. He hadn't laughed at the time though, so as not to hurt Mike's feelings. School had broken up the day before and now he had the summer holidays to look forward to, which was fantastic.

As always, at the start of the vacation, his own birthday approached too. It was only two weeks away; excitingly, he would be seventeen this time around, on Sunday August 1st.

Nearly three years had passed since his first outing into uncommon realms of the space-time continuum and he was content, to a large extent, just to forget about it. As for his second adventure in outer space; that hadn't actually happened yet and so he knew nothing of it. However, every now and then people would still come up to him in the street saying, 'Hey! Aren't you that kid who got struck by lightning?' It was annoying at first but he'd grown used to it.

With nothing much to do for a couple of hours, Jay folded his arms behind his head and gazed thoughtfully out of the window. The sky was bright blue and the breeze felt warm as it wafted into his room.

A digital beep came from the watch on his left wrist as it chimed on the hour. Making a discreet smile, he remembered that he did not treat time in the same way as most of his friends. Past experiences convinced him that it was not linear, not absolute and not even certain. In reality, he had great doubts about it; and this black wristwatch was the very same that he'd taken into the rift with him in his fourth year.

He would probably still be wearing the same scruffy old trainers too, but he had grown quite a bit in the intervening three years and so they no longer fitted his feet. He was still rather weedier looking than Mike who was turning into something of an athlete, and he had given up all hope now of ever catching him up in stature. His other best friend, Dave, had begun to get markedly plump, and Jay was glad that he was not growing in that direction at least.

A drifting fluffy cloud sent a brief shadow into the street below and it came to pass across Jay's face. The battle scar on his right cheek had not faded at all. Still visible, still testifying to something that children in South Fields Comprehensive would ask him about, but Jay would never tell them; he and Mike had sworn to keep it secret - for the good of everyone.

Jay was wearing a red chequered shirt that he could never be bothered to iron. His mother, Carol, had long since delegated this and other household duties to Jay and his younger sister, Alice.

The illegal, military-spec computer had not been confiscated by the police or MI5 as yet, and thus remained in pride of place on top of his work desk opposite his bed. The black casing gleamed at him as if the machine were brand new. He had not had trouble falling through the monitor recently... thankfully.

Again he thought of this and chuckled to himself. In truth, he did forget about that adventure the majority of the time. *But sometimes it's fun to cast my mind back there occasionally,* he told himself.

Tea in the dining room was a subdued affair. Jay sat at the table with his mother and father. Alice had been spending the day in Oxford with the Hampton's from next door and would not be home until later. Robert Romero had resigned from his position at *Smartsoft Inc.* the year before, feeling uncomfortable about their secretive and underhanded deals with various Government Departments. He now worked freelance as a programmer and software engineer. Self employment turned out to be more rewarding, but it did cause him considerable stress, the chief concern being the irregularity of the income. In a brisk week he could bring home a thousand pounds, but in a slow one he'd earn nothing.

The white cloth lay over a beech topped table and there were places enough for six people. Mr Romero was keen on pasta and they usually ate it twice a week; wine was normally served with the evening meal too. It was customary and from his fathers side of the family.

Anxious to meet up with his friends after tea, Jay sat and marked out parallel lines in the residue of the gravy on his plate, holding his knife like a paintbrush. Mrs Romero had served up roast chicken and he'd finished his helping before his mum and dad were halfway through theirs.

Jay started to get impatient and his eye fell upon his father's plate. He still had quite a decent pile of potatoes to get through and it was nearly quarter to seven. Jay had arranged to meet Mike and Dave at seven and the talk was set for half past. He did not want to be late for it. Although Jay made no comment his father noticed where his son's eyes strayed. Taking a swig of wine he looked up from his meal.

'Mother and me eating too slow for you, Jayjay?' he asked kindly, wiping his lips with a napkin. Jay grunted in a non-committal sort of way.

'We could keep some dessert for you, if you want to leave now,' his mother suggested.

'I didn't make any complaint,' Jay answered, defensively.

'I know you didn't, son, but I saw where your eyes were going. If you're going to be late— '

'What *is* for dessert?' Jay interrupted, turning to his mother quickly.

'Ice cream, dear,' she replied.

'Think I'll skip it,' Jay decided, looking at his watch. 'Can I leave the table?'

'Yes,' said Mr Romero. Then he added, 'Enjoy your talk; who have the astronomy club got coming tonight, anyone we know?'

Relieved, Jay sprung up from his chair. 'Dr Percival Seymour from the Royal Observatory, Greenwich. He's quite famous actually,' Jay informed them.

'Never heard of him, son,' his father replied with a smile.

But Jay was almost out of the doorway. 'See you later, bye Mum, bye Dad,' he called out over his shoulder.

In the hall he pulled on a beige coloured jacket and then went upstairs to grab his wallet. The friends expected to socialise for a while after the meeting and Jay would probably need some money. It was difficult to socialise without any.

He regularly earned pocket money by stripping down old computers for his father, who would service them as part of his business. Jay could remove and install new disc drives and replace burnt out mother boards and other circuitry without knowing what everything did. A few minutes later he set off down Westbury Drive.

In his sixth year at secondary school, Jay was taking Maths, Physics and Chemistry at A-Level. Most people referred to these as the 'hard three,' the subjects that required the most brain power, but Jay himself had no shortage of this and his year had been thoroughly enjoyable.

Mike was doing an NVQ in Sports Science, fancying himself as some kind of whiz in this area; though career options were rather restrictive. Due to the light weight nature of *his* school time table, he had also been forced to undertake an A-Level in General Studies. This most boring of subjects, the pupils were convinced, was invented by the sixth form teachers purely to fill out the time tables of those who had rather too many free periods in their week. Like all the others in his year, except the geeks, Mike hated it. Furthermore, he found to his delight, that he could regularly skive these lessons and nobody seemed to notice his absence. He preferred to join in with a fifth year swimming class at the local pool and would concentrate on improving his fitness instead.

Dave was in the same year as his two friends and taking Physics, Geography and German at A-Level. He hoped to end up working abroad somewhere, but for the present he had the same Physics assignment to be getting on with as Jay. He himself had a moderate interest in the subject nowadays, but not nearly the fervour that his friend had.

Mike had very little time for it, especially as it now involved more maths. So he was only going along to the meeting tonight because his two best friends were going and Susie Parker, whom he'd been eyeing up for years, had refused yet another one of his invitations to a date.

Coming from different parts of the town, the three friends met each other at the top of Market Hill, the main street through the centre of Brackthorpe.

They were moving past the traffic lights by the junction of Westbury Road. This was close to where the three of them had stood for Mr Robert's funeral procession three years ago; but since the time line was now changed, he had not actually died. Jay loved having his old teacher back again and it was he, in fact, that had set them this innovative project to do over the holidays.

The clock on the tower of the town hall read twenty five past seven; they were only just going to make it to the astronomy club meeting on time. Crossing over the road opposite the pub car park at the top of the hill, they marched down the high street at a quickening pace.

'So how did you get to hear about this meeting, mate?' Dave asked Jay, puffing slightly as he hurried along beside him. Mike was tailing the other two, a few yards behind.

'They advertised it in the Bampton Guardian last week. I wouldn't normally have bothered with the astronomy group otherwise,' Jay responded.

'Why?' came Mike's voice from behind him.

Jay turned back and said rather wittily, 'Because, generally, they're a bunch of old fogies, mate.'

Mike smirked.

'But this Seymour chappie sounds interesting,' Dave put in.

'Yeah, but it's his cosmology that I'm really keen to hear about, and that's why I'm going,' Jay explained.

Mike had begun to type a text message into his mobile phone at this point, and so did not add anything further to their discussion. They

7

continued on down the hill towards the town hall. It stood at the bottom of the market square, ringed on all sides by the main road. The small car park outside the entrance was already filled and it looked as though the meeting was going to be well attended. The visiting speaker had an international reputation, particularly for his championing of unorthodox and anti-establishment ideas. For this reason also, it was rumoured, he was about to get the boot from Greenwich.

Three storeys high and rectangular in form; the old town hall was built in masonry and its proud sandstone walls were amongst the most ancient in the town centre, dating back to the 1700's. Three carved arches supported the northward wall which stood adjacent to the market square and also faced up the high street from where the friends had come. The tower sported a small bronzed dome at it's very top and the roof over the main hall was pitched. All along the edge of this there was a narrow walkway and parapet, which was off limits to the public and used only by the caretaker for maintenance work. Jay, of course, was all too familiar with it. He had seen more of this building than anyone else ever had.

Beneath the arch structure there lay a walkway, and through this the public could ascend the short flight of steps to the double, glass-panelled doors in the entrance. A large white poster had been taped up inside one of these doors advertising the night's meeting in gaudy lettering. One of the Councillors was acting as usher for the evening and waited by the entrance for any last minute stragglers. He beamed when he saw the three teenagers come striding into the car park. Most of his clientèle hitherto were more senior members of the local community.

Dave said a polite, 'Good evening,' as the three of them made their way past the gentlemen in his grey suit and into the entrance hall.

A wide staircase led the way up to a balcony and a further set of double doors opened into the debating chamber where the town council met in plenary session. Mike looked disdainfully at a display board at the foot of the stairs pointing them upwards, as if all of tonight's visitors were perhaps a bit thick.

Arriving at the doors to the inner chamber leading off the balcony, they heard the low rumble of chatter coming from the room ahead. Jay went in first and discovered that they were indeed the last to get there.

The chamber resembled an old chapel, with close rows of benches set around three sides of the room facing a raised platform in the centre. A narrow public gallery spanned the width of the chamber on the rear wall, above their heads, and Jay promptly turned towards the steps that accessed this upper level. All of the seats in the lower circle were full.

Rows of pointed Gothic windows added to the impression that the lads had just marched into a rustic church somewhere in a village in Cornwall. This perception was soon corrected however, by the presence of a lectern together with an overhead projector and screen on the platform. A laptop computer suggested that the speaker was also bang up to date with PowerPoint presentations.

The capacity of the lower chamber was about sixty persons and Jay reckoned that there were another thirty five or so in the gallery, as he and the other two squeezed themselves on to a bench at the back by the wall.

A veritable sea of grey heads was not quite comprehensive but they were the only teenagers in the room, for certain. Mr Roberts, their Physics teacher, had plumped for a front seat and he turned and waved up at them cheerfully when Dave blurted out his name from the gallery.

Within a minute or two of their arrival, a certain Mr Bainbridge, Deputy Chairman of South Northants Astronomy Club whom Jay recognised as the proprietor of the local newsagent, stood up and called the assembly to order.

While his mates looked on keenly, Mike examined his reflection in the LCD screen of his mobile phone. When convinced his hair was just right, he photographed himself with a bored expression on his face and then proceeded to send a picture message. His correspondent was a certain 'Fit Sue' whose number he had permanently stored in the phone's memory.

A round of applause jerked his attention away from the text reply on the little silver screen, reading, 'NOT THIS TIME HERO, C-YA.' Jay then leant over and said loudly in his ear, 'Listen carefully to this guy, mate. He's got some really cool ideas, you know.'

Mike gave his colleague a mild scowl and then turned his attention to the platform in the chamber below where a middle aged gentlemen had taken the floor to a warm welcome.

Dr Percival Seymour was South African by descent and well tanned in complexion. He had the classic, slightly mad-looking features that all brilliant scientists seem to have, and the signs of a pot belly present under his immaculate brown tweed suit.

Jay took one direct glance into his dark and frenetic eyes: they were blazing with a childish enthusiasm for the mysteries of the cosmos, and he realised immediately that he was dealing with a kindred spirit.

Feeling a mite upset for the disinterest of his best friend, Jay nonetheless settled himself back into the hard wooden bench, expectant, ready to hear an amazing hypothesis. Dave, too, was paying his full attention to the speaker as he stepped up to the lectern.

Various papers and files were arranged over the small table to one side. On top of this also, an overhead projector was set up aimed at the portable slide screen at the rear of the platform. Seymour pressed the return key on the laptop and a blue window appeared on the screen with the familiar *XP* logo. His hint of Afrikaans made him still more interesting, as he thus spoke -

'Mr Deputy Chairman, Ladies and Gentlemen; thank you all for your most kind welcome. For those of you who are familiar with my work this will be tedious but for those who aren't, I should briefly explain my background to you. It is also worthy of mention that I am undoubtedly non-establishment and therefore somewhat of an object of ridicule amongst my fellows at Greenwich. However, - '

'Didn't you say this guy studies *Astrology* as well as Astronomy - as if they were both equally respectable and scientific?' Dave whispered.

'Yep, but I don't go along with him in that,' Jay hissed. 'Anyway, keep qui— '

'No wonder the guy's ridiculed,' Mike butted in.

A stern faced man sitting right in front of them wearing a dinner jacket then turned and frowned at them, wondering why on earth three rude looking teenagers had bothered attending this respectable conference in the town hall.

'Sorry,' Jay apologised. Then, as the gentlemen turned away, he added, '*Shut up guys!*'

Meanwhile Dr Seymour was moving on to the relevant subject matter -

'Now, my friend Mr Bainbridge has invited me to speak on my own specialist area of research, namely, the magneto-hydrodynamics of the Sun. Specifically, I would like to detail how the tidal forces of the planets in our solar system can account for the solar cycle that we observe every eleven years. I must inform you all at this juncture that my system is at variance with the established model.'

Someone politely interrupted from the front row at this point.

'And a damn sight better I'd say! Thank you, Doctor.'

A slight commotion greeted this vocal intervention and Jay gawped when he realised that it was none other than his own teacher who had spoken. Dr Seymour nodded appreciatively towards Mr Roberts but Dave called out, '*You tell 'em, Sir!*' right in Jay's ear. Jay winced.

Several people now turned around to face the guilty party in the balcony and Dave smiled at the consternation he'd just caused. Mike suddenly began to find the meeting rather more interesting than he'd first anticipated. He pocketed his mobile phone in his jacket and watched attentively.

'My apologies, Mr Speaker,' Mr Roberts continued. He gestured towards the boys in the gallery. 'They are pupils of mine at the school. Pray continue, Sir.'

Jay was flushed with annoyance and mild embarrassment at his friend's attempts to liven up proceedings. He did not want to find himself evicted from the chamber as this talk promised to be highly engaging. The disturbance soon died down though, and before long the speaker continued with his presentation.

'I have further been invited to discuss another subject, this being one of my own choosing. I have therefore determined to cover a little known but profound idea that is perhaps on the brink of credibility in the minds of those in the profession. However, even if this hypothesis turns out to be more myth than truth, it does at the very least demonstrate what fascinating potential discoveries we have yet to make, and for that I make no apologies to my sceptical fellows if any be here present tonight.'

Jay's eye's lit up. What could possibly warrant this kind of introductory fanfare? It had to be something really incredible, surely? Dave chewed his thumbnail and Mike looked bemused. Mr Roberts straightened his hairpiece and then was the expectant silence ended.

'Tonight, I'm going to propose to you the theory of *World Lines!*' the Doctor announced, grippingly.

'Eh?' burped Mike

'You what, mate?' Dave added.

'Whoa, boy!' Jay exclaimed under his breath. 'I'm glad I came here tonight.'

'What are Wor—— ?' Mike started, but the irate gentlemen in front of them interrupted him with a loud and angry sounding, 'SSHH!'

The speaker went on, 'Imagine drawing a graph of me, here, in space. What would you see?'

Nobody responded to this question, assuming it to be rhetorical. Though two people in the room at least knew the answer: one at the front of the room and the other in the balcony.

'As I am not moving, it would just be a dot. There would be no displacement along either axis; agreed?'

This second question was neither rhetorical nor difficult and a slow murmur of assent rose up from the ranks of his listeners. Jay however had not answered. He was clutching at the edge of the bench seat, hoping that this talk was going to go where he wanted it to.

'Of course the Earth is moving around the Sun and also rotating about its own axis every twenty four hours, but I am leaving that out of the equation at this stage. Therefore, consider my graph with respect to this building, Brackthorpe Town Hall. Do you all agree that the plot of my position would simply be a single point?'

'Yes,' came the general response.

'Consider now,' Dr Seymour went on, ' how my graph would look if I were to stroll around and around in a nice, even circle. Thus - ' He demonstrated walking in a circle on the platform, moving round the table and the lectern until he returned to his starting point.

'How would my graph appear now?' he asked.

'A circle!' someone called out from the lower part of the chamber. Jay looked down and saw what had to be the only other person under twenty one in the hall, a ginger-haired chap looking decidedly pleased with himself, sitting beneath one of the Gothic style windows.

'Precisely,' the Doctor replied. 'But we must now consider that we are not just living in three dimensional space. There is the fourth dimension of our world to consider - *Time!*'

'Yes, yes, yes!' Jay whispered to himself. '*Trek* magazine did an article about this last year, but they described it by another term. This is it; this is the same theory.'

He was gleeful and not only that; his interest began to rub off. Now Mike was actually becoming intrigued with it all. His own tortuous experience of space-time anomalies may have left him scarred also, but the old fire began to catch in him again, and his face too, cracked into one of excitement.

'While I stand stationary with respect to space; yet am I still moving forwards through *time*. Time is passing as I stand here. Therefore, even though I am not moving anywhere *spatially*, I am moving *temporally*. The stationary dot on my graph, showing my track, becomes not a dot, but a straight line. Remember, we are disregarding the pre-existing motions of the Earth and Solar System for the moment, yes?

'While I am not moving with respect to space, I am progressing with respect to time. My track is presently a straight line therefore.'

This increasing detail had already begun to stretch the minds of a number of the astronomy club but the good Doctor had hardly got started.

'Think carefully, friends. What would my graph then look like, if I walked around once more in a circle?'

He clicked a button on the laptop and a new slide appeared on the screen that was partially obscured. He kept the diagram covered up to allow his audience time to work out the answer for themselves. Sooner than anyone else Jay thrust his hand into the air, bursting with exuberance.

'Our young friend here seems to know the answer, yes?' the Doctor prompted.

13

'It'll be a spiral shape, sir!' Jay called out boldly.

'Well done!' said Dr Seymour, revealing the remainder of the diagram and straight away the screen behind his back lit up with the requisite drawing. Everyone in the room was now staring at a four dimensional plot, reduced to a 2D representation on a graph. A swirling green line against different coloured grid axes clearly showed that Jay had answered correctly. A number of the astronomy club applauded him politely, others just took Seymour's word for it as they couldn't understand the diagram.

'Congrats, mate,' Dave encouraged him. 'We always reckoned you were the smartest of us three.'

'We're not in school though, mate. Leave out the 'Sir' bit can't you?' Mike complained, sitting on Dave's far side.

Meanwhile, the series of illustrated plots and graphs that kept appearing on the projector screen were growing ever more interesting and complex. Thirty minutes later the speaker had reached the heart of the theory in question.

'So twins, particularly identical twins, will share the same World Line for nine months of their life, while together in the mother's womb. Then, of course, these tracks will stay closely aligned for the majority of their childhood years. In adulthood, it is likely that their World Lines will diverge completely. However, because they were so closely associated for so many years, it is plausible that a residual link survives between them.

'Not only this; the potential of World Lines to explain phenomena such as telepathy and empathic feeling is very great. I propose that every living person here present has a trail through space-time streaming out behind them. This track or... plot, or... World Line, is a memory within the very fabric of the universe itself of where they have been and *when* they were there.

'With all of these strings of World Lines stretching out behind us, as the world rotates about its orbit, won't some of them get tangled up like wool? Grasp a handful of string and twist it in your hands. Will it not get tangled up?

'The question therefore before us is: What will happen when your own World Line crosses somebody else's? Some kind of short circuit in space and time will occur, but what exactly? When two opposing magnetic field lines interact, they cancel each other out in an annihilation event. Will the same not occur with World Lines?

'Ladies and Gentlemen; what are your thoughts? What do you suppose? The reason for my asking: I do not know the answer!' And thereupon he rested his case - to an astonished silence.

Unashamedly, and not caring who frowned at them this time, Jay whistled loudly in admiration as applause rattled through the chamber.

'I understood all that!' Mike gasped. 'Can you credit it?'

'Impressed, eh, Mikey boy?' Dave muttered.

Jay didn't speak however. He felt too radiant with excitement and needed a moment or two to re-gather himself.

The following presentation on magneto-hydrodynamics had yet again been way over the heads of most of the amateur astronomers and, from Jay's point of view, rather bog-standard and boring. He was, however, quite enthralled with the plain and straight forward proposition of World Lines in the first talk of the evening. These speculative entities were by far the more intriguing and tantalising, particularly so as they could be genuine. Jay felt that the cold shouldering from the academic establishment gave these Lines a definite relief. He appreciated them as a rebellious counter culture within science and it appealed to his teen aged temperament. There is something enjoyable about counter culture.

As the audience spilled out of the meeting two hours later, Dave and Mike found themselves waiting together in the car park outside the arched entrance way. Jay had inevitably joined the crew of avid members thronging the Doctor at the end of the talk, hoping to pick his brain about sundry other queries.

Nearly all of the cars had driven away into the night-lit high street before, forty five minutes later still, Jay emerged from the building smiling broadly. He skipped down the steps underneath the arches and went over to his friends waiting by a series of concrete bollards. These had been erected to stop market traffic from encroaching on to the town hall car parking area, and one or two of them showed signs of contact with passing lorries.

Mike's feelings had turned rather ill again. 'It's gone quarter past ten Jay, mate,' he complained. 'That's almost used up the whole evening!'

'No it hasn't,' Dave responded. 'The night's young; tomorrow's Sunday after all.'

'Sorry guys,' Jay said, 'but I just had to ask Seymour a couple of things and, being at the back of the hall, I was virtually the last one in the queue.'

A group of passing girls dressed for a night out - probably in Bampton - whistled at Mike standing there in his black jacket and looking like a proposition. They were walking along the pavement and heading towards the bus stop nearby.

Magneto-hydrodynamics seemed to be working on Mike as his friend watched amusedly. Jay could tell by the strange effect in his eyes. At least two of the female party were blonde, like Mike himself, and another one of their number beckoned him teasingly. They were only across the other side of the main road by now. Dave was getting impatient.

'So, what're we going to do tonight folks?' he asked, eyes flitting between Mike, Jay and the ladies.'

'I've got some cash,' Jay replied. 'We could catch a late show in the Warner Village Cine— *Hey!*'

At that moment, Mike began drifting out of the car park and wandering over towards the girls on the opposite side of the road. Excited chatter broke out amongst them and they appeared to be half mocking, half disbelieving at their luck.

Jay then recognised a few of them from the fifth year at school, but without blazers and uniforms they looked much older. He called out to his friend, in considerable unease.

'C'mon, mate; they're just taking you for a ride.'

'Go home, mummy's boy! This man's ours,' shouted a girl with a short red dress and high black boots. It was fortunate for her that she hadn't said '*Gyppo,*' as that might have switched Mike into his defensive mode. He always stuck up for Jay against that kind of abuse.

Instead, now that they were growing up, Mike turned and shrugged rather hopelessly at his two colleagues in the car park and then walked right up to the huddle of girls. Grabbing him by both arms, they frog marched him into the bus shelter. He was gone for the night.

Just as the late bus pulled in to the stop, five minutes afterwards while Jay and Dave were still talking, Dr Seymour and Mr Bainbridge came through the doors of the town hall into the orange-lit car park. All but two of the cars had gone by this time.

As his friend boarded the bus, surrounded on all sides by his new female companions, Dave yelled out across the street, 'You're thinking with the wrong head, Murkin!'

'*Dave…?*' Jay cringed. 'Keep your voice down!' He nodded towards the respectable departing figures of Mr Bainbridge and Dr Seymour.

'So?' Dave demanded. 'You know as well as I do; he's not thinking his brain, but with his di— '

'Shut up!' Jay hissed frantically. 'We're still in earshot.'

The bus pulled out of the stop with Mike and the party of girls aboard and Dave stared mulishly over at the two gentlemen talking near the entrance to the Town Hall. He grunted and then said rather too loudly, 'What's wrong with saying 'dick' in public; it's not even a swear word?'

'I'm off to the cinema,' Jay yelped, and with that he darted out of the embarrassing situation just as Dr Seymour turned to face their way.

Chapter 2

The Morning After

Dave's house was in a close off Ellesmere Road at the top end of town. His parents had bought a bungalow many years earlier when they'd first moved into the area and they still lived in the same place. Due to the increasing value of the property market, his father often talked about selling up, as their home was now worth five times what they had originally paid for it. But for the present he had not acted on this intention and Dave felt glad because he hated the very thought of moving house. He was not that keen on change.

His own bedroom overlooked the small front lawn and he and Jay had just finished bacon sandwiches for elevenses and were surfing the Net together on Dave's computer. It was the next morning and the two of them were trying to come up with information for their Physics assignment. Jay had a continuing reluctance to use his SM7 too often, in case it sent a coded signal back to the ISP and the Secret Services came bearing down upon them in quiet Westbury Drive. While his friends thought this ridiculous and paranoid, Jay was not so convinced. He had, for a long time, entertained dark feelings about the powers that be.

They had decided to attempt the project together, but had not yet come to any agreement about what subjects they ought to look into. Normally Jay would have preferred to work at it alone, but he figured that Dave could use a hand and so he'd suggested a joint effort for this one, to help him out.

Neither had seen or heard a hint of Mike and were not particularly worried about it; he was big enough to take care of himself. But his absence began to play on their minds somewhat as they pored over screen's full of potential research material on the Internet. Dave had drawn up another chair at his desk as Jay sat at the keyboard. He was marginally the quicker at typing.

Dave had a good deal of books of all kinds, and a combined TV and DVD on top of a chest of drawers beside his wardrobe. Studious at his work, his only fault was his dislike of sport and a sedentary lifestyle, which began to show up around his waistline. The three friends however, continued to share many things in common, albeit not to the same extent that they had in their earlier years at secondary school. It was true to say that the most significant common factor between them was the friendship itself, which had not failed.

'UCAS forms next year,' Jay muttered, scanning down a list of News Groups on the computer monitor.

'Yep,' Dave answered beside him. He pushed his plate further out of the way and asked, 'Still want to go for Cambridge then, or have you changed your mind since we last talked?'

'You know,' Jay replied with a wistful glaze in his face, 'I don't seem to have the same motivation that I used to have.'

'What d'you mean?' Dave queried. 'You're not thinking of...'

'What, mate?' Jay turned to him in interest.

'Dropping out!' Dave whispered, as if he were worried his mother might hear him from the kitchen where she was busily doing the week's laundry.

'Course not,' he said disdainfully. Then he added, more honestly, 'I can't say it's never crossed my mind though.'

'Nor mine,' his friend confessed. 'D'you think all this work is worth it? Does it all mean something?'

'Definitely,' Jay stated. 'But I tell you it isn't about pulling top grades in Physics or getting into Oxbridge—'

'Where's that?'

Jay smirked. 'That means Oxford and Cambridge, mate; biggest red herring if ever there was one, if you ask me.'

Dave knew Jay well enough to spot when his friend went all philosophical and it really intrigued him. However, he did not get much of a chance to ask him about it because his mother then called out from the kitchen and simultaneously the doorbell rang.

'David, your friend Michael is walking up the drive. That'll be him now!'

Jay guessed that he would be distracted for a few minutes. So he disconnected the dial up and went off-line to save the cost of the phone call. They could not use broadband as the coverage in Brackthorpe was not yet complete. Dave hurried out of the room to meet their friend.

Mrs Baker's voice sounded through the hall offering Mike a cup of tea and then, with a shuffle of trainers on carpet, the pair of them arrived in the bedroom. Jay swung round in his seat, looking up expectantly as Mike appeared through the door, worse for his night on the town. His clothing was dishevelled and he behaved quite sheepishly.

Dave gave Jay a wide-eyed stare as their friend moved over to a white chest of drawers and slumped against it, round shouldered. Mike looked miserable.

Wincing for a second as Mike's right arm knocked the TV DVD a bit too close to the edge for comfort, Dave then asked, '…erm …so, what happened then, mate?'

Jay watched sympathetically but said nothing to begin with, not wanting to aggravate Mike in his obvious distress. Before, however, he'd started to give an intelligible account of his evening, Dave's mother came into the room carrying a tray with three cups of tea and half a packet of digestive biscuits.

'Nice one, Mum,' Dave said.

'Thanks, Mrs Baker,' Jay agreed.

She handed the tray to her son and then paused to consider Mike. Both of Dave's friends were more than well known to her, so she could not help but notice his significant change of demeanour.

'Are you all right, Michael? Have you been in another fight or something; you don't look very well dear?' she enquired.

'No. I'm fine, thanks,' Mike mumbled.

Mrs Baker did not seem to be remotely convinced, but she knew better than to question three teenagers about personal issues if they hadn't the mind to talk. Smiling pleasantly, she left them to it and went back into the kitchen, where the noise of the washing machine going into its spin cycle could be heard.

When Dave's mother had safely left the room, Jay got up and very deliberately closed the bedroom door behind her. He then turned to face his friend, hunched against the chest of drawers.

'What happened, Mikey?' he asked, making no judgements.

'I… '

'Yeah?' Dave encouraged, not so adept as Jay, nor as skilful in dealing with delicate circumstances. Whatever was troubling Mike was causing him acute pain.

'I… er… I-I g-got jumped,' Mike stuttered. He glanced at them fearfully as he said this, and paled significantly.

Dave had been lounging casually against the wall but, upon hearing this, he jerked upright and his mouth fell open. Jay frowned more deeply than normal and made a silent gasp within himself.

'You *what?*' Dave repeated.

'I got jumped; I know I did,' Mike answered, unwilling to meet his friend's eyes.

Jay got up out of the swivel chair at the desk and picked up two mugs of tea. He kept one for himself and handed the other to his dejected friend, who grasped it without looking directly at him.

'Cheers,' Mike mumbled.

'Are you going to tell us the whole story then, mate, or d'you just want to forget the whole thing? But… if you were assaulted or something, you ought to… you know…' Jay let the words hang in the air.

Finally, after a frustrating couple of minutes, Mike decided he wanted to let it all out. He plonked the untouched mug of tea down beside the television and rubbed an angry red mark on his neck, just above his untidy shirt collar. Jay, who was swigging a mouthful of tea at that moment saw it, but did not know it for what it was - a love bite. Dave though was less naïve. He recognised it at once and gawped, but made no audible comment.

'We went to Bar Zooka; you know, that place in Castle Quay? It's the hottest spot in Bampton.'

'Everyone goes there,' Dave observed, 'or, at least, they *talk* about going there.'

'How did you get past the door security?' Jay asked. 'You can pass for eighteen but some of those girls wouldn't… Did they?'

'Must've done,' Mike responded. 'Anyhow, we joined the queue and piled on in to the club. No trouble at all.'

'So what happened next?' Dave urged him, keen to hear the whole sorry saga.

Mike grimaced and said, 'Well… That's the weird part… I can't remember much after that.' His two friends exchanged glances. This was not good news.

'What *do* you remember?' Jay asked, feeling more than a hint of concern.

'We hit the dance floor. I had maybe three drinks, no more than that. Music was too damned loud, as usual, could hardly hear what this girl was yelling at me. Then I can't remember anything much after that…' Anger flashed across Mike's face.

'Did some bastard crack you over the back of the head, maybe?' Dave suggested.

Distractedly, Mike ran his left hand through his untidy blond hair and felt the rear of his skull. All seemed to be in order.

'Nope,' he declared. 'Meh' head's OK; I reckon somebody slipped something into one of my drinks. *Damn it!* Three units of alcohol will never lay me out - twenty would do.'

'Are you sure about this?' Jay gulped.

'Look! I only had three drinks, and no one smacked my head in. What else could it be - random amnesia?'

'That date-rape drug!' Dave shuddered. 'What's it called, Jay?'

'Can't remember; listen mate, I think you ought to pay a visit to the cop shop.'

'Don't be daft,' Dave argued. 'He's only seventeen and so were all the others. The cops will have a field day if they get wind of that! Bar Zooka will be forced to shut down.'

'That might not be a bad thing,' Jay pointed out.

Dave snorted in disagreement but he turned to Mike again. 'Tell us the rest, mate. What happened this morning?'

Mike shivered nervously, then he continued with a rather panicky string of words.

'I came to myself - or, woke up - at about ten o'clock, in a strange bedroom in a house on the French Estate. Nobody else seemed to be there except me and I was in pieces. I could tell it was a girl's room because there was girlie stuff everywhere in it. I sat up, feeling pretty ill, and when I looked around I saw my clothes chucked all over the floor. I got out of this bed, got dressed and let myself out of the front door. There was not a soul in the place so I just scarpered. Then, after I rung your house and found you weren't in, I guessed you'd be round here with Davie. So I walked straight over...I've been *had* guys... someone jumped me!' Mike nearly wailed these last three words to his friends.

Jay was simply horrified, but Dave needed to be clear about something first.

'It was a girl, yeah? Not... Not a bloke, yeah?'

Mike shuddered as he leant against the chest of drawers, and then he put his hand behind him and felt around, nervously. After a short delay to make certain of it, he answered, 'Definitely a girl, m-mate.'

Relived about this, Dave suggested rather slyly, 'Wasn't it - er - fun?'

Mike groaned and he sunk his head a little lower. 'I - don't - remember - it!' he said, testily.

Jay slapped his friend across the arm, furiously. '*Idiot!* The poor guy's just been done... jumped... Don't you get it?'

Dave went quiet, and Jay forced himself to ask calmly, 'Mikey, if you were out of it, are you sure it actually happened?'

'Trust me Jay, mate, it's pretty obvious; it happened.'

'We tried to warn you,' Dave put in, adding a plaintive note to his voice to avoid furthering Jay's anger.

'I guess I'll listen to you guy's next time then, won't I?' Mike replied, sadly.

Jay smiled sympathetically at him and gripped the shoulder of his jacket. This had proved an unexpectedly nasty start to their summer holiday. The only question was: would it get better or worse?

Mike's unpleasant rite of passage had been a real shock when it happened, but a week later there was little damage to show for it, and the friends were almost ready to joke about it. None of them had told the Police or their parents and were content to chalk it down to experience. Mike had got himself checked out at the GUM clinic and was all clear, and everything was well on the way to getting back to normal.

Jay had spent quite a lot of his holiday so far pondering the hypothesis of World Lines and also whether he could perhaps use this as the basis for his project. The concept had really caught his imagination and he had been rehearsing Dr Seymour's lecture in his mind many times. But with his seventeenth birthday looming ever nearer his attentions became somewhat divided.

On the Sunday following the incident at the night club, Dave called up Jay in the evening. He was frantic with excitement. Coming downstairs to take the phone from his father, Jay had no idea of the news he was about to receive, nor that the news was not going to be new.

Mr Romero passed the receiver to his son and left the hall as Jay sat down on the staircase a few steps from the bottom. The telephone cable, stretched to its limit, reached to a small table by the front door. The vase resting on top caught Jay's eye and he remembered vaguely that his mother had once thrown it at him in fright. Now, of course, it was no longer broken; *Time* was altered.

'Yo, Dave mate, what's up?'

His friend's reply rang with the fervent anticipation of a young child wanting to tell of a brand new toy: 'I've found something... on the Net.'

'What? Something to get us started on Roberts' project?' Jay asked, keenly.

'No, mate, much better than that, a hacker's kit... including a worm you can e-mail to someone you don't like and it'll— '

'Whoa! Hey, hold on mate!' Jay gasped and almost slipped down a step in surprise.

'What?' Dave said, breathlessly.

Jay once again cast his mind back in time. 'Did it come from a link to that weird cyber-cult group in the US? What did they call themselves?'

'*The Cult of the Sacred Moose?*' Dave prompted.

'Yep, they're the ones.'

'Yeah, but how did you know about them?' Dave demanded, completely taken aback.

'Sorry to disappoint you, mate, but I discovered that crazy bunch in the summer of our fourth year,' Jay said, apologetically.

Although he made no sound at all, Jay reckoned he could almost hear Dave deflating miserably on the other end of the line; after all, he'd been so excited.

Feeling entirely sympathetic for his friend, Jay did not realise himself to be moving towards a state of mind where openness could prevail over discretion. Soon afterwards, Dave's voice grumbled down the telephone line again.

'I'm always playing second fiddle to you and Mikey. Why can't I ever do something first or best? It's just not fair,' he complained.

'Don't get upset, mate; I deleted the stuff after using it once - on Colin Davis.'

Dave baulked. 'Great! Why didn't you tell me? I'd have loved to hear that *that* thug got done over. You should have said something. Why didn't you?'

Strange things began to swim their way through Jay's head and he briefly lost control of his eloquent tongue. Suddenly, almost as if it were meant to be, as if it were forced out of him, he blurted out, 'Because I changed the future, so it didn't actually... *oh no!*' He stopped short in mid speech, looking horrified at what he'd said.

At the same moment the telephone line crackled with static energy and immediately Jay was hit with a blinding headache. Instantly he knew he'd probably started something in motion that he should not have done, but he also felt that it had not been entirely voluntary.

'What's that? What *are* you talking about?' Dave demanded, in irritation and bewilderment.

'Please,' Jay hissed, 'just forget I said it, mate; just forget it, Dave.'

'No, I won't,' came the antagonised answer. 'What d'you mean you changed the future? Are you feeling all right mate? Jay...?'

Reeling with giddiness by this time, Jay pulled the receiver away from his ear, staggered to his feet and slammed it back down on the phone. To make sure of the job he also yanked the cable out of the connection socket on the wall below. That would let the caller think the phone was ringing when, in fact, it was not - or so he thought. Anyway, it would give him a brief respite to compose himself.

Hoping his parents had not heard anything suspicious from the lounge, he dashed up to his bedroom again only to find his mobile phone ringing. His friend was being persistent. The infamous Nokia jingle made him feel like a hunted animal. He fumbled in the pocket of his jacket which he'd slung over the back of his chair and saw Dave's number flashing at him on the illuminated screen.

Desperately, he hit the 'off' button and the mobile went dead in his hand. Then he lurched over to his bunk and collapsed on to it, shaking with fear and anguish. That sensation of pain he had not felt since entering the rift three years ago, and it was not an experience he wished to repeat. Filled with little short of panic, Jay lay on his back and gazed up at the ceiling, running his fingers through his jet black hair, and breaking out in a cold sweat.

The transmission to Dave of knowledge he should never have had could risk untold repercussions throughout the continuum. As his immediate discomfort receded, Jay was then struck with an awfully morbid train of thoughts: *I'm a danger to myself and others; if I keep letting stuff out that I shouldn't do, all hell could break loose; maybe it already has done; did Davie actually get what I said over the phone?*

Nothing less than terrified, Jay rolled over on to his side and shut his eyes, feverishly hoping that he had stopped short of plunging the entire world into another temporal Armageddon. That had almost happened last time, and he could not face it again.

All the while and unbeknown to him, a future career as a deep space Captain - something he had always dreamed about - passed from the realm of 'unknown' into 'never could have been'. Such was effect of the World Lines jumbling up, a number of them snapping and then reconnecting themselves.

Soon his thoughts became nightmares and, having fallen asleep, he found no place of haven from his own imagination. Worst of all, he even thought he heard his own malicious voice laughing at him, as if in some kind of brutal revenge from the other side of the grave. All in all it was not a pleasant night.

Chapter 3

The Late Birthday

There was something wrong with the wall paper, there had to be. Jay knew he was asleep but this was not like a normal dream. He wanted to get up out of his chair and examine the room more closely but found he couldn't do it. Some great unexplained effect pinned him to his seat and, try as he might, he could not shift himself. Perhaps it was just old age?

Finally giving up, he let his focus drift from the indefinite coloured walls and over to the furniture in the room. He knew it to be a hotel room, but where was he? He tapped his fingers on the table beside him and looked down at them. He was startled to see they were not youthful and fresh skinned like he knew them to be, but old and wrinkled. His wasn't the flesh of a teenager, more that of an eighty year old man. What did it mean? The shock of this discovery distracted him from the little black diary-like book under his hand.

There was something important he had to do, but he could not remember what it was. Then again, he could scarcely recall what he was doing there at all - or who in fact he was.

The only thing he really remembered, was hearing an irritable grumble from his father some time the next morning as he awoke.

'I don't believe it; no wonder I didn't get that call. Jay's gone and tripped over the phone cable. *Why didn't he just plug it back in?*'

Jay spent another bleary minute or two between the waking and sleeping universes. But in a shiver of consciousness, the worry of the previous night's outburst fell upon him anew. 'What have I gone and started?' he mumbled to himself, squinting at the brightness coming through the windows. He hadn't drawn the curtains the night before.

The day Jay became seventeen by his body clock, seventeen according to the calendar, he was actually somewhat older in terms of existence. Exactly three months of his life had bypassed the normal reckoning of time due to a short circuit. The dimension rift altered the future from what, originally, it would have been and Jay was approximately seventeen years and three months old when his birthday came around on Sunday August 1st.

At ten o'clock in the morning two teen aged friends from South Fields School walking up Westbury Drive turned into number twenty four. They opened the gate and marched up the path. Lance Beveridge and Paul Metcalf were friends with the other three, and invited to the party.

Paul was curly haired and pock marked and in the same year as Jay and the rest. Lance was dark and slim and very fit. He, being two years older, was re-taking his A levels in order to achieve better grades. He had his mind set upon a career in the Army, and wanted to enrol a step up from the lowest rung of the ladder. The decent grades would ensure this. His father was a Detective with Thames Valley Police and had had dealings with Jay's father in the old time line.

Paul rung the doorbell enthusiastically and moments later footsteps bounded down the hallway and Jay pulled the front door open.

'Great! You're here. Come on in,' he beckoned to them.

'Hi, Sport; this is from me,' Lance said. He smiled and pulled an envelope from inside his leather jacket. Jay took it eagerly and Paul, who had been carrying a plastic bag, offered it to him as they stepped into the hall. He then smirked and turned away to close the door behind them.

'Lance and Paul are here,' Jay called. Then he stopped abruptly, halfway down the hall on the way to the kitchen, staring into the plastic carrier bag. Lance bumped into him and peered over his shoulder too.

'So, what's the punk brought you then, mate? Oh boy!' Looking into the contents of the open bag in his friend's hands, he saw plenty of reasons to stop Jay in his tracks, including... 'flavoured Durex... cigarettes... vodka'...

Paul was biting his nail and looking mischievous as the hold up continued. Jay turned around to face him with an irritated expression on his face.

'I know I've just turned seventeen, Paul, but this is a joke... isn't it?'

28

he whispered angrily.

He knew his parents would find these 'gifts' even less amusing than he himself did. Paul jerked backwards in mock surprise and gasped, 'Oh, sorry Jay, mate.... wrong bag!' He stuffed his hand in his pocket and pulled out another scrunched up plastic bag, bearing the same supermarket logo.

Lance laughed as they exchanged bags, Jay frowning as usual.

'D'you lads want tea or coffee?' came Mrs Romero's voice from the kitchen.

It turned out that Paul had really bought him an handful of book tokens which he said were much more boring but they made Jay happy. Lance's present had been a voucher for the local cinema allowing ten free visits. Jay only rued the fact that he had not had these prior to the release of the third instalment in the Lord Of The Rings trilogy, which he had viewed with a passion the previous years' end. Sci-Fi was still his favourite pursuit but, for a month or two, he had definitely fancied living life as a hobbit in *The Shire*.

The three friends sat and drank coffee at the kitchen table, waiting for Mike and Dave to appear. For some unknown reason they were late. Jenny Hampton called around for Jay's sister, Alice, five minutes after the friends arrived and they left for next door. She was being rather annoying by calling Lance, *Lancelot*, and by pointing out that that was where his named derived from. He would have none of it.

Meanwhile Jay's father had been lounging against the worktop reading an article in the Daily Mail. During a lull in the boys' conversation, he looked up and pitched them another topic for discussion.

'Have a read of this, lads,' he said, passing Lance the newspaper.

'What's it about?' Paul asked, casting his eye over a double page spread on which were horrible scenes of stranded and dying whales on a muddy beach.

'Strange,' Mr Romero answered. 'A whole school of whales washed up on a beach in Scotland. Dozens of them. The reporter is wanting to know why; they don't seem to be hurt.'

Lance scanned the article in interest and stopped with his finger hovering over the second column. 'An RSPCA chap at the scene reckons that when a group of rescuers managed to get a few of them back into the water, they just turned right round again and floundered on the shore - like they wanted to die or something?'

'Maybe they lost their bearings. The marine wildlife experts are all perplexed,' Mr Romero replied.

'It might have something to do with pollution,' Dave suggested. 'Is that a chappie from Greenpeace in that photograph?' He pulled the newspaper nearer him. 'What do *they* reckon is the cause? They're always banging on about saving whales.'

'They're almost as clueless as the Scientists,' Mr Romero continued. 'But one thing has got them all wound up, it's happening more and more these days. Have a look at the table of statistics on the second page Lance. You can see that more and more of them are dying each calendar year.'

Jay had been listening to this talk with a glum face, but lifted his chin off his hand at this point and said, 'The reason whales and other creatures like dolphins are washing up on beaches is not because they're lost!'

'Really?' his father enquired.

'Nope. It's because they *want* to get washed up.'

'What d'you mean?' Paul demanded.

'Marine mammals are highly intelligent,' Lance added. 'Are you saying that they're actually committing suicide?'

Jay heaved a sigh. 'Yes.'

'Suicide dear?' said Mrs Romero, coming through from the lounge with a can of air freshener under her arm and a magazine in her hand. 'That's a bit depressing.'

Paul had a sceptical look about him, and he said, 'Why would a fish just— '

'Whales aren't fish,' Jay interrupted.

'Whatever,' Paul brushed it aside. 'Why would they just top themselves?'

'Because they're being driven to do it, driven mad by noise pollution in the oceans,' Jay explained forlornly.

'That's news,' Lance exclaimed.

'Indeed,' Mr Romero added, gazing intently at his son.

As Mrs Romero disappeared again leaving them to their discussion in favour of housework, Paul asked warily, 'Is this a recognised theory, out of some text book?'

Jay shook his head. 'No one else even knows about it.' Then he added, 'I did seriously consider writing to Greenpeace or Friends of the Earth... even to the Daily Mail itself. I guess I never got round to it.'

'No one else knows? It sounds like you've decided that you know for certain, Sport,' Lance responded, sounding a hint sceptical, 'despite the fact marine biologists and oceanographers are all bewildered.'

'You know old Jay,' Paul teased, 'has a theory for everything but no one else ever believes him. Isn't that right, mate?'

'I'm right about this,' Jay said, determinedly. 'But it's my birthday and I don't want an argument, so let's forget the whales and plan our day. Shall we?' He reached over to shut the paper but Lance noticed an underlying seriousness about his demeanour which intrigued him no end.

He put his hand out and stopped Jay from closing the newspaper and gave him a questioning look. 'I'm not taking the P—. Tell me about your idea,' he said.

Paul snorted quietly in the background and took another gulp from his mug. Jay looked up at his father, thinking.

Mr Romero smiled and folded his arms, pleased that he had provoked the teens into a thoughtful conversation. Then he said, 'If my son knows something that experts worldwide don't, I'd love to hear it... Tell us, Jay.'

Aware that all attention had focused on him, Jay resigned to the fact that a full explanation would now be required. He adjusted himself in the chair, took a deep breath and proceeded to detail his hypothesis. It was something that had occurred to him quite some time ago, but with the various events of recent years, he had ended up keeping it to himself.

'The mass suicide of marine mammals,' Jay began, 'is a comparatively recent phenomenon as far as I'm aware. If one checks the records, more whales and dolphins are ending up on beaches than ever before. No one knows why, or they didn't until the answer struck me like an inspiration. Clear as daylight I saw it: the problem began with the invention of Sonar. You know what that is?'

'Yep,' Paul said. 'It's underwater sound.'

'Sonar?' Lance repeated, thoughtfully.

'It's gotta be; I know how it works.'

Then his father looked startled and said, 'You know, Son, I think you're spot on there.'

'Thanks.'

'So, you're saying that sonar gadgets on the bottom of ships are making noise pollution in the oceans?' Lance prompted.

'Yeah,' Jay answered, running his eyes over the drying corpse of some species of whale pictured in the paper and the angry looking Greenpeace activist standing beside it. 'Every single ship in the world and most small boats have sonar - *transponders* they're called - on their hulls. The sound waves can travel for hundreds of kilometres. Any marine creature which can hear the sound can't get away from it. It drives them mad.'

'Speculative... if that's the right word for it?' Paul responded.

'No it isn't, Paul,' Jay's father breathed, catching hold of his son's idea. 'Imagine it: wherever you went, whatever you did, all you ever heard was a ringing in your ears - in your brain. Imagine it here, now if the very air around you was screaming, beeping and buzzing. Sometimes loudly, sometimes softly, but it's never-ending. You could run, hide, go to any room in any building but always you'd hear the ringing in the background... and these creatures are intelligent like you say, Lance. Jay, here, is right you know. He's cottoned on to something so obvious that the whole maritime world is oblivious to it.'

Paul was looking faintly puzzled, but Lance began to appreciate the full horror of the consequences of what had just been proposed.

'Flippin' heck! What d'you reckon the environmentalists will make of this when they hear it? They'll do their nuts!' he suggested.

'So it means...' Paul ventured, thinking very deeply.

'...that there is untold torture and suffering going on day by day in the seas all around us,' Jay interjected, 'and nobody knows a thing about it. Pretty gloomy stuff isn't it? Now you know why I was moping a bit when dad showed us the article.'

'Write to the paper!' Paul insisted. 'You could explain your idea in a letter to the editor. It might get to be 'letter of the week' or something. Might even get you famous!'

'You might change the world, Son,' his father commended him.

Distaste for the sorry fate of sea life then evaporated as his friends found this highly amusing. Jay, however, was tempted to mutter under his breath - *I already have* - but thought better of it.

In the back of his mind this roller coaster of a summer holiday was proving to be nearly as worrying as that of three years ago. Jay began recounting things while the others laughed and joked around him: hearing about World Lines and wondering if they could be real; Mike being date-raped later the same night; blurting out to Dave knowledge which Jay knew he ought to have kept secret; by another weird coincidence, Dave having just discovered the same website that he himself had found three years ago...?

Not for the first time in his life, Jay began to wonder if some strange and intricate plan was being unfolded around him. Then the doorbell rang again, jerking his mind back to the here and now. Lance jumped up and offered to get it. A second after he'd disappeared into the hallway, he bellowed through to the others from by the front door.

'Wise up! It's Goldie and the Spud. What kept you lads?'

Mike and Dave's voices sounded in the entrance along with a clink which Jay recognised as a large crate of bottles being dumped on the mat. He leapt from his seat at once and charged into the hall.

'Don't let your mother see that, if it's what I think it is,' came his father's hushed voice as he hurried out of the kitchen.

Dave in fact had been quite troubled since the previous Sunday night, when Jay had made the strangest of comments over the phone; that is strange, even by *his* otherworldly characteristics. Then he'd simply hung up on him and refused to answer his mobile as well.

Wondering whether his friend was feeling all right and considerably worried about his state of mind, it was with great relief therefore that

Dave arrived with Mike at Westbury Drive this morning. Jay had proved unwilling to communicate with him all week but his birthday was a useful and unavoidable opportunity to meet up.

They had indeed requisitioned an entire crate of bottled beer from somewhere - Jay didn't ask where - and were tired and sweaty from humping it halfway across town. Mike slumped on top of the load just inside the door, red faced and smiling. Dave, completely out of breath, leant against the banister and looked anxiously up at Jay as he appeared in the hallway.

Lance made some remark about the crate sitting on the door mat that sounded pretty much like what Mr Romero had also said but Jay hardly heard it as he pushed past his older friend. He hurried up to the others; an earnest glance from Dave told Jay that his spilt beans were not unforgotten, so he turned to Mike, hoping awkward questions could be staved off until a more convenient moment.

'What kept you?' he said.

'This,' Mike replied, pointing downwards. 'Damned heavy! We had to lug it all the way from the King's Head. You know, Davie's Dad's friends with the Landl— '

At that instant Mrs Romero called out a greeting from the bathroom upstairs and Jay ceased worrying about what his friend might ask and returned to the immediate problem.

'Hide it somewhere, quickly; if mum sees it...'

He beckoned Mike to his feet who looked disgruntled at having to get up again so soon. Lance, quick off the mark, then decided to employ some diversion tactics.

'I'll go upstairs and talk to her about wallpaper and cheesecake,' he whispered.

'Smart one,' Dave murmured, but his eyes remained on Jay, as Lance stepped past them and charged upstairs towards the sound of the bathroom sink being rinsed out and the smell of Oxy-bleach.

'We'll heave this in the garage,' Jay urged, bending down and grabbing one end of the plastic crate, half lifting it off the ground. Mike reluctantly made to help, but Dave saw his opportunity and snatched up the other end first. Jay saw what was coming.

With Mrs Romero safely detained upstairs by their senior colleague's charming patter, Mike held the front door open and the other two dragged the beer out of sight.

'Give us five minutes, mate,' Jay hissed in Mike's ear as he crossed the threshold and followed his friend's lead down the path between the house and the block wall of the garage. Mike snorted and left the front door on the latch, heading to the kitchen for some coffee.

He could tell that Jay had something to say to Dave but had no idea what. He, of course, knew virtually all the same details that Jay did about the adventure two summers before last, details which, he too had sworn to keep secret. Being the only living witnesses to a re-ordered future felt strange, and although the initial excitement had long since worn off, the two of them were always on a different level to everybody else. It produced an unusual bond between them, that none of their other friends or kindred could understand or break in to.

While his friend had been fully transformed by the rift, into something like a saint in his eyes, nobody else except Mike remembered the original, more selfish and childish Jay. In the new time line, people obviously understood that Jay had always been this - good - for want of a better word. Mike, however, had spent fourteen years with the other Jay and often compared them in his own private thoughts.

There was a clear difference between the old and new Jay and although Mike could see which was better, it made him feel rather uncomfortable. It wasn't easy having a near perfectly moral best friend. And although Mike himself had suffered a partial split, plenty of his old self still remained. However, his amazing double memory at least gave him the chance to compare things in life in a way that nobody else could. This attribute also made *him* unique in fact, though he did not realise it at the time.

Dwelling on these and other thoughts he wondered through into the kitchen and took up the newspaper article.

'*Noise pollution killing off marine life?*' Paul remarked. 'Where does he get these ideas from?'

'What's that?' Mike enquired, having not been a party to the conversation.

Back in the garage, Jay and Dave shoved the beer crate under the work bench and covered it with a dirty blanket his father would use when working under the car. Mrs Romero had sold her green hatchback six months previously and Mr Romero no longer had the company van. The family now owned a blue MPV (multi person vehicle) which, in the good old days, used to be called a minibus.

Jay dusted off his hands in the darkened space between the wall and the car, looking thoughtfully at the concrete floor. Dave wiped his brow on his right sleeve and neither of them spoke for a minute. Then, after a short and uncomfortable delay, Jay decided to bite the bullet and he turned to face his curious friend.

'Go on, then,' he said roughly. 'Ask me what the hell I was going on about last Sunday; ask why I've been avoiding you all week!'

Dave should have been upset by this undue unpleasantness, but his anxiety left no place for offence. He was just desperate to find out what was up.

'I… er… I was worried about—' Dave began, but Jay cut across him.

'Look, I'm sorry I'm being foul. It's just that you're bound to ask stuff that I can't answer and I don't want to spoil things today, and with our friends— '

'There's no need to apologise,' Dave reassured him, sitting down momentarily on the work bench and then springing up again suddenly when he realised how filthy it was.

'Yeah, best not to sit down, mate, dust everywhere,' Jay advised him, as Dave lamented the cloudy patch on his trousers. 'Anyway, is there something you want to know? We don't have long before the others come looking for us.'

Jay glanced at his watch; that *same* watch.

Dave bit his lip, then said, 'Well, we were talking about that hacker software and that cyber-cult. Then you said something about changing the future so something never happened. I thought you'd got your words mixed up or something. But then you went a bit crazy and hung up on me. What was happening?'

'Yeah,' Jay sighed. 'I guess it came across as rather strange.'

Dave stared at him and Jay wondered where and how far he ought to go. Maybe he'd already gone too far? He looked through the single pane window at the path outside. It had weeds growing on it, but so far no one was coming to investigate their delay.

'Jay, what are you hiding? It must be something serious because you hardly ever take the piss; you're far too genuine. C'mon, mate, tell me…'

Still unsure of what to do, Jay decided to make a brief explanation, which he hoped would not cause any more temporal ructions. He wanted to play for time and perhaps have a consultation with Mike, seeking *his* counsel. Talking to Mike of course would be safe, because he already knew all about it.

Considering his pal carefully, Jay said, 'There is a grave secret that only me and Mikey know about - in the whole world. Nobody else has a clue about it.'

'You're kidding. Come on, I'm really serious…'

'*So am I,*' Jay responded, adding a menacing bite to his voice.

'No?'

'Yes! Now listen up; I'm not going to tell you about it - it's dangerous to spread it around, mate. But I can— '

'What! Why?' Dave argued. 'You're freaking me out you know?' He was glaring at Jay through the semi darkness and, indeed, his friend's expression was noticeably more intense and frightening, made worse in the dingy surroundings.

Jay held up his hand to calm Dave down a bit, and continued very impatiently. 'I'm *not* going to tell you what it is - not yet. But I promise, I'll have a chat with Mike and then we'll decide if it's safe to let you in on it too, mate.'

'But why wouldn't - whatever you're going on about - be safe, mate?'

'Things happened in the summer holidays of our fourth year that shouldn't have happened. So we have knowledge that we should not have. If we go around blabbing about it, the future could really get screwed up; it almost did the last time. When I cracked up last week on the phone to you, I might have let the cat out of the bag. D'you follow what I'm saying?'

'Absolutely not, er, has it got something to do with the lightening

37

strike? I mean, the fact that you survived it... everyone knows about that?' Dave enquired, feeling all at sea.

'Yes it has got something to do with it. That is where it all started.'

'Where *what* started? C'mon mate, you're talking riddles with me,' Dave implored.

Jay however shook his head determinedly.

'No,' he said. 'No more now.'

Dave made a pleading look.

'Davie give me a break!' Jay shouted. 'Not telling you the truth is doing my head in, mate. *Listen* to me,' - he calmed himself - 'I want to tell you everything because you're my mate. But I know that if I do, all sorts of trouble could result. But I care about people and don't want them to get hurt by it. So I'm torn between telling and not telling. Just trust me on this all right?'

Jay noticed as his colleague seemed to relent. As was the entire neighbourhood, Dave was well aware of the lightening strike and the public aftermath that had followed, but knew nothing of the three months detour that his two friends had taken. Though Jay's story made little sense to him he finally gave in, but not in a very good mood.

'Fine,' he grumbled. 'Don't tell me then. You and Mr Wonderful can keep your little secrets...'

'*Davie!*'

'If you weren't the, '*Miracle Kid of Northamptonshire,*' in the Advertiser and Fortean Times— '

'I don't read that magazine any more— '

' —then I wouldn't even believe you! I'd say you were a crack pot,' Dave muttered.

Jay suffered a momentary surge of anger, but it was immediately assuaged when Dave added a postscript as he turned towards the steel garage door, ' pity you're my friend.'

Anger gone, Jay grinned and slapped him on the back and said, 'Keep stum mate, and we might talk more later.'

Business sorted, they went back inside.

The warm evening breeze blew through the park from the direction of the cricket ground in Westbury Village. This quiet spot, two miles outside Brackthorpe Town, was a common haunt for young people wanting some rare peace and quiet.

The Reindeer Inn opposite the park was often filled with local trade but tonight it was especially quiet, and the chatter inside barely carried across the grass to where the six teenagers sat together by the swings. There were six of them, because Mike's younger brother Matt had wanted to come along and the others, in surprisingly charitable mood, had allowed him to. Matt was still only thirteen and something of a nuisance, being in awe of his older brother and even more so of Jay. Lance sometimes referred to him as a fly he'd love to swat.

After a fun day in Oxford exploring the old town centre, the colleges, the museum and having a punt along the river - and almost crashing the boat - the birthday party returned home and then took a bus out to Westbury Village. With copious amounts of alcohol stuffed into their bags and coats, they had settled down in the play park and chilled out at about nine o'clock.

Jay was completely sober, having had only two drinks. Mike was merry enough, having had four or so. The others however, Matt included, were beyond meaningful conversation. Sprawled in a talkative heap on the grass, blithely solving all the country's political troubles, their two other pals left them to it.

As Jay and Mike sat side by side on the swings looking out over the silent cricket field, Mike munched his way through his sixth pack of crisps. Jay had switched to coke, determined above all things never to be drunk - much to the misery of the rest of them.

A little distance away from his strewn colleagues, Lance lay flat on his back looking intently up at the moon through a huge pair of binoculars. Wincing slightly at the brightness, he giggled happily as he zoomed in and out, making himself dizzy. These magnificent night vision binoculars were Jay's gift from his dad, who always managed to find the most superb birthday presents. They were current military stock and should hardly be in civilian hands.

Fitted with various heat sensitive filters and an infra red chip, these binoculars could allow the user to focus in on a single body trace up to a mile away - given the right conditions - and showed everything up in a range of green coloured light.

Lance finally made himself too sick and stopped his game, letting the night vision bins fall to the grass beside him, his head spinning. He managed to stifle a retch and then laughed out loud setting off Paul and Dave.

'Oi...! They're worth a lot of money!' Jay barked.

Mike jumped to his feet, reasonably securely, marched over to where Lance lay and picked up the fallen binoculars. He brushed them off and returned to Jay at the swings.

'You always get top presents,' Mike complained, sitting back in the seat and rocking it gently to and fro. 'What did you get last year?'

'That 'Build your own Laser kit' from Maplins,' Jay replied. 'Yeah, dad's presents are really cool sometimes.'

'Wish my dad was cool. Didn't even give me a cool name...'

Jay ignored one of the others being sick loudly into the grass. 'What d'you mean?' he asked, slightly bemused.

Mike examined his own trainers close up, with infra red vision. Then he said, '*Murkin*...! Rubbish or what?'

'Nothing wrong with that,' Jay answered.

'Hmm! But you don't know what the name means, do you?' Mike responded, glumly.

Jay was doubtful, 'It doesn't have any meaning... does it?'

Mike grimaced. 'Well, not exactly, but there's a word which is spelt differently but pronounced the same that means something... well, something rather un-cool, put it that way. Good job Matty doesn't know...'

'Know what? What *does* 'Murkin' mean?' Jay asked, intrigued.

'I'm never telling you,' Mike hissed. 'And now I'll make sure I stay off the rest of the beer so you can't wait till I get drunk and trick it out of me then.'

Jay shrugged. 'Fair enough, but I don't see what the big deal is. Anyway, you had some decent things on your birthdays didn't you?'

'Can't remember,' Mike said, stuffing the crisp packet into his pocket and licking the grease off his fingers.

'You got that mountain bike for your fourteenth,' Jay reminded him.

'Yeah! But what's that compared to that supercomputer your dad nicked for you?'

'He didn't nick it!' Jay argued. 'He rescued it from a skip at work, remember?'

'Maybe.' Mike frowned and yawned; then, looking at his watch and seeing it was now eleven o'clock, he said, 'We'd better think about calling a cab for this lot, or they'll be spending the night out here in the park.'

'Warm night tonight,' Jay mused. 'Let's sleep rough, I fancy a change. How about these concrete drainage pipes the kids play inside?' He pointed to three large bore pipes behind them that had been embedded in the earth that served as a makeshift tunnel to explore. Some time ago the Council had condemned them as hazardous but they had not, hitherto, been removed from the park.

'I'm not kipping in there,' Mike bawled. 'They're full of graffiti and Dave went for a piss in one of them earlier!'

'More than that boy!' Dave roared, tuning in to their conversation at that point, while lounging on the bank below the swings. He had just opened another bottle of beer and began to drink noisily.

'I wish you hadn't drunk so much,' Jay complained, 'I really wanted to have a talk, but I'm not going to go taking your advice if your— '

'I am not pissed,' Mike interrupted. 'I've only had four drinks.'

Jay eyed him carefully and saw that Mike was quite coherent even with the alcohol. He was right; he wasn't drunk, but he was hardly in a state where Jay could seek his counsel over important issues.

'So,' Mike announced cheerfully, 'what do you want to know Jay, mate?'

Jay considered broaching the subject of his indiscretion with Dave the previous Sunday but thought better of it. When Mike therefore raised his eyebrows to enquire further what Jay had in mind. Jay diverted him.

'Er... I wanted to know, er, have you finished with the night vision bins yet? I wouldn't mind having another go, you know... *with my own birthday present.*'

Mike gasped, 'Oh yeah; sorry, mate.'

He passed them to him, and Jay got up and carried them over to the chain link fence at the edge of the park. Paul called after him something about abandoning their excellent party but he wasn't listening. Instead, he put the binoculars to his eyes and trained them northwards to find the pole star, Polaris.

Finding the correct altitude he gazed through the greenish haze of the milky way, examining the constellations he recognised on his way to Polaris. He had a great appreciation for the night sky, and his long held desire to Captain a deep space freighter went hand in hand with it.

For a time, he was blissfully flying through the solar system. Then, quite suddenly, he saw a shimmering snakelike formation of light dance down from the northern latitudes. Astounded, he refocused the lenses, wondering if he'd become worse for alcohol than he thought.

Jay swallowed intensely; it made no difference. For several more minutes the dancing, snaking light in many shades of green hovered just around the northern horizon.

'The northern lights,' Jay muttered, 'the Aurora… but it shouldn't be visible from here. I'm nowhere near the Arctic Circle?'

Struck and confused by this unexplained anomaly, Jay continued to observe it for many minutes until it eventually retreated towards the pole once more and vanished below his horizon. As swiftly as it had appeared, it had gone. Puzzled no end by this, he lowered the night vision binoculars and stared out into the galaxy with his naked eyes. Without the enhanced vision, it was astoundingly black; he could barely see anything at all.

'What're you gawping at,' Mike yelled, 'those heavenly bodies?'

Jay shook his head but did not turn around, naively wondering why his friend had used that old fashioned terminology, seeing that he had no time for astronomy. Yes, that was what they used to call the stars and planets in the old days, he thought.

'Nope. I've just seen something weird, something which I shouldn't be able to see from here, but… whatever it was, it was beautiful,' he said, remembering again the dancing lights in shades of green and how they seemed almost alluring.

'WHAT? There really are girls up there?' Mike bellowed, in disbelief.

Jay groaned and turned back towards his friends in the middle of the park. They were little good for company now or, indeed, anything else.

'Mikey, just go to the Reindeer and call a cab, mate!' he ordered.

Chapter 4

The Hacker's Software Again

The intriguing and unexpected sight of what appeared to be the Aurora Borealis thousands of miles off course, was constantly on his mind for the next two days. Jay knew perfectly well that this dancing formation, often called the Northern Lights, was generated by particles from the solar wind careering through the upper atmosphere and ionising things as they passed. A similar light display, the Aurora Australis, also occurred in the southern hemisphere. The reason for the light being seen at both the polar regions was due to the overall shape of the earth's magnetic field, which deflected incoming solar rays towards the poles. The effect of this was to shield the earth from harmful radiation, but the bonus was the entrancing phenomenon of the two Aurorae.

Before long Jay also realised that in order for the light display to become visible at his lower latitude, namely, Westbury Village, a humongous shift in the earth's magnetic field would be needed. Remembering how the light had arrived and then, several minutes later, just disappeared, he reckoned that the earth's magnetic field must have taken some terrific jolt from somewhere... Perhaps an ionic storm had erupted on the surface of the sun eight or so minutes before he'd gone over to the fence that night? Then he wondered if any *man made* event could cause such a significant interference to the planet as a whole. He doubted it. The consequences of some earth-bound, man made cause were unthinkable. Could man ever hope to possess the power to alter the very core of the planet?

Dr Seymour had mentioned disturbances in the earth's magnetic fields during his second presentation at the Town Hall, and the possible reversal of the poles. Could that be what was happening? No, Jay thought; the odds of it occurring so soon afterwards were quite ridiculous and, anyway, a full magnetic reversal would lead to utter chaos. In the end, he decided that it had to have been some unusual astronomical event.

However, he did have his project set by Mr Roberts to be getting on with, and so, sitting at his computer on the Tuesday after the party for one of his late night sessions on the Net, he searched for potential topics.

Eating his way through a bowl full of pistachio nuts one handed, he read through a web page all about a certain late scientist called Nikola Tesla. He was familiar with the name from his GSCE Physics textbook, but knew little more about the man other than the fact he gave his name to a unit of magnetic inductance. It was almost by accident that he'd discovered this page after typing the surname into the search engine – his preferred one being Netscape Navigator.

He might not have bothered reading the article at all, but the headline caption, reading – '*A WEAPON TO END ALL WAR; DID TESLA REALLY HAVE A DEATH RAY?*' - grabbed his attention.

Pistachio nuts taste great but they're a pain to have to eat because it takes so long to prise them apart without crushing them, that you simply can't guzzle them fast enough to quell your appetite. As the article about Tesla and his possible discovery of the ultimate weapon became more and more engrossing, Jay gave up with the nuts and pored over the text instead. Stopping only to refocus his tired eyes once in a while, it made for intensely interesting reading.

The final paragraph said -

Whether Tesla ever actually came up with a viable weapon we shall never know. He certainly took it to the grave with him if he did, and his notebook, alleged to contain all his most formidable discoveries, was never found. Detectives and family searched his room in the New Yorker Hotel the morning following his decease but to no avail. Rumours abounded that FBI agents secreted it away in the early hours but these remain mere speculation. Who knows; apart from the Weapon to end all War, had the man lived, we may also have witnessed Atmospheric Lighting and the means to control our own Weather? One person I know actually had the gall to suggest that he was 'taken' early, to avoid mankind getting his wicked hands on technology so potent, it could have spelled doom for civilisation if misused... Perhaps the Almighty did not want anybody else stealing his thunder - only joking. Jojo signing off :-)

' "*We may have witnessed Atmospheric Lighting?*" ' Jay repeated to himself. 'Are you trying to tell me something computer?'

He ruffled his hair, which was already quite untidy, and wiped his brow on the sleeve of his old red shirt. A cool breeze wafted around his bedroom through the window which he'd left open for refreshment, because the computer screen filled the air with positive ions and it made him feel sleepy.

Leaning on his desk, he puzzled over the web page. This material certainly counted as 'innovative' which was the qualification for their Physics assignment. But for this night at least, Physics had to take the back seat. The strange apparition on Sunday evening was now followed by this: an amazing yet possible link to something he just read about on a website. It was devoted to 'speculative discoveries in science,' and Jay reckoned he might have just made one for himself.

Putting two and two together quickly, as he always did, he immediately began to suspect that something might be in store for him this holiday, something which could be even more testing than his previous nightmarish adventure.

The only trouble was, he had no idea what it might be. There wasn't even proof that any of this had been planned at all. The mysterious diversion of the magnetic field could have been a fluke of the solar wind, and finding this web page containing Atmospheric Lighting could be nothing more than coincidence. Yet, some gentle but distinct feeling in his gut told him otherwise. He knew he had been singled out to help the world once before, so was it that ridiculous that he might be called into action again?

He looked at his watch and realised it was already the next morning. Making a note of the web address, he yawned and shut down the computer. Tomorrow, he decided, he would go over to Dave's house and make a start on Roberts' project.

And if his services *were* called upon between now and then...

'...they just better not be called upon for the next eight hours,' he grumbled.

Next morning after breakfast, Jay set off for Ellesmere Road.

Walking past the newsagents for whom he had once worked a paper round, he had a number of things on his mind. These mysterious portents aside, there were the mind boggling discoveries on that web page he was keen to show Dave. There was also the *Cult of the Sacred Moose* web site that Dave would almost definitely want to show him - even though he'd seen it all before.

On top of all this - and also Mike's unprecedented hassle from his strict parents, who were livid that they'd all been out getting drunk in Westbury Park, doubled by the fact that Mike had helped buy the beer - there was also the likelihood that Jay would find himself pressed yet again about his outburst over the phone.

His brain weighed down with heaviness, he marched along Market Hill where a row of small shops opened out on to the main street. He halted abruptly outside one of them when he noticed a blond head he thought he recognised. Peering through the glass of the shop window, between posters advertising that month's special offers in blue and yellow, he did recognise him.

It was the mini-market and young Matt Murkin was standing, looking bemused, in the fruit and vegetable aisle. He was holding two different kinds of melon, one in each hand, as though not sure which was which. Jay tapped on the window and grinned at him. Matt looked up and gasped, then beckoned him into the shop urgently.

Jay pushed through a crowd of shoppers milling about with baskets and children by the entrance, and caught up with his friend's younger brother. Matt looked quite relieved to see him, as if he felt like reinforcements had turned up. Shorter than Mike and rather puppy-faced, he was unmistakably his sibling, and Jay immediately wondered why - his mother, presumably - had him out buying fruit.

'Hi, Matty, what's with the melons, mate?'

Matt shrugged and said, 'It's for this new pavlova thingy mum's trying tonight. She's never tried it before and doesn't have half the stuff she needs.' He dropped the large red and green melon back into a cardboard box on the display shelf and put the yellow one into another box nearby.

'I really don't know what this Galia thing is, do you?' he asked, pulling a crumpled piece of paper out of his pocket and showing Jay a hastily scribbled list of items.

'Why didn't she send Mike?' he responded. 'Normally he gets sent out on these errands of hers doesn't he?' Matt goggled at him for a second and then made a worried face.

'What?' Jay said, moving aside one step to allow a young woman with a trolley move down the aisle. She was humming to a Carpenters tune being played quietly in the background over the tannoy system.

'Haven't you heard?' Matt gasped, going more wide-eyed.

'Well, I know your mum and dad had a row with him about buying all that booze, and then letting you get razzled with the guys in the park. You're under age!'

'It was worse than that,' Matt mouthed. 'Dad threatened to hit Mikey and so he just decided to leave home!'

'You're joking?' Jay baulked.

'Nope,' - Matt shook his head - 'this morning we went into his bedroom and he'd gone!'

Jay panicked for a moment but then reconsidered. 'Bet he's gone to ground at Dave's place,' he said. 'Davie's folks always were much easier going than yours.'

'Can you go and find out if he's OK, Jay, I don't want him to be in trouble... please, I can't go there I'm not allowed. I'm grounded too apart from this emergency trip to the shop, you see?'

'It's OK, mate, I was on my way there anyhow. Davie and me have got to do a Physics project for Roberts and we ought to be getting on with it, so it's no trouble.'

'Thanks,' Matt breathed, returning to his shopping list.

'Er, better go and ask an assistant,' Jay advised him, 'and you might want to grab a basket from by the entrance while you're at it.'

'Thanks,' said Matt again, and they parted.

Jay left the mini-market and headed up towards the top end of town with increased urgency.

The first thing he saw upon arrival at his friend's house in Ellesmere Close, was Mike sitting gloomily in the front garden on a plastic chair. He was wearing shorts and a T-shirt and reading the Baker's newspapers.

If he hadn't been sulking, he could have been enjoying the pleasant morning sun before it got too hot.

The front garden itself was square, and fronted by a smart brick wall. Modest herbaceous borders surrounded three sides of the lawn and the grass was striped neatly by Mr Baker with a traditional cylinder mower. Being semi detached, one edge of the garden joined the next door neighbour's property, while on the opposite side there was a shared driveway to the two garages. Dave's other neighbour, a middle aged plump fellow, was in his garage at that moment. Jay saw him inside buffing up the chrome headlamp of an historic motorcycle.

Not bothering with the gate, Jay hopped over the low wall adjoining the pavement and advanced across the lawn.

It took a long while for Mike to acknowledge him - or perhaps he'd just been too engrossed in the sports section of the newspaper. He usually followed Manchester City's progress avidly.

'Making yourself at home, then; I heard you'd moved?' Jay called, nonchalantly.

Mike threw aside the paper and raised himself painfully out of the chair. Jay cringed, thinking that his friend must be carrying some parental injury, but his apprehension turned out to be quite unfounded, as Mike spoke again.

'Slept all night long on the settee; think it's put my back out, mate.' He grimaced as he said it.

Jay walked up to him smiling, in some measure of relief, and said, 'You all right? You didn't get knocked around, did you?'

'Nope. Sore throat from yelling all yesterday afternoon. Nothing more than that though.' Then he added under his breath, 'Reckon I'm more than a match for dad now, anyway.'

Jay swallowed awkwardly and thought it best not to pursue this topic, but he glanced at his friend's physique and, tacitly, he agreed with him. To Jay though, striking his own father would be tantamount to murdering him, and he would rather die than do that. Nonetheless there did seem to be a violent streak running in the Murkin family and Jay was not altogether untroubled by it.

In himself, Mike looked rather dishevelled and pitiful this morning, and seemed to be in need of a change of clothes, a bath and someone to give him a hug. So Jay did the honours and gave him a comforting grasp around his shoulders, saying, 'Met Matty on the way up here, bro; he's frantic, but I'll tell him you're here and that your safe.'

They broke apart and Mike waved the comment aside with a gesture of his hand. 'Thanks, but little bro will be all right. He'll just do what he's ordered to and knuckle down. Me...? Well, I reckon I've had just about enough of it; d'you think Davie's parents will let me stay? They've got a spare room.'

'Yeah, but we keep that one reserved for my Gran,' Dave called out, appearing in the doorway with three mugs of tea on a tray. 'What's up Sport? Heard your voice from the kitchen.'

'That's one of the Corporal's labels,' Mike muttered, 'Sport... Goldilocks he calls me, and you're the Spud, well, that one's pretty accurate.'

'Hi Davie,' Jay replied, glad for the offer of tea and disregarding Mike's comment. 'I'm fine. Mikey here has a few things up by the sound of it though. Are you taking care of him while he convalesces?'

'I don't need taking care of,' Mike grumbled, examining his dirty fingernails. Meanwhile, Dave plonked the tray down on a outdoor dining table by the bay window, from beside which Mike had drawn the chair, and carried *it* and the drinks over to his guests on the lawn. Then Jay, with a nod from Dave, brought over two more of the chairs and set them in a ring around the table.

'Top of the morning,' Dave said, offering Mike and Jay mugs of tea.

Jay stole a glance at his watch and saw it was half past ten already. The morning seemed to have gone by faster than normal. Perhaps it had been the sheer volume of concerns buzzing around in his brain. At least Mike's safe, he thought to himself; that makes one down and.... how many more to go?

Safely ensconced on the green front lawn with mugs of tea apiece, they made idle conversation for a while with Mike being rather distracted to put any effort into it. At the same time, Dave's gaze kept flicking from one to the other, hopefully, while telling them that his mother was out for the day with friends in nearby Bampton.

Then, during a lull in their talk, he blurted out with, 'So, did you speak to Mike about— '

'No!' Jay said firmly, spilling some of his drink in his rush to get the answer out swiftly enough. Dave halted in mid sentence and Mike looked up.

'What?' he demanded.

Jay glared at Dave who raised his eyebrows in defiance.

'You *said* you'd ask him about it.'

'Not now!'

'*Ask me about what?*' Mike urged, more loudly.

Not sure whether he ought to fume or cringe, Jay confessed weakly, 'I'm afraid I let slip something about our deadly secret *secret…*'

Mike was silenced by the shock of this unexpected statement. Immediately the memories of that life and death fight came flooding back to him and, unsurprisingly, his present predicament became less of an issue. But he wasn't any the happier for it; instead, he turned faintly white and Jay hoped it wasn't rage.

'What did you tell him?' Mike said, very deliberately facing Jay and ignoring Dave, who was bursting with interest now. This was a secret he'd never been allowed into.

'I mentioned changing the future - but not any of the details. I was hoping he'd misheard, or else wouldn't believe me, but— '

'But what?' Mike demanded.

'But I was hit with a killer headache at the time and what with all the pain I was in and the noise I was making, there was no way he'd accept it was simply a joke. He's not thick!'

'You got those *headaches* again?' Mike repeated. 'You know what that meant the last time; damn it! It's not happening all over again is it?'

'I don't know. So then, d'you think it'll cause another temporal rift if we tell him all about it?' Jay asked.

'Stop talking about me as if I don't exist!' Dave shouted out, unable to contain himself any longer.

'Shut up, will you? This is deadly serious,' Mike barked.

At this, Dave bristled alarmingly. He had just been insulted by someone he'd been trying to help. 'You ungrateful arse! You can sod off and sleep in a ditch tonight - if you're going to speak to me like that, mate.'

Mike drew himself up to his full height and turned on Dave. 'You've no *idea* what you're talking about, or how serious this thing is...' He lowered his voice to a threatening whisper: 'Let me tell you Davie boy, I'd gladly kip in a ditch, a pig sty, or pretty much anywhere rather than live to see... that...' He stopped himself with a great effort, so as not to reveal anything further.

'What?' Dave protested, still very irate.

Jay however, relieved that his two friends hadn't come to blows, and that Dave still had all his teeth in the right place, decided to take charge. He stood up and suggested, calmly, 'Let's go inside, shall we?'

It was an aggravated procession that entered Dave's bedroom a short time later. Mike had sworn that Jay was making the wrong choice and, furthermore, that if he succeeded in plunging the world into chaos - this time he'd be on his own. Mike had no intention of risking his neck again. Jay himself was squirming at the thought of what he had agreed to do, though was no longer tormented by having to keep his friend permanently in the dark.

Dave found himself halfway between disbelief and unbridled fascination. He knew these two had shared a strange, esoteric life experience together, but, on the other hand, could it not simply be one of Jay's more ingenious and spectacular wind-ups? They didn't happen very often because Jay hardly ever wound people up. But maybe... just maybe...

Dave itched with excitement and could barely contain himself as they sat down on the bed. After a very long and jittery pause, which served as the ultimate introduction to a thrilling account of some kind, Jay took a deep breath and said, 'Everything began Davie, in the summer holidays prior to our fourth year, on the twenty first of July.'

'When you survived that lightning hit?' Dave said, gleefully.

'Yep. Well, something happened that night that set a whole train of events in motion, and— '

'—it's a train that's still rolling down a slope out of control!' Mike interrupted and, shaking his head in despair, he washed his hands of them and got up. Without so much as asking, he then stomped over to his friend's work desk and flicked the computer on.

Dave opened his mouth to protest again at Mike's total lack of respect, but Jay gestured for him to let it go, and so Mike, now with his back to them, set himself to ignore the rest of their discussion.

As a matter of fact, he spent the next three quarters of an hour playing *Worms: Armageddon* on the CD ROM, with the talk going on in the background. Possibly, the slaughter of these creatures being practised on screen represented the holocaust he expected in the real world hereafter. Now that Jay had fully broken their pact to keep the affair hidden, who knew what would happen?

Racking his brain to drag out every last detail from his memory, Jay recounted his story from three years ago. In the end, it reeled off so nicely, it was as though he read it from an adventure book.

Dave, listening in awe to every word of it, had long concluded that this was not a hoax. For starters, Mike was not that good an actor and Jay, well, he wasn't really the type to wind one up. As for the adventure itself; the abject horror of what he was hearing had turned Dave sickly pale by the end of it.

When Jay, tear glistening in eye, told him how he had at last destroyed his terrifying alter ego, Dave gripped his arm in fright. He forgot that it made him look rather young.

'…and so I came out of hospital for the second time. The first thing I wanted to see, then, was whether the time line would take the same course as before - which would have been an absolute nightmare.'

'*As if you hadn't already had one!*' Dave exclaimed.

'Yeah, but very quickly I realised that we had set the future off on a different course and my Dark Side was gone for good.' Jay shivered all the way down his spine as he thought on it.

'So, in the *old* future I knew all about it, but in the *new* future I, er, I didn't; but, hang on a sec, you just told me all about it just now.'

'That's right,' Jay said, 'and I'm not sure what that means for us.'

'It must have been tough not telling a soul for three whole years,' Dave concluded, letting go of his friend's jacket, after finally realising what he was doing.

'Yeah,' Jay murmured, 'you could say that.'

'So, it's only you, me and Mikey who know a thing about this; is that right? 'Cause all of this time travel stuff does my head in,' Dave complained.

'Until Jay mate goes and blabs it all to someone else,' Mike grumbled, bludgeoning another helpless worm with an axe, taking away half of its energy in one fell swoop. 'Whatever happened to the absolute sanctity of the blessed future?'

This gripe was directed at Jay, who said vaguely, 'I just felt tha— '

'Whoa! *My God*,' Mike yelped, interrupting him suddenly.

The computer screen had scrambled and lines of distortion and interference were tumbling down the monitor. Mike leant back, away from the keyboard, as a loud crack burst from the hard drive and the computer died instantly. The screen went dead and, with all three lads watching anxiously, a wisp of smoke spilled from the machine's casing.

'You broke it!' Dave gasped, leaping up from the bed and diving over to his desk.

'I…I d-didn't do nothing,' Mike stammered, prodding the dark LCD screen with his fingertip.

'You've blown it up!' Dave shrieked. 'What did you do to it?'

Jay, equally alarmed, hopped over to the desk and stared at the defunct PC, still smoking quietly on the white work top. Dave punched Mike in the shoulder, but he was too shocked to retaliate. Instead, he gawped blankly at his hands, wondering if he had suddenly developed magic powers.

Dave, stricken with angst and desperate, turned to Jay.

'What am I supposed to do?' he wailed. 'He comes round here in the middle of the night, homeless. I persuade mum and dad to put him up. Next day he swears at me and blows up my computer. I really can't take it, mate!'

'I was only blowing up worms, mate, not your PC. I don't know what happened to it, all right,' Mike hissed.

'Yeah…?You still owe me a new computer,' Dave hissed at him.

'Cool it!' Jay ordered, moving himself in between them for safety. He cast his eye over the contents of Dave's desk top, but could see nothing at all amidst the pencils, books and notepads that could account for a catastrophic failure of the computer's hard drive. Then he noticed Mike's empty mug.

'Did you spill your tea over the keyboard?' he asked.

'Probably!' Dave snorted.

'No, I didn't,' Mike argued, 'and you can shove off too,' he added in Dave's direction.

Dave tried to swear at him but was prevented from doing so by Jay jamming his left hand over his mouth. While Dave wrestled to free his face again, Jay grabbed Mike around the collar as he sat in the chair and shook him hard.

'Listen! This is Davie's house, mate! For Heaven's sake watch your tongue... and calm DOWN!'

Mike had not taken kindly to Jay's hand around his neck, and was apt to explode at him too. He leapt to his feet, kicked the chair across the bedroom and glared furiously at Jay, who had lost his grip on both protagonists.

Usually, when the two of them stared each other out, Jay won. On this occasion though, Mike had the ace up his sleeve.

'Watch my tongue? *Watch - my - tongue!*' he repeated, faintly. 'When you're happily blabbing all manner of dangerous information to Spud? How many times did you lecture me about keeping things secret, eh? Talk about hypocrisy!'

Rather defeated, Jay pleaded, 'Mike, I'm just trying to prevent— '

'Prevent what, me thumping him? Don't know why; he's being such a prick. The computer probably picked up a bug or something.'

'Get out of my house, Murkin,' Dave bellowed, red in the face and neck.

Mike gave a derisive snort and turned and marched towards the bedroom door. 'Glad to,' he muttered.

'Fuck off and sleep in a ditch,' Dave shot at his departing back.

Mike froze and clenched his knuckles so hard the cracking sound could be heard on the other side of the room. Jay saw him grit his teeth and shake with fury. But with a massive effort, he brought himself under control. He opened the door and left without any further response -

except to slam the door so hard that a split appeared in the paintwork around the architrave.

Jay felt horribly tense, but Dave was utterly beside himself. He wondered aimlessly around his room in circles for quarter of an hour, muttering things about Mike that kept annoying Jay. Then, he vainly tried to resurrect his computer but the whole thing was dead as a door nail. It was no use, and so, in a fit of passion, he swept all the contents of his desk, keyboard and all, into the bin. The bin was rather full and some of it fell out again onto the floor.

He could still be heard sobbing from the kitchen, where Jay had gone to make them both a fresh pot of tea. Arriving back in Dave's room with the drinks and some cake he'd found in a cupboard, Jay found his friend head-in-arms on the desk, moaning to himself indistinctly. Jay placed the tray on the surface and drew up a chair to sit down beside him.

'Cheer up, mate,' he said, comfortingly. 'We might still be able to save the motherboard and the RAM. Far worse could have happened, couldn't it?'

'Like what?' Dave groaned, reaching out for his drink and taking a great slurp from the mug.

'Er, the thing could have exploded and killed Mikey, or— '

'No, that would have been better, not worse. You got that one wrong!'

Jay did not answer that, but chose to try a more logical approach.

'Listen; have you been doing anything dodgy with it recently?' he asked, glancing down at the battered remains of the PC lying beside the bin. 'Anything that could have caused it to get a bug?'

'Nope - unless you call visiting that cyber-cult web site every day for several hours at a time 'dodgy'.'

Jay considered this for a while; then he said, 'Yes, mate, I think I probably would. Did you download anything from them - that worm, or some of their other - er - goodies?'

'Yes,' Dave admitted, 'quite a lot of stuff actually.'

'In that case, I'd definitely say it was dodgy,' Jay said.

'I was going to show it to you,' Dave continued, 'guess I can't now

56

though, eh?'

'No, pity; you do realise, mate, that Internet security firms keep tabs on groups like *Cult of the Sacred Moose* to see what they're up to. It's part of the constant war waged between the Corporations and the hackers. Each side is trying to outdo the other. The hackers are always inventing new ways to attack the corporate systems while the security people keep finding new ways to spy on the hackers... and everybody else!'

'Crikey! I never considered that,' Dave gulped.

'Obviously not,' Jay said, 'but nowadays the Western Governments are so frightened of terrorism that they're also deploying people from the Secret Services to scope the Net, looking for potential terrorist networks, as well as wanting to catch the usual hackers, stalkers, virus writers and paedophiles.'

'D'you reckon? You mean MI5 and those guys?'

'There are agencies worse than MI5,' Jay answered, sounding quite foreboding. 'There are agencies which have no name, and powers that can't be seen.'

'Wonderful,' Dave replied, ironically. 'Let me think now... a faceless security swine in some underground bunker sent an e-bomb into my hard drive did they?'

'I don't think so,' Jay responded. 'They haven't invented them yet, as far as I know, but I must say it really wasn't wise spending so much time on line with the Cult. You know, it *could* have brought you to the attention of the Authorities.'

'But they're based in America,' Dave reasoned, 'why should they bother with me? Anyway, you said you'd logged on once before.'

'I wasn't so clued up then but, still, your house hasn't been raided yet; so we can be thankful for that at least.' Jay bent down and picked up the damaged computer tower from the floor. It rattled unpleasantly as he shook it. 'Drive's busted, I reckon,' he said.

'Will I have lost all my files?' Dave whinged, gazing fearfully at his wrecked PC.

'Depends, mate,' Jay replied. 'Things might have been corrupted before the power died.'

'Great!' Dave moaned, sinking his face into his arms again.

'Everything I've ever done is on that hard drive, and not all of it was backed up.'

'Um, we'd better decide how we're going to break this news to your parents, without starting a full blown feud.' Jay would have gone on to explain how, seeing that Mike was already in big trouble at home, it might not be a good idea if Dave's father were to ring them up this evening and create uproar about his son's blown-up computer.

Instead, he was halted by Dave sitting bolt upright in his seat and trembling with terror.

'My folks!' he cried. 'They'll have my skin for this. It cost them a grand or more.'

Now Jay's temper got the better of him. He dumped the dead computer back into the bin and kicked the carpet in frustration. On top of all his current worries - this too?

'Being friends with you and Mike,' he thundered, '*It's just too much*! You're asking too much of me. Why couldn't the damn thing have blown up and taken out the both of you; boy...! You folks really know how to spoil a guy's day, you know that?'

Dave couldn't answer. He was dumbstruck and afraid.

Chapter 5

The Man in the Suit

A few years ago, during a major refurbishment of their house, Jay's parents had allowed him to furnish his bedroom more or less as he pleased - with some exceptions.

He then thoroughly disappointed his mother by opting, for the most part, for that which was purely practical. His desk, chest of drawers and filing cabinet were all ex-Government surplus stock from a local warehouse. Plain and drab; Jay loved them because they were solid and useful for standing on without breaking, as the need arose.

In truth, the need had arisen often these last few months as Jay, bored with the cream coloured ceiling, had decided to augment it. He'd bought some luminescent paper from the Art and Crafts shop in town and proceeded to draw and cut out replicas of the Sun, Moon and planets. Bit by bit, he was manufacturing a not-to-scale reproduction of the Solar System and attaching it to the ceiling of his bedroom.

He relieved himself from the stress of that day by cutting out Neptune and sticking it into its orbit with a dab of contact glue, the fumes of which made him feel rather high as an added relief. This was probably the closest he ever came to taking drugs.

Lying back in his pillow, around midnight, he surveyed his nearing complete star system and smiled in the darkness. The dim yellow orbs above his head made him feel peaceful, as though his true destiny lay somewhere up there - amongst them. One day, maybe, he would live and work in deepest space? But for now...

Content to let his imagination delve into interplanetary euphoria, he drifted off to sleep without realising it and, later, he returned to a very unsatisfying dream.

...It was a hotel room, and he was sitting in his armchair, drumming his fingers over that little black book again. The sepia leather of his chair had faded, like much of the other décor about the room. But where was he....?

Jay felt a source of heat on the side of his face and turned to see where it came from. Straight away, he was pricked by a stabbing pain in his neck. His aged old joints were not akin to moving so quickly and they protested.

An electric radiant fire with art deco surround blazed red and sent its crimson glow to all corners of the apartment. But inside him, Jay felt cold and tired. Rain drops began to pelt the window and his mind became more distracted. What was he supposed to do? How could he keep the people safe? What was he even doing here? Who was he...?

A bird chirped loudly on the window sill next morning and Jay awoke, bleary-eyed. He saw his alarm clock reading eight o'clock but was not too upset about the time. Whatever he'd dreamed of the night before he couldn't remember, but it had left him with a mild migraine.

'I thought sleep was meant to be restful,' he grumbled.

He sat up and rubbed his eyes. Pulling open his curtains, through which the summer sunshine was already spilling, he saw a tiny speckled bird take off in fright, disappearing into the trees at the bottom of the garden. Before summoning up the energy to get out of bed, shower and go down to breakfast, he decided to make a plan for the day.

Sympathetic as he might be to their difficulties, he could not face another round of Dave and Mike bickering; also, he reckoned that each should sort out their own domestic affairs for themselves. He himself had enough to be going on with.

It's not as though either of them is in any great danger, he told himself and, still, he hadn't written down anything for his project, which, at the start of the vacation, he had been keen to get on with. All in all, Jay thought it would be best to spend a good part of that day in Waynefleet Library, researching material for Mr Roberts' assignment.

Mid morning, Jay turned off Waynefleet Ave and approached the glass foyer of a single storey building with pebble dashed walls. This uninspiring sight was the larger of Brackthorpe's two libraries. There was another, privately owned one, on the High Street which boasted a clientèle of arty types and toffs, but Jay wanted to try out the County Council premises first; it was for more normal people.

Only a five minute walk from South Fields School, the sign outside this establishment announced, *South Northants County Library Services*, and a series of telephone numbers followed.

Feeling somewhat warded off the Internet lately, by its ominous size and doubtful security, Jay marched through the entrance and past the alarm system guarding the exit door. (The books were all tagged with magnetic bar codes which needed to be deactivated before you took them away; otherwise they would trigger the alarm. Though some of the school pupils would 'accidentally' forget to do this and set it off - just for fun.)

He was faced with rows of bookcases and a study area where six large tables were set out, and he smiled amiably at the staff counter where he was reasonably well known. There was something deep inside compelling him to find out more about the amazing Mr Tesla and his coveted inventions - which was fine by him; the material had to be perfect for his assignment. He just knew Mr Roberts, being an anti-establishment man himself, would simply lap it up.

The only asset Waynefleet had over the other place on the High Street was a superb air conditioning system, visible below the headlining panels. Shiny steel ducts blew a cool, dry breeze around the corridors and the sweat of the summer morning evaporated swiftly from Jay's skin.

He searched carefully through the Biographical Section but, alas, his subject wasn't there. Next, he tried looking through the shelf entitled 'Popular Science,' but again, to no avail.

Two hours after beginning his enquiries, Jay began to wonder whether everything about Tesla had been removed from the public record - just to frustrate him. He come to think that way in recent years because of his experiences.

Sitting cross-legged on the carpet tiles between two untidy piles of books, he slammed shut another hardback compendium and furrowed up his brow and then it came to him... the Encyclopaedia Britannica!

'Of course!' he whispered, 'everything's in there.'

Leaving the book on the floor with all the others, he rushed over to the Reference Section at the back of the building with renewed enthusiasm.

The Reference Section was a separate reading room, a library within the library. It contained books that were too valuable, too rare, or plain too big for customers to have out on loan. None of the books were supposed to leave the Reference Section, let alone be taken out of the building. Many of these volumes were very large indeed and looked to be over a century old, with cracked leather covers and faded imprints.

Jay opened the door and let himself into the room. There were three wooden tables inside but they were all empty, as no one else was studying in this area. He quickly found a current set of the Britannica and pulled out the volume covering 'Te'. If he wasn't in here, Mr Tesla wouldn't be anywhere, Jay thought.

A minute later he struck gold. But he had to admit it was a bit of an anticlimax. Leaning his elbows on the table top, he pored over a rather small paragraph about the man in question and, feeling deflated, he learned very little new information about his subject.

The article revealed more about Tesla's place of birth and family circumstances, but nothing more about his supposed ultimate weapon. Jay was disappointed; perhaps he would have to rely on the Internet after all, which, as everyone knew, was the world's largest pool of knowledge.

The hydraulic hiss from the door closer stirred behind his back as someone else came into the Reference Section. The quiet footsteps, the slight chill upon the air; they did not distract him from his task.

Not long after this he finished his reading, biting his lip in disappointment. There seemed little more he could do, and Jay shut the volume of the Britannica pensively. But...

A moment later, a sharp hand gripped his left shoulder without warning. Jay started violently, jerking round to see who it was that might be accosting him.

An elderly man in a very dark suit and a bowler hat stood over him, looking down from on high with a supercilious smile. He withdrew his arm in recoil at Jay's physical intimidation and simply bored down upon him with unfeeling black eyes.

Jay stared back into a face that was devoid of all emotion, all sensibility, an inhumane visage that was disturbing to say the least.

Breathless with the surprise and alarm, Jay tried to assess this stranger's intention. Was he about to be kidnapped?

The mouth in the pallid face cracked open. 'Jay Robert Romero?' the man enquired, softly.

'H-How do you know my name?' Jay gasped.

'You needn't worry about that,' the stranger hissed, straightening up to his full stature, which was considerable given his age.

'Who *are* you?,' Jay demanded, squeezing himself out of the seat. It was difficult because his chair was tucked in, and the man in the suit stood so closely behind him, that there was barely enough room to manoeuvre. All of a sudden the rows of heavy books began to feel like bars of a prison cell, or maybe it was solely the presence of this mysterious individual.

Jay wondered whether he ought to run for it. This fellow had to be the best part of sixty or seventy, and should not be able to keep up with him… unless he had special powers… or a gun. Jay couldn't help but think in these devastating terms. There was something awesome about this man. He had an unpleasant spirit, one that provoked Jay badly.

He felt he was being mocked, mocked and despised. Worst of all, Jay felt terribly threatened, even though he was standing in the middle of a library building with dozens of witnesses only yards away in the main reception area.

'Sit down!' came a commanding voice.

Jay fought this order in his mind, but found he was somehow compelled to retake his seat. He sat down again, filled with ice-cold dread in the pit of his stomach.

'I come here to bring you a message,' the stranger declared, unmoved it seemed by his daunting influence upon this young man.

'And what's that?' Jay said, shortly. He did not want to show his discomfiture, but he really wanted to escape from the Reference Section and, indeed, the library building altogether.

'Do not meddle in things which don't concern you!' the man warned. 'That is all.'

Jay, gob smacked, could barely avoid letting his mouth gape open. Who did this fellow think he was? Then, the very same words forced their way out of his trembling lips.

'W-Who do you think you are…?' Jay blurted. 'Hey!'

Silent and implacable as a cold brick wall, the dark suited stranger had just turned away, not doing him the politeness of a reply. Jay glowered after him as he slowly approached the door to the main library, walking stiffly upright. Then, as if he'd forgotten something mildly important, he turned again and faced Jay with a pallid white gaze. The tension in the air was palpable.

Waving a claw-like finger vaguely in Jay's direction he said, 'Your friend has been taken care of, by the way!' The voice almost sang, an ethereal and derisive melody.

'What?' Jay demanded. 'Who? What are you on about.'

He felt as though he wanted leap out of his seat and grab this arrogant old man around the neck. He wanted to wring an explanation out of him. How dare he drop a challenge like that and then just walk out? Waltzing around this place as if he owned it? A sudden burst of youthful vigour and protest swept over him. He felt a strong urge to thump this sinister old bully, to rise up and teach him a damn good lesson. Respect for his elders would just have to go on hold.

Either Jay's intents showed on his face as he made to stand up, or maybe his mind was read. All he knew was that, as he got to his feet in anger, the stranger snapped his fingers at him and he suddenly blacked out…

Leaving him on the floor, the man in the dark suit departed without the least commotion. Meanwhile the library continued to bustle with activity.

Jay came to at the sound of the alarm system, which rang out as another student 'forgot' to take their book to the counter before leaving. He was slumped on the carpet beside the table, with the volume of the Britannica beside him. He must have caught it as he fell; some of its pages were creased. He noticed how far the sunlight had shifted in the window and guessed he'd been unconscious for the best part of half an hour. He lay there musing how few customers must use the reference books – otherwise someone would surely have found him?

Jay pulled himself up and replaced the book on the table, still wondering why no one had come to his aid, called an ambulance, called the Police or even noticed him lying there on the floor. They couldn't have even looked through the window! Maybe this terrifying individual had put some spell on all the staff and visitors.

Most of his energy was drained, as if something had sucked the life out of him, and his headache had come back with a vengeance. He moved shakily to the door and peered through it. Everybody else in the building seemed to be OK and the man in the suit was nowhere to be seen. But who had he been?

His heart thumping loudly, Jay made his way cautiously into the main library, trying hard to return an innocent smile to the lady serving at the counter. She plainly hadn't noticed anything untoward.

Then he remembered a part of the old man's message… *'Your friend has been taken care of.'*

What did this mean? Was it a threat? Jay had to find out; he knew he had to do something. As usual, his careworn predictions of impending doom were rapidly taking shape.

Throwing all caution to the wind, he hurried across the room, scattering one or two people who were queuing up to take out books and charged out of the library and into the car park. There was no sign of his erstwhile assailant – not that he'd expected him to still be around.

He pulled his mobile phone from his pocket and dialled up Dave: no one was in, or, at least, nobody was answering the phone. He tried Mike's house next, but Mike's mother told him he wasn't at home either and whatever the cause - it was likely to be their continuing row - she was not a little distraught over it. More bad news!

Turning and walking briskly up Waynefleet Avenue towards his home in Westbury Drive, Jay desperately tried to raise one of his friends. He needed to speak to somebody. He called Lance's mobile phone number but, most annoyingly, it was his girlfriend Joanne who answered and she sounded rather too busy doing something to chat. She apologised and hung up straight away.

'It's hardly the time for *that*!' Jay muttered.

Angry, exasperated and frightened; Jay made a bolt for home, using up what little strength remained within him by running flat out all the way. He felt like a startled rabbit and wasn't the least bit ashamed to admit it. All he wanted to do was get to refuge. Everything was ganging up on him it seemed.

As he arrived at his house, he all but collapsed on to the grass verge beside the garden hedge. He thought it not good to turn up gasping for breath. It took a full five minutes for his heaving chest to return to normal and for the chance to talk rationally to himself once more.

With his mind in overdrive, he sat with his head on his knees on the grassy bank, listening dimly to the occasional car travelling along Westbury Drive. Now, at home, he felt a mite safer, but he was filled with confusion about what was happening. This holiday had started going weird ever since he'd let slip his secret to Dave on the phone and, from then on, whatever was occurring seemed to be snowballing alarmingly.

He considered Mike's analogy about a train running downhill out of control and conceded that he may actually have been right. That was painful too: admitting that his less-than-perfect friend might just have taken the wiser part.

'Space-time chaos again,' he murmured, rubbing his forehead into his sleeve.

When Jay judged he was ready to go inside without drawing too much attention to himself, he hauled his exhausted body to its feet and plodded up the garden path to the front door. He let himself in quietly and slung his jacket over the banister, heading for the kitchen. He was feverishly hungry by this time.

His sister Alice had heard him coming in and she burst around the kitchen door at the end of the hallway and smiled pleasantly.

'Michael's staying with us, Jay,' she said in an excited tone of voice. Then she added, 'Are you all right?'

'Pretty much,' he answered, wishing the strain on his face wasn't so obvious.

'Mum said he could camp here for a day or so while - um - while things get sorted out back at his place; isn't that good?' she continued.

Jay, who had lived most of his life on Mike's doorstep did not feel so enthusiastic, but at least it explained why he had not been at home earlier on. Mrs Romero then joined them in the hall bearing a healthy looking plateful of salad. She pushed this kindly into her son's hand and then said, 'Are you all right my love; you look ever so upset?'

'It's OK, Mum,' he grunted, though he didn't actually mean this. What he meant was: I'm desperately worried about strange and bizarre things that are happening to me but I just can't tell you because it'll make things worse, and because the future's changed, you have know idea what happened last time.

A familiar laugh then carried into the hall from the lounge, where a familiar someone had evidently been watching a humorous programme on the TV. Jay poked his head around the door. Mike was sitting in the sofa watching the box with a large grey holdall at his feet. He must have been home for a brief visit at the very least, but had brought most of home back with him - judging by the size of the bag on the floor.

Jay wandered into the room. He was seething with anxiety about the information he had to off-load as soon as possible. To his irritation, Alice accompanied him into the lounge, while he munched a handful of rocket and lettuce leaves.

'You get around, mate,' he said, addressing his friend who'd taken up two and a half places on the sofa.

'It's not my fault,' Mike whined, half looking at him. 'I'm having grief at the moment.'

'You're not the only one,' Jay replied under his breath.

Out of the blue, Jay realised why Mike had not looked him in the eye. He whipped around and glared at his sister who stood, carefully positioned, at his right shoulder. She blushed, suddenly, and giggled behind her hand. Jay turned back to Mike who quickly glanced away towards the TV in the corner of the room. A teasing smile flashed across his cheek - and Jay saw it!

'My sister fancies you... I wandered if she'd ever...' But Jay tailed off; he was too distracted to care very much. Instead, giving Alice a firm shove towards the exit, he said, 'I need to speak to Mike in private; give us some space!'

'Hey, don't push me! Mum... Jay's pushing me around!'

'Mum, I need to talk with Mikey. Don't come in the lounge. Thanks.'

'You're a pig, Jay!'

'Go away... Thank you!'

Forced to concede ground to her older brother who pushed her out of the room, Alice stomped off to the kitchen to whine at her mother about Jay's unfriendly behaviour. Meanwhile, Jay shut the lounge door smartly and locked it just to make certain. Then he moved over to the smaller settee of the three piece suite, upholstered with floral motifs, and sank into it - facing his colleague of old.

Mike's programme had ended so he reached for the remote control on the coffee table and switched off. He considered Jay, as he munched through the remainder of the salad and a piece of chicken breast. Mrs Romero had gone beyond the call of duty and glazed it with honey and mustard. This was Jay's new 'favourite flavour in the world'. Although this was endlessly updated – rather like Micro$oft computer programs.

Throwing his plate down with a relish, Jay sighed appreciatively. But his grievous upset could not really be disguised, and Mike knew the worried look as well as any of his other friends.

'Something bad happen at the library?' he asked, shrewdly.

Jay flinched a bit. 'Er, yeah, you could say that. How did you know I was there by the way?'

'Your mum said,' Mike replied.

'Did she? That's OK.'

'What happened then?' Mike urged, sitting upright in the cushions - as his back still twinged a bit. 'Another temporal rift get you, did it?'

A momentary rage erupted inside Jay upon hearing these words and his forehead went bright red. For a moment it looked as though he were about to breath fire.

'I'M SERIOUS,' Mike insisted very loudly, although it was unlikely that that had been the case. 'Are you having some kind of trouble again?'

It was like releasing the pressure valve on a steam boiler. Knowing that Mike was no longer making light of him caused the fury inside Jay to drain away like a great ebbing tide. He relaxed and leant back in the sofa.

Jay stared at the only confidant he really had, the only person he knew that could appreciate who he really was and his whole world view.

Mike's eyes told him that he, too, was bearing pain and guilt. In the gravity of the circumstance, both of them seemed to come to a common understanding before they started discussing anything. But Jay, for his part, knew he'd have to share this burden. So, after a brisk trip to the kitchen for a glass of orange juice, he returned and began telling Mike everything.

Chapter 6

Where's Davie?

The Romero's house had four bedrooms, one of which, being spare, they had converted into an office when Mr Romero went self employed. Mike bedded down for the night in a sleeping bag on the carpet and spent an awkward few minutes trying to get comfortable. He feared what might be around the corner, but in a resigned sort of way. What could he do about it?

Whereas Jay spent hours on his knees that night, leaning over his bed and grappling to come to terms with the situation. He openly sought counsel, overawed by events of the last week or two. Barely more than a fortnight ago school had broken up, and he'd been hoping for a month's respite before his coursework results came out. He was halfway through his A-Levels and hoped for top grades.

Now though, life had thrust an altogether bigger hurdle in his path. His experiences in the past had taught him one thing above all: that was, when destiny came calling he shouldn't try to fight it, just keep his heart true and follow the way of compassion. Providence would deal out the judgement in the end. But then he remembered that cruel snap of the fingers, and a power that had knocked the breath out of him - leaving him unconscious. His heart faltered. This was worse than what he'd faced the time before.

'Last time I only had to battle with myself,' he informed the duvet cover, with his face buried in it. 'This time the whole heavens are on the move. I saw the Northern Lights; is every dark power in the earth lining up against me. What could I have done to deserve *this?*'

He continued in a cold sweat for two more hours, after which his joints ached painfully. Finally, in the early hours of the following morning, not long before dawn, he climbed into bed and slept.

The smell of fried breakfast wound its way upstairs and through the crack between Jay's bedroom door and the frame. This most excellent tonic chivvied him out of sleep and gave him a small amount of renewed hope for the day. Jay had overslept - quite understandably - and it was half past nine when he emerged from his room, following the inviting scent of breakfast that was under way in the dining room.

'Morning, son,' his father greeted him as he appeared in the dining room still wearing his pyjamas and looking ruffled.

His father, mother, Alice and Mike were seated around the table making their way hungrily through a full course English breakfast: toast; marmalade; cereal; fry up; it was all there. Jay's mouth watered considerably as his eye roved over the delicious looking spread.

Then he glanced over at Mike, who sat with his back to the dining room wall, facing the hallway. He winked, as if to say, 'OK, mate?' but his expression was such that it made for a grave pleasantry as he, too, felt fearful.

'Thought we'd let you lie in. Mum says you were looking rather ill yesterday. Sorry I got home late, important job in Bedford; someone's system went down unexpectedly - that blasted URKEL virus again! Thought they'd nailed that one years ago; anyway, feeling better are we?'

'A little bit,' Jay answered. He made his way over to the empty place and pulled out the chair.

'Yep, the PC no longer recognised its own hard drive as a hard drive... Had to re-format the whole damn lot to clear it. Good job the guy had a backup,' Mr Romero continued, mostly to himself.

Neither Jay nor Mike had any time for computers blowing up today. Not after the day before yesterday, and they hadn't yet mentioned *that* to Jay's father yet.

'Sorry we started without you, dear,' his mother said, offering him a round of toast. 'But the food was going to get cold otherwise.'

'It's no problem,' he assured her.

For several hours that Friday, Mike and Jay discussed the strange events so far that holiday, wondering whether they were indeed in store for another life-changing summer. In agreement that something odd was definitely up, they both reckoned that their best course of action would be to take the same approach as last time. On that occasion, they had kept silent about it while trying to fix things for themselves, scared that talking too much might upset the future course of the entire world.

Keeping the whole affair under wraps and waiting to see what came of it all, sounded by far the more realistic option to Mike, who also pointed out that, as before, they were little more than pawns in a much bigger game and so should not try too hard to understand it.

In some respects Jay had already settled upon the same idea, though it did not rest comfortably with him. Mike, after all, hadn't just got threatened and then zapped unconscious in the local library. Again those ominous words crossed Jay's mind: *your friend has been taken care of!*

A sudden desire or impulse caught him in the chest as he sat there in the settee, waiting for Mike to load a new DVD. It was the latest Harry Potter film and they were going to watch it for the evening.

'We've got to go to Davie's,' Jay said, suddenly.

'What?' Mike said, looking over his shoulder from beside the television and DVD player. 'I thought you wanted to see *this*.' He waved the inlay card at him. 'Not that I'm that fussed about it myself. They've cut far too much stuff out of it. Everyone knows the book was far better!'

'I still want to watch it,' Jay said, reconsidering. 'I'm just concerned about him.'

'What for?' Mike protested. 'Just because that old geezer in the library gave you the creeps.'

He made his way back to the settee, bringing the remote control with him as the DVD loaded up. Jay felt irritated again.

'Have you forgotten? He hit me with something that laid me out. I'm not joking, mate, one moment I was standing up, the next I was flat on the floor.'

'OK,' Mike conceded, unable to counter this rather pointed and disturbing fact. 'But it's easy to frighten someone by threatening their friends. Anyway, how d'you know which friend he meant? You've got loads... well, quite a few... er... some - '

'Thanks,' Jay remarked, as Mike flopped into the other half of the sofa, watching the opening trailers for other movies.

'Davie's been calling up a dodgy site on the Net. I'm really worried,' Jay added.

'Stop pestering me about Spud,' Mike grumbled. 'You've been

bugging me all day to go and apologise to him and I've agreed to do it. We can go round to his place tomorrow - stop fretting about it! You wanted to watch this childish stuff. It's starting now, see - '

Jay reluctantly let his concerns drop, but it troubled his conscience all evening, spoiling what was otherwise quite a good film. Before they retired for the night, some two and a half hours later, Jay made Mike swear he'd accompany him to their friend's house straight after breakfast the next morning. Mike agreed and they went to bed.

The long, sweeping run of Pavilion Way saw it rise from the lower western part of town, up through the French Estate, to where it joined Halse Road. This made for a pleasant alternative route avoiding the town centre, and allowed the two friends to get a view of the fields on the outskirts of Brackthorpe.

Over the previous twenty years, the town had undergone a marked expansion, and thus its boundaries had encroached significantly into the surrounding agricultural land during this time. Jay could well remember that a large sector of housing on his left hand side used to be a hay field. The majority of this estate, in fact, was only a few years old.

As he walked along the gently rising slope of the wide street, he recalled the summer of his second year at school. The annual Brackthorpe fête had chosen the theme of 'The Rock & Roll Years', and South Fields had entered a float of their own. An old lorry trailer, drawn by a clattering farm tractor, had been driven through the town by Jay's old maths teacher, Mr Hopkin. The float was bedecked with music paraphernalia, including a gigantic cardboard guitar painted all in blue which had been put together by the Art Department. Beside this the school's very own jazz band sat, huddled together, playing music to the watching crowds as the parade drove through the streets.

This year's event had been cancelled late, due to a crippling shortage of sponsorship, and insurance worries. A disgruntled spokesman for the Brackthorpe Fête Steering Committee had complained bitterly in the local Advertiser how the requirement to have 'this ridiculous' Public Liability Insurance would be likely to kill off all such public festivities before too much longer, if things carried on going the way they were.

He had also mentioned something about the EU bureaucracy strangling this country.

Gazing away at the tightly packed dwellings and landscaped driveways and borders, Jay pictured the time when all this red and yellow brick was merely empty space. The tarmac passing beneath his steps had once been vibrant green grass and meadow.

If memory serves me correctly, he thought to himself, the school float parked up somewhere... around... here!

But now all traces of the long standing field pattern, dating back to mediaeval times, had vanished beneath the suburban overlay. So it was very difficult to know for sure. He paused for a moment to take a breather, squinting against the brightening blue sky. Mike noticed that he'd stopped.

'What's up?'

Jay continued taking bearings from the distant hills around him, trying to locate the site in question.

'Remember coming down here to watch the fête in our second year? You know, when the school entered that musical float with the big guitar on top, which Mr Johnson had filling up his classroom for weeks?'

Mike stopped too and scratched his head, thinking, then said, 'Yeah, vaguely, but this was all grassy fields back then.'

'Yeah, pity really,'

Mike surveyed the rows of houses on either side of them: regular, detached and semi-detached properties with their small, square front lawns and box-sized garages. Pavilion Way was modern, tidy and clean, but the developers had had only one motive on their minds, as ever - the profit margin.

Though not as aesthetically articulate as Jay, yet Mike could still express himself admirably.

'Doesn't have much heart does it? Reckon I preferred the meadow too.'

Resuming their journey to their friend's house, the pair of them strode on once more towards the French Estate. The air felt unnaturally refreshing today, as if someone had enriched it with negative ions. But that would be just barmy, Jay told himself. How could anybody produce enough ionised air to make a difference all over the county?

His mind returning to the present concerns, Jay fixed his gaze northward over the horizon of the town. The broken, woolly clouds drifted left to right in the summer breeze. At least *they* were behaving normally.

Jay wondered anew about the extraordinary appearance of the Northern Lights the previous weekend. Had it really been a unique occurrence, a one off fluke of nature? He strained his eyes, scanning the undulating hills in the distance and the skyline above them. A distant glint of white reflected off a speck high above him. Squinting harder still, he recognised it as a glider, probably from the nearby Turweston Aerodrome, which was a remnant of the patchwork of small airfields that had been built in World War II. They were now mostly used for agricultural storage and flying schools.

The glider pilot was circling high above brown, uncultivated fields, using the thermal to gain height. Jay watched until the speck grew too small to see, rising on the up-welling air currents.

He found himself brought down to earth once more by an anxious poke in the ribs from Mike, who'd been keeping quiet next to him.

'What?'

Mike was now pointing at a nondescript house on the corner of an adjacent street. The junction with Halse Road lay just ahead of them, and Ellesmere Crescent, Ellesmere Road and the old soap factory were a short walk beyond that, where the disused railway line crossed under the main road.

There was nothing obviously unusual about this house. Jay had no idea who lived there, but maybe his friend did. For Mike, he now realised, was biting his lip uncomfortably while indicating the same address opposite them.

Looking downwards he mumbled, 'That's the place, mate.'

'What place?' Jay asked, quite bemusedly.

Mike cringed and looked straight ahead again. 'The place where I came to... you know, the morning after I got jumped!'

'Oh!' Jay gulped, remembering at once the whole sorry affair. He gawped at the house in question, and read the number on the door.

'Number fifteen. Which road is it? Ah, Sportway Drive, I wonder who lives there, then?'

At that point, Mike gave his jacket a sharp tug to keep him moving.

'Don't know. Don't want to know! Just keep walking,' he ordered, quickening his pace noticeably.

Jay grinned at him, but Mike stared determinedly in front of him, not caring to dwell at the site of his past embarrassment.

'I forgot how close it was to this road,' he complained. 'Why did we have to come this way?'

'To get away from the town centre,' Jay reminded him. 'It was your idea actually.'

Mike decided to jog the remainder of the way to the junction. He clearly wanted to around the corner as soon as possible and leave Sportway Drive out of sight.

Puffing to a halt beside the Leylandii hedge on the far side of Halse Road, Mike waited, leaning over and drawing deep, recovering breaths. The nervousness, it seemed, had sapped the youthful energy from him. Whereas Jay strolled up to meet him on the pavement, quite casually, a minute or two later. He kept his face impassive, but inside still felt like grinning.

Belittling the unpleasant nature of the assault somewhat, Jay mused over it. Here was great big macho Mike, running scared from a nasty memory.

A moped raced past them giving the impression that the rider thought he was doing at least 90 mph. It was one of their fellow pupils from South Fields. Head bent low over the handle bars, he hooted at them, yelling, 'See ya, Blondie... Gyppo... Ha ha!'

Sounding more like a gnat than a proper motorbike, it swerved down the boulevard from where Mike and Jay had just come, leaving a cloud of oily fumes in its wake.

'Dean Forren!' Jay muttered angrily.

'Hope you crash, mate!' Mike called out after him, but it was too late; he'd disappeared around the corner.

'D'you really hope he has an accident, mate?' Jay asked, sounding surprised, as they set off again heading eastward, sun shining into their faces.

'Yep!' Mike declared, unrepentantly. His mind had been taken off his cruel rite of passage completely by this point. 'He's the biggest tosser in our year!'

'In the school?' Jay added, light-heartedly.

'In the world,' Mike insisted, quite adamantly.

Five minutes later, they arrived in Ellesmere Road. Usually Dave's house showed abundant signs of life but, strangely, not today. All the windows were closed and the curtains drawn.

The man who lived next door had brought his classic bike out of the garage, and was oiling part of the engine when the pair turned up outside his drive. The chrome work gleamed in the sun light. He looked up when he heard them approaching.

Mike and Jay slowed down as the man gestured at Dave's house, recognising them both as his younger neighbour's close friends from school.

'Fraid your pal's out,' he informed them, wiping a piece of metal tube with a dirty, grey rag. This bike had to be his devoted passion. Jay wondered whether the man was married or not.

'Dave's out?' Mike asked.

'They're all out... must be; not a peep so far this morning!' He pointed at the front door of the Baker's house. A copy of the local Advertiser was jammed into the letter box, which had not been taken out; also, Jay noticed, there lay a small pile of letters inside the entrance, obscured by the frosted glass pane.

A disturbing feeling came over him, as if he had just received news of something awful, but could not quite tell what...

'Any idea where they are?' Mike persisted. It had taken a fair bit of work on his part to summon up the resolve to come here and apologise. Now that he'd gone this far, intent on offering some kind of humility, Dave's absence was frustrating. He continued, trying hard to avoid facing the fact of a wasted trip.

'Did they leave any messages?'

'Nope,' the man replied.

'Er...Gone on holiday?'

'Doubt it. They left the car!' the neighbour scoffed, indicating Dave's father's estate car parked neatly on the other side of the road.

'Baker's garage is full of old tat,' he explained. 'That's why he parks up in the street. Daft if you ask me. I mean, what's the point of havin' a garage eh?'

'Er, yeah, thanks mate,' Mike responded.

Jay, meanwhile, had come over all pale and clammy. The colour blanched noticeably in his cheeks. He pulled Mike aside as the portly man returned to his beloved old bike.

'What's up?' Mike demanded. Then he saw the expression on Jay's face. 'A-Are you feeling OK?' he faltered.

Jay felt as though his world was caving in again. Even in the warm August sun, a cold sweat broke out upon his brow, and made a tell-tale glistening.

'Mikey… the message!' he gasped.

'Which message?' Mike hissed, distracted from his all-consuming quest to restore a friendship. He had been working so hard to humble himself; it was tragic.

'Your-friend-has-been-taken-care-of!' Jay mouthed, looking fraught.

Mike began by making a derisory noise in the back of his throat, but he quickly swallowed it before it emerged, a realisation dawning upon him: this might not be a joke. Coughing it down, he turned to face Jay, aghast.

'D'you think?' he choked.

Jay couldn't speak. He merely nodded while endeavouring to squeeze a look of sheer terror out of his face.

'They keep a spare key in the greenhouse out back!' Mike urged. 'Let's go in and investigate, shall we?'

This was another question altogether and Jay hesitated badly, glancing back and forth from the lifeless Baker residence to the neighbour working keenly on his shiny motorcycle. He, himself, paid them no further attention whatsoever… as if someone had virtually turned him 'off'. Certainly, he'd heard nothing of what the two lads were discussing.

Feeling as though he was trembling in his shoes, Jay stammered, 'O-

OK then?'

'Follow me,' Mike ordered, and he climbed over the low garden wall and traipsed across their front lawn. He made for a gate at the side of the house which opened into the back garden. Jay followed, anticipating the worst.

Just as he stepped through the timber framed gate, smelling faintly of wood preserver, the neighbour's voice called out behind his back.

'Ain't seen nothin' of 'em for... must be two days now, at least!'

Jay then heard him unscrew something, apparently unconcerned that the two teenagers were intruding in his next door neighbour's garden. Inwardly, Jay marvelled at the fellow's couldn't-care-less attitude.

Though he'd now been delayed for about half a minute and, abruptly, Mike called out from the Baker's greenhouse at the far end of the back garden. 'Got it! Let's get inside. They might need our help.'

'OK,' Jay answered, hoping dearly that no one was about to report them for trespassing.

The key proved to be a spare for the door to the rear utility room. Mike had initially tried it in the large, sliding patio doors, which led into the lounge, but these were fitted with a cylinder lock and not the dead bolt type. They let themselves in, hoping no alarm was set.

All was very quiet.

Chapter 7

The Police Station

'But... there was no sign of a scuffle; nothing's damaged,' Mike pleaded.

'There's a full mug of cold tea on the kitchen table,' Jay argued. 'The washing up in the sink is half finished. There were computer catalogues open on Davie's desk - he's obviously looking for a new one - even his TV was on standby!' he added, sounding frantic as he talked.

'Exactly,' Mike contested, but it was without much conviction. He was trying desperately to find an alternative explanation. 'There's no sign of trouble or anything!'

But Jay was certain what it meant. 'Exactly! No sign of *anything*! It's as if they all just vanished in the middle of whatever they were doing. Everything in the house is perfectly normal, except— '

'No one's at home,' Mike interrupted. 'Yeah, freaks you out doesn't it?'

Having made a thorough search of the Baker's house, only to find that the place was deserted, Jay and Mike quickly realised that the mysterious threat Jay had received in the library the other day was no laughing matter. The entire Baker family had either taken a trip by taxi without packing any belongings - at incredibly short notice – and then forgotten to come home, or else, they had been snatched from their house against their consent in such a precise operation that it left no signs of a struggle.

It wasn't really an option, especially after what Jay had witnessed the other day when accosted by that dark stranger.

'They've been taken!' he spat, kicking at the ground as they walked.

'Who by, do you think?' Mike cringed, unwilling above all else to embark upon yet another hair-raising adventure. The first one had been bad enough!

'I don't know,' Jay answered. 'But I'll tell you one thing—'

'What?'

'Something *really* nasty is going on.'

'Let's go to the cops,' Mike suggested.

'Yeah, good idea,' Jay agreed; then he added, grimly, 'Ha! I won't be trying to stop you this time, mate!'

But in the stress of the situation, Mike had forgotten all about that.

Leaving Ellesmere Road apace, Mike and Jay decided to head directly down the High Street towards the Ring Road, which was built in the late eighties so that through-traffic could bypass the town centre. A brand new Police Station had been opened here only last year, beside the roundabout at Charles Cross. This was now the regional headquarters for Thames Valley, having taken over from the station at Bampton, although that building itself was also fairly new. The whole enterprise seemed like a waste of money to some people.

Neither Jay nor Mike said very much as they both hurried down Market Hill, passing the old Town Hall and then the impressive stone frontage of a turn-of-the-century building that housed both the museum and a number of the County Council departments all in one.

In the years before the Ring Road had been built, the enormous volume of cars and lorries driving through this part of Brackthorpe had often brought it to a standstill in rush hour. The black grime from the traffic fumes of those days remained as a witness in many places, around the lower courses of masonry. Jay picked some of it with his finger as they marched by, tense and yet determined.

Approaching the Charles Cross roundabout, Jay and Mike had to take the underpass to get to the other side of the road, which was all dual carriageway now and too busy to cross safely. The large circuit of the roundabout encompassed the ruins of an old church which had been blown up by a stray bomb during the Blitz in the Second World War, and traffic could use one of the four exits: north into the town centre; south into the multi-storey car park; east towards Buckingham and Aylesbury, or west for Bampton and the M40 motorway.

Rising before them by the road side, opposite the Northbound exit, Charles Cross Police Station stretched upwards to five stories. Jay counted them automatically just to be certain. This imposing wall of concrete cladding, steel and glass surveyed the boundary of the traffic island in all directions and beyond from its raised ground-floor level, which was accessed by a flight of broad concrete steps. Disabled access had not yet been installed, much to the embarrassment of the Police Authority.

Jay halted halfway up the steps, making a note of the time - it was half past ten - and gazing up at the tinted glass doors and windows of the foyer. The large sign above the entrance, embossed with blue and silver metallic lettering, announced boldly what the premises were, as if anyone was in any doubt, and Jay wavered as he stood there.

But Mike was at his shoulder now, and he was adamant.

'We've got to go in, mate; look, I know you don't trust them, but— '

'All right!' Jay protested. 'Davie's in trouble, *I know!*'

Steeling himself to do something that, subconsciously, he'd always feared, Jay squared his shoulders and marched up the last few steps heading straight for the double sliding doors of the foyer. Mike followed closely behind.

An expansive public service counter, rather like the ones you find in banks and building societies, greeted them as the doors slid shut. No one else was in the room apart from the Officer manning the desk. Behind him, through a half partition, a busy operations room was working away for the good of the community. Apart from a yucca plant in a large ceramic pot in the corner, the foyer was sparsely decorated. There was a fire exit on their right hand side and a number of easy chairs arranged by the tinted glass walls.

From the ceiling panels, an array of pin-point spot lights sent small pools of illumination over the carpet and showed up the sweat on the Police Officer's forehead - the room was quite warm.

The man was large and broad, with a thinning head of short brown hair and a chunky, protuberant forehead; also, he was possessed of an unforgiving face, Jay felt.

While engaged at his computer console behind the counter, he barely noticed as the two white-faced teenagers entered the room. Mike had his beige leather jacket on, covering a lurid yellow T-shirt. Jay was wearing a faded black top over his old red chequered shirt. They didn't feel like delinquents, but the pristine atmosphere in here along with the Officers neatly creased uniform certainly made them feel that way.

The man looked up briefly as they approached the counter. He completed whatever he'd been doing on the computer and then looked up again to scrutinize them properly.

'And what can I do for you two lads?' he enquired, sounding pretty bored with the duty roster.

'Erm... We've come to r-report a m-missing person,' Jay ventured, gripping the edge of the laminate desk top as he spoke.

'A Missing Person?' the Officer repeated, sounding rather more interested now. He leant towards them slightly, as if to check they were the genuine article.

'Actually, it's a whole family...' Jay explained.

'What?' the man responded.

Mike took over at this juncture. 'Our friend, David Baker from 16 Ellesmere Road. He and his whole family seem to have been - er - abducted, by the looks of it.'

'You don't say?'

'Yeah, the neighbours haven't heard a peep from them for two days now. We went inside their house just an hour ago to check if they were all right, but— '

'Hold on!' the Police Officer ordered. 'One thing at a time, please.' He pulled out an incident report book from a drawer beside him and reached for a pen beside the computer keyboard. This report, it seemed, was worth writing down.

Mike and Jay were in earnest, wishing the man would sympathise with them in their worry, but he maintained a stubbornly formal procedure.

'Right then,' he informed them both. 'Before I fill out a report, I need to know which one of you is making it?'

'Both of us,' Jay replied.

'Fair enough, who are you then, sonny?'

'Jay Romero.'

'Who?' the Officer remarked, pausing with the tip of the pen hovering over his note pad.

'Romero,' Jay repeated, seeing how far the man had got with trying to spell his name. 'R-O-M-E-R-O...Yep, that's it.'

'Address please?'

'Why?'

'For procedure. Nothing to worry about!' the man said, in a bored voice again.

'But our friend's in danger!' Jay argued.

'He'll be out of danger quicker if you answer my questions then, won't he?' the Officer retorted, not far from making mockery. He wiped his brow on a handkerchief and resumed.

'Address?'

'24, Westbury Drive,' Jay answered, capitulating.

'And you, lad?'

'Michael Murkin; I live at 12 Grosvenor Place,' Mike said.

'Righto then. I'll just pop your details on here and then you can make a statement concerning your friend's alleged abduction.' He turned to his console and flicked the mouse to bring it out of standby.

Jay, feeling suspicious all the while, watched intently as the man called up a new display window on the screen. Mike, though, cast his eye over the ceiling panels, having found nothing on the service counter to occupy his attention.

But... perceptibly... about a minute afterwards, the Police Officer drew a sudden sharp intake of breath and a tingle rippled up Jay's neck as he did so. The man stared briefly at his computer, as if it, like Dave's, were about blow itself to smithereens. But it didn't...

'Well I never,' he exclaimed. 'And they just walk right on in here... My shift an' all!'

He turned to face Jay, who now picked up an unearthly delight about the Officer's hard smile. Something was up, and Jay knew it.

'Is there a problem?' he suggested, as Mike returned his attention to the business in hand.

Glancing from one to another, dangerously, the Officer said, 'Would you mind confirming your names for me boys, just for the record.

Bewildered as to what this may mean, Jay replied, 'J-Jay Romero.'

'Of number 24, Westbury Drive. Yes, that's the fellow,' the Officer interrupted.

'Michael Murkin of—'

'12 Grosvenor Place, yes, you're both here... on the warrant. It's only just this minute come down the wire from London. Isn't that strange, just as the pair of you happened to come by?'

Jay's mind began to race. What did it mean, 'on the warrant?' Mike however, did not comprehend the situation quite so fast as his friend.

'What are you talking about?' he demanded, scowling at the fresh pressed uniform behind the desk. The Officer, in response, let his eye peruse his young catch.

'Warrant?' said Jay, looking blankly at him.

'Yes, sir,' the Police Officer replied. 'Awfully sorry lads, but there's a warrant out for your arrest, with immediate effect. I'm afraid we'll have to discuss your missing fr— '

'Arrest?' Mike wailed, nearly leaping off the ground in surprise.

'Fraid so,' the man said, smiling. 'I suggest the two of you take a seat over there and wait a minute. I'll call a colleague round to take care of you!'

'What's going on?' Mike hissed, turning and gazing fearfully at his friend.

Jay stood there, rooted to the ground in shock and anger. He glowered at the imposing, uniformed man behind the counter. The face was implacable, supercilious and hard. Jay knew he would show them no mercy, not allow them to leave, not allow them to give their side of the story until they were firmly apprehended... and then what?

Almost as if he were acting on some kind of ruthless autopilot, the Officer gestured for them to take a seat in the chairs opposite the counter, while he moved over to a trapdoor in the top of the desk.

'What are we going to do?' Mike whispered under his breath. He was staring wide-eyed at Jay, who swayed distinctly on his feet at the thought of their impending doom. They stumbled vaguely towards the soft upholstered chairs, set against the tinted glass wall of the foyer, with the Officer watching them carefully. He buzzed an intercom on the desk top and then raised the trap door, which allowed him access to the entrance area.

Jay's mind was working away furiously. Should he submit to the power of the Establishment? Under normal circumstances, yes, of course, but this was a different matter altogether… and what Powers were really operating behind this man? He appeared to be reacting like a machine! The whole gamut of circumstances began to feel like a terrible, cosmic trap!

'Jay?' Mike whimpered, halting beside a chair.

A momentary pause ensued, and then…

'RUN!' Jay yelled, charging towards the double set of sliding doors. Mike didn't need telling twice. He took off after him.

'Oi!' the Officer yelled, scrambling through the trap door into the foyer. He pressed a concealed button on the work top and, as the two friends skidded to a halt in front of the sliding doors, a red warning light flashed on above the door controller and the sound of a lock engaging itself, clicked…

'He's locked it!' Jay cried, knowing instantly what happened. They were trapped like rats in a cage.

'This way!' Mike yelled, grabbing Jay's shoulder and hauling him off in the other direction, towards the fire exit.

The Officer lunged after them as an alarm bell rang out through the building, and the operations room behind them came to a standstill as a number of uniformed staff gawped over the partition to ascertain the cause of the commotion in the entrance.

In the ensuing scramble, the Officer managed to catch hold of Mike's left arm as he and Jay dived past. Jay tore on ahead, crashing into the emergency bar across the fire exit door. It burst open with a clang. Meanwhile behind him, Mike exerted all his strength and wrenched himself free before the frantic Officer could get a decent hold on him.

The pair of them sprinted out of the building and raced down the concrete steps towards the underpass. Seconds later, the perspiring Officer bundled through the door after them, yelling into a radio set, but they had disappeared into the underpass, running flat out.

More alarms and sirens, including the fire bell which had just been triggered, wailed throughout the entire Police Station. The noise was deafening. Out of nowhere Police cars began converging on the scene - three of them within half a minute.

As Mike and Jay emerged from the echoing tunnel, into the ground floor of the car park, they both caught a glimpse of a patrol car racing around the roundabout towards the Police station, lights flashing and cutting a swathe through the other road users.

The underpass linked all four exits on either side of the road. Jay knew that gave their pursuers eight different possible escape routes to block. For the first few minutes therefore they would have the advantage. But...

'We've got to get out of the town centre,' Jay gasped, grinding to a halt beside a huge square pillar holding up the many decks of the multi-storey car park above them. The low ceiling was barely higher than Mike's head, giving a very claustrophobic feel to the place - especially with the entire Police Force on their tail. But the forest of regularly spaced pillars gave them ample places to take cover behind, and they used them.

Another patrol car came tearing around the far side of Charles Cross as the hunters converged on their prey. Meanwhile oblivious shoppers continued driving slowly into the multi-storey car park, and the three people queuing by the ticket machine nearby barely paid them any heed.

'We've got to keep moving,' Mike whispered pulling Jay out from their hiding place. 'Try and act casually.'

'Yeah right!' Jay panted, adrenalin pumping through his system.

Ignoring one or two suspicious glances from passing ladies with young children in pushchairs, the two friends jogged across the open-plan deck of the car park, weaving in between ranks of vehicles in order to take the most direct route to the far exit. The Police Station became more and more obscured as they moved further in to the complex.

A narrow road behind the building served only for access to the small number of shops in that street and the rear exit of the car park. Jay and Mike bounded into this dead-end road, having jumped the barriers fixed at the exit.

Emerging outside a shop selling traditional Chinese remedies, they were about to make a bid for freedom when yet another Police siren screamed around the corner at the end of the street. Mike pulled his friend towards a telephone box and they both dived for cover. But the strain was beginning to tell and, as the tension mounted, Mike began to freeze. So Jay took charge - they had to know what was going on.

Peering out from around the kiosk, Jay watched, heaving for breath, as a Patrol car pulled up at the junction at the far end of the road.

A Police Officer in the car, wound down his window and stared up and down the street; evidently he was searching for the two runaways. The Patrol was holding up a queue of traffic, it's lights flashing blue shadows everywhere. One or two folk going about their business looked mildly curious at the scene, wondering whom he might be searching for.

There was a private hire cab attempting to make a three-point turn halfway along the street, having delivered a groups of lads to the pub opposite the photographic shop. Meanwhile the Officer's gaze ranged to and fro, scanning the Saturday morning shoppers milling about with their goods.

Finally, after a fruitless two minutes searching and with a growing tailback behind him, the Officer gave up, turned back on to the main road and raced off again.

'All clear,' Jay hissed, noticing that Mike had sunk down against the glass side of the phone box, making as though he'd rather be a death's door than right here, right now.

'C'mon, get up! We've got to go, mate. They'll have the whole place surrounded in five more minutes.' Jay tugged his friend's collar, desperately.

Shaking, Mike raised himself to his feet again, white with panic.

'Hey! I've got an idea,' Jay shouted. 'Follow me.'

Leading the way, he ran quickly over to the middle of the street where the white, private hire cab had just finished turning around before setting off on another job. It was a Ford Mondeo.

Jay banged on the window, still considerably out of breath. The driver, an Asian man, wound down the window and gawped out at him.

'We need a ride,' Jay gasped, indicating himself and Mike, hoping he could get away with this, in fact almost praying that he could.

The driver shook his head faintly and then, with heavy Southend accent, he explained, 'Sorry lads. Can't pick up folk off the street.

Private hire, see - '*Advance Bookings Only.*" He gestured to the unmistakably large lettering on the side of his car door, together with the company phone number.

'Please,' Jay groaned. 'We're in a h-hurry…'

'What for?' the chap replied. 'Convicts on the run from the Cops are ya? Crikey, there's a load of them out today, wonder wassup?'

Jay then faltered but Mike recovered the situation and burst out, 'We're late for a film at Warner Village. It started five minutes ago and we're supposed to be meeting friends, see.'

The man eyed them suspiciously.

'Look, I said I can't pick yer up; it contravenes the Licence. Now, if yer don't mind— '

'Wait!' Mike interrupted. He thrust his hand inside his jacket and pulled out his wallet. The driver watched with interest as Mike then unrolled a bundle of five-pound notes right under his nose.

His expression changed. He leant over and checked his rear view mirror. Jay, beginning to think he might live this down after all, reckoned he could be checking for Hackney Carriages - who'd be very quick to report him. There had been a long-running dispute in the town between the black cabs and the private hire firms.

Then the driver said, furtively, 'All right. Jump in quick.'

Without further ado Jay ran around to the passenger door and climbed in. Mike leapt into the rear seat. The driver, shaking his head in amusement, then indicated and pulled out into the street. They were off.

Thinking desperately all the time, Jay swiftly removed his jacket, hoping to change his appearance.

'Warner Village Cinema, is it?' the man asked, just to make certain.

'Yes, please,' Jay replied, forcibly controlling his breathing.

They turned out on to the main road; at the other side of the car park the imposing Police Station came back into view.

'Gee! The boy's in blue are busy today!' the driver mused. 'There's four of 'em round the Cross now!'

While waiting at the traffic lights on the southern exit of the roundabout, Jay stared over at the developing scene outside the Police headquarters. The Duty Officer was still standing by the Foyer. He was gesticulating to a colleague who was standing next to him on the steps, looking over at the car park. Two Patrol cars had parked up in the side street in front of the building itself and two more were stationed on the hard shoulder of the East and West bound exits. Uniformed Officers were already conducting searches of the surrounding area, but there was no way they could seal off the Ring Road altogether. That would cause a gridlock. Also, judging by the fact the Police had taken to setting out on foot, they did not expect Jay and Mike to be escaping by car.

The lights changed and the queue of vehicles in front of them pulled away. Then, with a thrill of horror, Jay realised that their route around Charles Cross would lead them directly past the Police Station and the officers standing by the entrance, one of whom had seen them up close and even grabbed Mike. He'd recognise them both… straight away…!

The driver of the cab had to stop again, halfway round the roundabout, at another set of lights. He turned on the radio and mentioned nothing about Mike or Jay's awkward behaviour, or teeth-gritting silence.

Jay then glanced into the vanity mirror inside his sun visor. Mike appeared to be attempting to remove his own jacket without attracting the driver's attention - it was halfway down his shoulders. He caught Jay's eye, who was suddenly startled.

'Leave-it-on!' he mouthed furiously into the mirror.

'What?' Mike said, surprised, thinking he'd just come up with an ingenious idea to help prevent them being captured.

'*Your T-shirt is yellow!*' Jay said, throwing all caution to the wind. 'It stands out a mile!'

'Oh!' Mike gulped. 'Yeah… Sorry.'

'Wassat?' the driver asked, as the lights changed to green again, and they continued with the agonising crawl around the roundabout. Surely they were going to be spotted, Jay thought to himself. Surely?

'Oh… I was - er - I was just telling my mate. His shirt's yellow. It's a trash colour really *and sticks out a mile*!'

'S'pose so.'

But Mike had long since got the message, and he began pulling his jacket back on properly again.

The situation then moved from mere agonising to brain-numbing. Just seconds later, the cab driver was forced to pull up yet again behind a red Rover 100 whose driver had stopped rather too keenly at the last set of traffic lights before the Eastbound exit road. If only she'd put her foot down, they could have squeezed through too, Jay fretted.

As the cab drew to a rumbling halt, they were all but twenty nail-biting yards away from the very steps where Mike and Jay had fled minutes earlier.

The two Officers had been joined by another colleague by this time. Unfortunately the Duty Officer who'd so nearly apprehended them was still there detailing what had happened.

Jay held his breath and kept his hand ready on the door handle, in case he had to get out of the car in a hurry. None of the Police were looking in his direction, but undoubtedly, inevitably, one of them would turn around soon enough. They had to? They must do?

Jay counted the seconds. He could hear Mike's rasping breath behind him above the idling car engine. They were done for surely? Jay fingered the door handle, getting ready to wrench it open in one last, desperate bid for freedom. And still the big, broad Officer with his protuberant forehead was gesticulating to his colleagues, trying to explain how he'd managed to allow two lads to escape his clutches when, of all things, they'd only just presented themselves at the Station. Jay thought he detected a measure of incredulity about the Officer's fellows.

The seconds crept past. It was pure torture; even more so because the oblivious cab driver kept on making reference to the unusual numbers of Police on duty, wondering aloud if perhaps there were Al-Qaeda suspects in the neighbourhood. Jay tried so hard not to look at what was going on outside the window he felt his heart miss a beat.

As he reached the point where he thought that the stress would literally kill him, something happened, something that renewed his will to live. Never, in his whole life, had he been so glad to see one…

…A dirty, white transit van pulled up beside them on the inside lane and completely blocked the cab from the Officers' view.

Sweating profusely, Jay grinned bleakly into the vanity mirror.

Behind him Mike pointed fervently up to the ceiling, but Jay did not get his meaning.

Finally, the lights changed once again and they pulled off the roundabout heading for the outskirts of town and the Warner Village cinema. They'd escaped - for the time being.

Jay wound down the passenger window, cooling his flushed face in the breeze and listening to the diminishing sirens in the distance. At least I'm still alive, he thought to himself.

Chapter 8

Suits, Sunglasses and Guns

Mike stuffed two five-pound notes into the cab driver's outstretched hand through the open window. With an indistinct grunt, he pulled out of the drop-off bay and drove away across the tarmac expanse of the Barbican Leisure Park.

A new, purpose built site; the Leisure Park encompassed not only a multiplex cinema, but also two night clubs, a Mac Donald's, a Pizza Hut, a gym and a café-come-bowling alley. The derelict and run down precinct around the former Thistle Park Road had thus been transformed into one of the prime out of town leisure venues in the region. They'd even changed the name of the street to prove the point - from *Thistle Park Road* to *Barbican Approach*. With enough parking space for a thousand cars, the Warner Village was an instant hit with the public and Saturday mornings were the peak period.

Jay hated the commercialisation of the whole place. On one occasion, after going through a door he should not have done by mistake, he'd come across a memorandum pinned to the staff notice board which sealed his opinion for evermore. Amongst the figures, staff league tables and fire escape procedures, he had read the following commendation:-

This week's star prize goes to Jo Bloggs - the name escaped him - *for selling the highest number of extra large portions of popcorn, a whopping 1158 units. Remember team, ALWAYS ask the customer if they want to go EXTRA-LARGE! Cheers.*

While his convictions about the place were set in stone, he had to admit, however, that this cinema was still the best venue in town to watch films. It boasted huge screens, fantastic surround sound, wide seats... everything.

Today, though, nothing could be further from his mind as he walked with Mike towards the convex glass entrance, sporting glossy posters advertising which films were showing and some upcoming features. Overhead a rounded canopy stretched across the foyer area, providing cover for the customers on wet days. It was supported by industrial style, white scaffolding and large bill boards were suspended from its outer edge. A white mast with the famous 'WB' logo reached high above the entire complex which was lit with floodlights at night.

Jay and Mike joined a trail of cinema goers thronging the glass doors of the entrance. Inside, the busy ticket kiosk was doing a roaring trade, mainly dealing with parents and their school-aged children who were all enjoying their holidays. This nerve-racked pair of teens though, had very little to enjoy so far as the summer break was concerned. Indeed, it was more a nightmare for them.

'What shall we do, mate?' Mike muttered, looking in all directions as they progressed slowly through the foyer moving nearer to the kiosk. There were no signs of law enforcement anywhere obvious - unless a group of Policemen were hiding behind a large, cardboard standee of Sirius Black who was being auctioned off for Children in Need.

'Get inside and watch a couple of movies; lay low for a while,' Jay answered, trying to exude a casual attitude. He shrugged and added, 'At least it'll give us a few hours to think - for what it's worth.'

'How come they've put out a warrant for us?' Mike whispered. 'We haven't done a thing... except leave litter in Westbury Park, maybe...'

'There's something dark going on,' Jay replied, lowering his voice, not wanting his fellow cinema goers to catch what they were discussing. 'How nice it must be to have no worries,' he added as an afterthought, watching the children in front of them chattering excitedly in anticipation of a great movie.

'OK then, *why us?*' Mike urged.

'Don't worry, mate, it's not really *you* they're interested in. Yep, I've got that clay-pigeon feeling again. Pity really. Oh...? *What film?*'

The assistant had caught him off guard as he'd glanced at his friend and rolled his eyes to the ceiling. Turning back to the kiosk, Jay hurriedly read through the film schedule. The details were moving over the screen in flashing red dots.

'*Erm -,*'

'Two tickets for *Fahrenheit 9/11*,' Mike interjected. 'I've always wanted to see what Mike Moore's got to say about Bush's dubious war on terror,' he added quietly in Jay's ear.

'Y-Yeah, OK then, 'Jay stuttered. 'Two tickets please. I don't suppose I could use a Ten Film Special Deal I've got lying at home on my bookshelf could I?'

The woman's voice came over the loud speaker; it was altered by the microphone like that of a bank cashier's.

'I'm sorry,' she smiled.

'Why doesn't that surprise me?' Jay mumbled under his breath, pulling out his wallet.

Mike prodded him in the back, anxiously. 'C'mon mate. We're holding up the queue!'

Much of the next hour and a half, the two friends made themselves incredibly unpopular, but not with the Authorities, with the people watching the film. As they sat in the back row of screen number seven trying to work out how to cope with this strange new ordeal they were facing and plotting ways to get back home without being spotted by the Police, other viewers became irritated at their constant talking.

In the end, they only ceased from their fervent dialogue when a member of staff came over to them and warned them that they would have to leave the premises if they didn't keep quiet.

After *Fahrenheit 9/11,* the pair watched a special feature: a cinema presentation of the newly extended version of *Return of the King.* Jay had been keen to see this ever since making his eyes go square through watching the original film over and over again. With an extra hour of bonus footage, it was now more than four hours long.

By the time Mike and Jay emerged from the doors of screen number four, heading straight for the amenities, it was early evening time. After they left the Gents - feeling very relieved - they decided to go for a burger, feeling reasonably hopeful that the search for them would have died down for the day. Jay understood the philosophy of 'hidden in plain view' and had ventured to explain it.

It was half past six, and Mike was slurping up the last remnants of his milkshake; a mixture of banana and vanilla. Their table in MacDonald's was next to the window so they keep could their eyes peeled in case any Police cars appeared in the car park opposite.

While his colleague concentrated hard on sucking up every last droplet of his drink through the straw. Jay let his attention drift over to the people clustering around outside the restaurant. A pair of young boys, perhaps about six years of age, were pretending to shoot each other dead with imaginary guns while their mother talked to her friend.

Jay watched them in contemplation, feeling isolated from the bustle in the room around him and not hearing his friend's continuing drinking noises.

One of the pair flung himself down on his knees and imitated keeling over into the dust - until his mother dragged him up again and told him to stop messing about. Promptly, the imaginary finger guns were put away for the day and the duel was over.

A strange feeling came upon him whilst he watched. *Do they really know what they're re-enacting?* he wondered. *Do they know what death means...? Do I know what death means...?*

The children were outside and a thick pane of safety glass was standing between them and Jay. On the outside were two youngsters who did not understand what death meant, but were not afraid of dying - at least in pretence. On the inside were the two teens who also did not understand what death meant, but were afraid of dying - in reality. It was that serious.

Jay felt the cold glass surface with his knuckle; it was the transparent division between himself and the nearest child. Desperately... for that one short moment, he just wished he could change places. *Then again*, he thought, *I'd just love to change places with almost anyone right now.*

'Half past six,' Mike informed him, glancing up from his wristwatch.

'What?' he answered, not comprehending.

'It's half past six,' Mike repeated. 'Should we try to get home? We're going to have to tell our folks. It might be a mistake, mate, but perhaps they'll be able to help?'

'I'm not sure how,' Jay muttered, in contrast.

Mike winced. 'You're not making me feel any better, mate,' he complained. But Jay then continued, saying, 'Well, if your dad hears the

Cops are after you, it might make him change his feelings towards you, I suppose, and that can't be— '

'Damn it, Jay! Any more nails you've got for my coffin?'

Jay swallowed uncomfortably. Mike was distraught.

'Er, yeah, I mean… *No*, sorry, I was only thinking—'

'Forget it. Let's go,' Mike said, forlornly. He pulled his jacket from the back of the chair and got up. Jay followed and they left the restaurant after checking the coast was clear.

In order to be discreet, they chose to walk back to the town centre via the Ring Road. It was a circuitous route but kept them away from the more populous areas of Brackthorpe.

The evening sun kept them warm as they trekked around the perimeter of the dual carriageway passing the industrial estate on the south side of the bypass. It was not so busy now that the rush hour was over.

As they drew near to the Bretonside Bus Station, which served as an important terminal for the region's bus routes, Mike suddenly decided he ought to ring home and mentioned it to Jay.

The Bus Station lay in a huge recessed area below the flyover, just off the Eastbound exit of Charles Cross roundabout. It was basically a large section of concrete hard-standing, set on a lower foundation level than the roundabout itself, and with the flyover acting as a viaduct it gave one the impression of being underground.

The underpass serviced the bus station at either end, where a flight of stone steps rose up to pavement level of the road above. Often frequented by rough sleepers who needed shelter from the elements, and little more than an expanse of composite and brick, the bus station had been earmarked for an upgrade and refurbishment many times over the years. Thus far, however, the Council had not been able to identify sufficient funds for the improvement work.

'There are phone booths here in Bretonside,' Jay suggested, as they walked into the outer concourse of the bus station. A National Express coach was waiting in one of the bays with its engine chugging and black smoke bubbling from its exhaust. It was the 500 Service bound for London, stopping off at Reading; the journey took about five hours. The fumes carried over to the two friends as they walked past. A queue of passengers was lining up beside the coach, while a uniformed driver heaved their cases and bags into one of the side-loading compartments.

Mike couldn't help but feel jittery about going home this evening. Not only had he his own domestic troubles to contend with, now the Bakers' had apparently been kidnapped as well... and what on earth was happening with the Police? He had no idea how to broach this subject with his parents, but he wanted to speak to them anyway and to check if they were OK.

Attracting no attention whatsoever, the pair made their way over to a row of three telephone boxes in the middle of the station underneath the viaduct. Traffic rumbled past high overhead sending vibrations through the columns holding up the structure. There were one or two graffiti tags visible around the walls where bored kids had wanted to leave their mark, and some of the light tubes suspended below the ceiling were on the blink. A sense of dilapidation was palpable.

Mike stepped into the kiosk. Opening his wallet, he began shaking out the last of his change into his hand. Jay waited outside, keeping a lookout as he dialled home. No patrol cars came by and the two friends were not disturbed. Jay folded his arms and waited.

By the time the majority of the passengers had stowed their luggage on board the London-bound coach, five minutes later, Mike emerged from the phone booth. He was pale and shaking.

'No reply,' he mouthed. 'I tried loads of times... Dad's mobile's off too - no response!'

Jay cringed all over and turned away, scanning the limits of the concrete deck of the bus station. All seemed quiet, maybe it too quiet?

'Help?' Mike wailed, seriously troubled. 'Jay, I can't deal with this, mate!'

Jay turned back and saw that Mike was close to tears. He knew how he felt, but Mike seemed to be even less cut out for life threatening dilemmas than he himself. Jay racked his brain desperately and, very shortly afterwards, he realised their only available option.

'We need to get out of town,' he whispered. 'Somewhere... anywhere; we have to find a place to hide until we can work out what we're going to do. Remember, we've been in danger before. We just need time to come up with something.'

'There's nothing we can do!' Mike argued, hysterically. 'Not if the cops are after us. *Hell knows why?*'

'They'll be searching for us here in Brackthorpe, mate, so we have to go some place else,' Jay insisted, though he, too, felt awfully afraid.

'What about my folks?' Mike pleaded.

'The best thing you can do for them, mate, is to keep you alive. Do you want to stay alive - and free?'

'Course!' Mike snorted. 'But -' He cast his gaze wildly around the bus station, hoping to find deliverance from somewhere amongst its poorly lit recesses and grimy parking bays, but none was forthcoming.

A series of deep clunks rung in his ears and with that an idea suddenly hit Jay. He turned around to see that the bus driver had just slammed shut the side-loading doors of the coach and looked to be about to set off.

'When are you off, driver?' Jay called, his shout ringing over the platform.

The man in his blue uniform had been rolling himself another cigarette as he locked the luggage compartments - he would have to go without one for the next five hours.

'Ten minutes!' he yelled across the station in reply.

Jay turned back to his quivering friend; Mike still looked terrified.

'Have you got any cash left? We can buy standby tickets from the driver. This bus is going to London and I think it stops at Reading en-route.'

'What? No, I used it all in Warner Village. Are you serious?' Mike baulked.

'Yeah, I am!' Jay urged him. 'Listen, I'll go and use a cash machine. They've got one next to the booking office. Then we can hop off to London for a while. I know someone who lives in Kensington.'

'Flipping heck!' Mike exclaimed, shaking his head.

'Five minutes!' came the driver's voice from behind Jay's back. He threw the cigarette butt into the gutter at the edge of the loading bay and climbed into the coach.

'*Quick!*' Jay pleaded.

'OK!' Mike gasped. 'Give me a second, I need to use the toilets.'

He jogged away towards the far side of the station concourse and Jay turned and hurried off to use one of the cash points mounted in the wall beside the ticket office. The staff were just shutting up shop for the day as he arrived. It was seven o'clock.

With a wallet filled with his entire bank balance, Jay returned to the platform opposite the bus bays and waited. Mike seemed to be taking rather longer than he'd anticipated, and the bus driver blasted the horn impatiently.

Three minutes later, Jay gave up. He waved the driver on and made his way over to the amenity block. The National Express coach rumbled away across the hard standing heading for the exit gate. By the time he got within a stone's throw of the Gents, the door creaked open - at last!

'Talk about taking your time!' he muttered aloud. 'We've missed it.'

He stopped and made another quick reconnoitre of the bus station and surrounds. Then he faced back to the toilets just as Mike emerged.

Except that it wasn't Mike...

A figure in a plain, grey suit came out. Peculiarly, for it was evening time, he was wearing dark sun-glasses. Jay would have thought him ridiculous but then something happened which caused his train of thought to take a different course completely.

Two more figures exited the toilets: men in identical, grey flannel suits... *Also wearing sun-glasses...* Jay spoke to himself, teeth gritted.

The symbolic omen of this situation might have been lost on some, but Jay was a Sci-Fi fan and as the three silent figures lined up against him, staring him in the face, he knew at once that his friend would not be coming out of that door.

The very briefest of stand-offs ensued - as if the reel of the Film of Life had jammed for a moment in the projector - and time stood still for a couple of seconds. Then...

'Yep... OK, Jay, RUN!'

He turned tail and raced away from the men in grey suits at top speed. With a loud shout, all three of them immediately set off after him in pursuit.

Jay hurtled over the concourse; concrete pillars flashed past him. He dodged between them as he sprinted, with all his might, towards the staircase at the other end of the bus station. The underpass would lead him up and out into the street. He may be able to lose his adversaries there; it was his only chance.

Jay glanced at an overhead mirror above the ticket office. The three chasing figures in grey were closing in. One of them, the figure in the lead, plunged his right hand inside his suit and, seconds later, drew it out. Jay registered a short black barrel protruding from the man's fingers. He had a gun...

Hitting the lowest step at full tilt, Jay almost tripped over and only narrowly avoided going head over heels. Instead, with his breath tearing at his throat, he lunged up the steps three at a time and emerged out into the evening sunshine at street level.

The road was fairly busy with traffic as he came face to face with the massive concrete form of the multi-storey car park, lying off the Southbound exit. Meanwhile angry shouts echoed up the staircase - hardly any distance behind his own frantic steps.

He rounded the corner by the steel railings and dived out into the busy stream of cars. Immediately horns blasted and brakes squealed. Jay dodged in between swerving cars and vans. A bright white sports car screeched to a halt opposite him on the other carriageway. More horns sounded on that side of the road too. Jay scrambled over the central reservation as a Taxi driver swore out at him from somewhere nearby - he hardly noticed where the voice came from.

All his attention focussed on the footsteps of those suited men, who had now reached the last few steps of the underpass and would appear in moments.

Gasping for breath Jay lunged out into the opposite carriageway, causing more vehicles to hit their brakes. A hold up was already in progress in this lane, due to the white sports car - a Porsche 924 - blocking all the traffic behind it, sitting there with its engine growling. Jay noticed the driver's window had wound down.

One more step and *bang!* He ran directly into a burning red light - a laser beam - and everything around him was bathed in crimson. It was a targeting sight for a gun... and Jay saw what gun.

Staggering on his feet, he came to a jittery halt in the middle of the chaotic traffic. Jay found himself looking down the barrel of a large silver automatic, glinting at him from inside the car. A man, a man dressed all in white, was sitting in the driver's seat of the Porsche. He had an automatic pistol trained right at him. The pinpoint red light blazed from the dark interior of the car.

The laser beam marked a spot right between Jay's eyes. Everything moving around him remained a hazy red mist. The man behind the wheel of the sports car had got him - Jay knew it, and he sagged where he stood.

So this was it; it was all over.

'They got me!' he said blankly, as though apologising for some failure of his.

He stood there staring at the white-clad man expecting to be shot from the front or behind or, possibly, just arrested and detained without trial.

'Do you want to stay alive?' came a stern voice from the man in the white car.

'Yes,' Jay squeaked.

'Then get DOWN!' the man bellowed at him, not more than ten yards away.

Jay dropped to his knees at once, oblivious to the cars around him, as two ear-splitting shots rang out above his head. The leading pursuer in the grey suit - whose own gun had been levelled at Jay - caught both rounds in the chest. He sprawled, face forwards, on to the pavement.

The other pair of suits instantly drew their own weapons. A split second later, the second grey figure caught a bullet in the head and crashed sideways into the railings. His own shot blasted a hole in the tarmac. By this point people began screaming and running in all directions.

The man in the sports car fired again, but the third suited figure had dived back into the underpass and the round missed, blowing a fragment out of the stone pillar as he disappeared down the steps in flight.

Jay looked around; he saw the red dot hovering by the entrance to the underpass. Scrambling footfalls were echoing around the underpass and the public were scattering in panic. It was mayhem.

Some drivers had abandoned their vehicles altogether and simply taken flight. Others were cowering below their dashboards. One passer-by, hiding behind a steel waste bin further up the pavement, was making a frantic call on his mobile. There was noise coming from all directions.

'*Get out of it, kid,*' someone cried from the floor of his car, where he'd taken refuge. 'He'll do you in!' He waved at Jay vigorously to take cover.

'I don't think so,' Jay called, facing back to the man in the white car. He had grey hair, and an intense face. Who on earth was he?

In answer to his question, the man beckoned Jay towards him. Jay staggered to his feet again and picked his way through the mêlée all around him in the carriageway. He approached the sports car, staring at the old man behind the wheel. The large, silvery gun continued to guard Jay's back in case the last agent should make another attempt to get him.

'W-Whose side are you on?' Jay demanded, as a new sound echoed through the air. The Police Headquarters, in full view of the altercation, had now sprung into action. Patrol car sirens were blaring down the road once again.

The man smiled at him gravely.

'Yours,' he said, simply. 'Now get in.'

He gestured to the passenger seat and Jay, reckoning that he had no other option and that he had to trust this man who, after all, had just saved his life, nodded in agreement. Ignoring hysterical objections from numerous frightened motorists and passers-by, Jay ran around the front of the car and opened the passenger's side door. No sooner had he landed in the low-slung seat, than the old man dropped the weapon into his door well, and floored the accelerator.

The car swerved deftly between the abandoned vehicles and raced up the bus lane on the inside of the carriageway. Loud cracks and sparks suddenly rattled against the rear windscreen. On an impulse, Jay turned in his seat and gazed out the back.

The figure in the grey suit had re-emerged from the underpass and was firing shots at them as they drove away. The bullets pounded into the rear screen but - unbelievably - did not break through. Nonetheless Jay winced as each round clattered and sparked against the car.

'Nothing to fear,' the man reassured him. 'It's polycarbonate.'

They quickly left the scene of pandemonium far behind them, the confusion of noise and the blur traffic lights.

Chapter 9

Counter, Counter-Intelligence

Bracing himself in the plush fabric seat of the car, as the driver took a series of corners at unfeasibly high speed, Jay gawped at the unknown stranger who'd come to his aid.

There was little doubt about it; he had to be at least sixty years of age, Jay reckoned, with his silvery-grey hair and lined face. They testified to a minimum of six decades at the least. But it hardly made sense, Jay thought, not in the light of his deft skill - like that of a rally driver in the prime of his career. Jay winced as the Porsche slipped through a narrow gap between the pavement and a lorry turning right at the lights on Westbury Road.

Then there was that crack-shot marksmanship. He looked past the old man's seat and saw the butt of the gun poking out of the driver's side door well. Jay thought he knew what it was; he'd seen the same weapon once before in a film - a magnum 45 with long slide and laser sight. He did not know much about guns, but he appreciated the laser mounted on top of the barrel. It had all but dazzled him.

At that moment Jay suddenly realised they were heading back to his own house, but he wasn't happy; he wanted some answers first.

'HOLD IT!' he shouted, glaring at the old man. 'Pull over, please, I want to talk!'

The driver nodded and, obligingly, he pulled over to the nearside kerb and the car screeched to a dead halt. They were parked several houses down from number twenty four, and Jay did not want to get any closer to home until he'd got some answers.

Feeling as though he could have spent the last five minutes on a roller coaster, no, the whole day had been the same - a virtual death ride, but without the funfair - Jay demanded, 'Who are you? What do you want with me? Who are they? And what do they want with me?'

The Porsche's high performance engine continued to growl under the sleek white hood, and the old man in his luminous white suit and trousers turned to his frightened young passenger. His lined features were so *clearly* aged but also somehow radiant. Jay could not resolve the warmth he felt for this individual and the act of killing he'd just witnessed in his head; at least, he didn't manage it in those few seconds before the man spoke to him.

'Jay, I have been assigned to protect you.'

'Protect me?'

'Time is short. I will explain things as we drive— '

'Where?' he butted in. 'Who said I'm going *anywhere?*'

'You did, friend, at the bus station – remember? You said you wanted to escape to London with your friend Michael.'

Jay opened his mouth to respond but, abruptly, he stalled. *How...?* How did this old fellow know about that? Briefly, he was silenced. After a short time, however, his concern for his pal overwhelmed him and so he ventured, 'Where *is* Mikey? Have they got him?'

'Yes, they have,' the man replied candidly.

Jay was fell silent again. He stared at the dark brown fascia panel in front of his seat, examining its moulding and the profile of its curves, not wanting to respond for a time. The reality of the situation was beginning to sink in now - somebody really was after him.

'You need to gather your belongings quickly, and then I must take you away from Brackthorpe, away from Northamptonshire too.'

'Why?' Jay asked, feebly, finding no dust anywhere inside the glove compartment; the car was spotless.

'The Enemy's forces are mustering in this region. This location is no longer safe for you,' the man informed him.

'Who were they, the men in grey suits?' Jay asked.

'Secret Service personnel,' the man replied disdainfully. 'About as useful as a blunderbuss in the hand of a drunken man. They are nothing to fear, Jay.'

'But... you *killed* them?' Jay gasped. He shivered at the memory of it, though it had all been over so fast.

'Yes; their appointed time had come. Do not worry. *Forget* them; I have!'

'But... would they have actually shot me?'

'More than likely,' the man confirmed.

'Well, thanks for saving my life anyway - er - who are you?'

The man reached over swiftly and offered Jay a handshake. Jay obliged, but with reservations in his heart. This chap had just shot two people and would have killed the third as well, it seemed. Was it wise to befriend someone like that?

'My name is Raphael,' he said. 'It is a privilege to meet you in person, Jay.'

'T-Thanks,' Jay stuttered, shaking the surprisingly firm hand. There were still many many questions on his mind though, which weren't going to go away just because he'd shaken hands.

'My folks,' he asked. 'What shall I tell them? You see, I know enough about temporal mechanics to know that I mustn't—'

He stopped short as the old man's face fell suddenly grave. Jay's heart sank horribly. He knew what his expression meant and he felt sick about it. *Dave and his family... Mike... and now...* 'My family too?' he added, voicing his thoughts out loud.

Raphael nodded to affirm his fears and Jay felt utterly winded. Although it seemed to have been inevitable - given the preceding events - it was nonetheless a terrible shock to his system.

'*No?*'

'I'm afraid so; they have been taken, along with the Murkin's and the Baker household also,' the man explained.

'W-What are they after,' Jay stammered, gazing helplessly at his white-suited saviour. The man Raphael, however, was not the least phased by the morbid circumstances surrounding their meeting. Indeed, he gave the impression that he was working to some long foreseen and well organised plan.

Untroubled, he said, 'We cannot do anything for them now, Jay, but —'

'Why not? Where are they?' Jay pleaded.

'Listen to me,' Raphael assured him. 'If we succeed, they will be all right again; I promise.'

'Succeed in what?'

'Our mission together.'

'What mission?' Jay protested, quite un-reassured and dreadfully afraid of what might be happening at that very moment to his family and friends. 'I've already saved the future once.'

'I know. Now I shall take you home to collect your belongings - we must move speedily. I can explain more to you on the way.'

'On the way *where?*'

But the man Raphael had already pulled out into the road again and set off.

A hundred yards or so afterwards, they swerved to a halt outside Jay's own house. Gazing forlornly out of the car window, he saw few signs of life and, as with Dave's house, so there appeared to be no sign of a disturbance.

Ten minutes later, Jay came hurrying out of his front door with a large holdall stuffed with as many clothes and other personal effects as he could squeeze into it. He'd decided on an impulse to grab a load of camping equipment, too, which he'd already stowed in the boot of the Porsche. His parents had kindly bought him a new tent, as the one he and Mike had used on their first outing had got burnt to cinders in the storm.

Finally, he locked the front door to his deserted house, praying he'd be able to return one day when ominous Powers had stopped trying to ruin his life and, with the night vision binoculars swinging around his neck, he climbed into the car.

No sooner had he fastened his seat belt than he heard a distant wailing of Patrol car sirens. The Police were obviously heading for Westbury Drive. Having been unable to find him all day, they must have assumed he would inevitably go home at some point - needing food and shelter.

In contrast to the horror he'd felt upon realising that his family had been abducted, a strange new hope began welling up inside him. *Ha* - he thought, savagely - *they don't know I've got some kind of counter-agent on my side with a sports car at his disposal, and what a car...Whoa!*

'Exactly!' said Raphael, apparently reading his mind.

Jay stared bemusedly at the old man, lost for words yet again, and the car tore away down the street at a blistering pace leaving a trail of rubber on the tarmac.

After a considerable time on the road, Jay began to wonder if there wasn't something unusual about this white Porsche. Wherever it was driven, it never seemed to get held up, except for perhaps the briefest moment. Not only that; not a single other pedestrian or motorist paid them the slightest bit of notice, anywhere they went. A pristine example of an obsolete 924, in brilliant white, ought to fetch a few appreciative glances from members of the public - but this one didn't. In fact, people behaved almost as if it wasn't really on the road at all, as if they couldn't actually see it.

And what about the driver? Raphael had begun telling Jay all kinds of things as they headed north on the M1 motorway. His words had been captivating, yet also somehow elusive. Jay recalled some of their conversation and went over it again in his mind while the darkening countryside flashed past his window and the night drew in.

'So, who are you then?'

'I am their worst nightmare come true. I know all about them. I know all of their ways. There is nothing they can do that I won't be warned about.'

'Are you a freelance operator? An Agent who got disillusioned with the system and went self-employed? I've heard about rogue agents who become a law unto themselves. Now your old spy-masters are coming after me you've decided to interfere a bit?' He'd postulated at this point, braving a wild guess.

'None of the weapons they use can hurt me,' the old man had added, smiling, but not answering Jay's question directly - or even indirectly.

'Why do you use a gun?' Jay asked, mulling over this last thought and hoping for something more forthcoming. 'You said that their weapons can't hurt you; so why do you need a gun?'

'Ah, well, I usually use a sword, Jay—'

'A sword?'

'Yes, but who says we can't move with the times, eh?'

'Er... quite,' Jay agreed, having no idea what the man meant by this odd statement.

'My apologies for answering you in riddles, my friend, but it is not wise for you to know too much at this stage. After all, knowledge can be —'

'Dangerous! Yes, I know that much already,' Jay confirmed. At last, he'd understood something of what his chaperone was saying.

'In answer to your question then; you know that your Government deploys counter intelligence agents in an effort to catch the foreign spies who come into the country, Jay?'

'Yep,' he replied, utterly convinced about that.

'Just regard me, then, as a *counter* counter-agent for the time being. As I said before, I have been sent to protect you, to keep you from the clumsy hands of those incompetents, in the first instance, and someone will also need to keep you safe from the, ah, more deadly enemies... I shall accompany you therefore.'

'What?' Jay gasped. 'You mean, more dangerous than Government hit men who are prepared to draw their guns on an unarmed teenager?'

'Oh yes,' the man answered, chillingly, 'far more dangerous!'

'You're a freelance agent,' Jay repeated, scowling at him in frustration, 'I just know it.' He grinned sardonically and added, 'You've got a gripe against the system and now you're working against them, aren't you?'

The man Raphael did not answer this time, and so he took it to mean, 'yes.' But it wasn't a happy thought. Although he'd been in the situation before of seemingly having the world on his shoulders, of having his family absent and in grave danger, and of being faced with all manner of things which he couldn't nearly explain, this time it all felt much *much* darker.

The countryside disappeared into the darkness and as the endless stream of motorway lights and blue signs passed by his window, a tangible, engulfing fear gripped his chest as he sat there. Like the crushing feeling of a heart attack - except that it wasn't; it made it difficult for him to breathe. This oppressive atmosphere seemed to have become a regular if depressing occurrence. The white sports car cosseted him in a frail shell, while racing through this universe of gloom, and the only apparent source of warmth and comfort emanated from the old man beside him in the driving seat.

That was the confusing part. Jay stared at the gleaming cuffs of the arm holding the steering wheel. Why should being in the presence of this elderly stranger make him feel better? Perhaps it was because he'd saved his life?

Jay stole a glance at the speedometer and smirked defiantly, refusing to give in to the panic that would willingly overtake him. That was just ridiculous he told himself; they had to be doing more than *that!*

He'd long since lost track of where they were as Raphael had turned off the motorway an hour before. The white car was now plunging into the heart of some rural countryside. Jay reckoned they'd done about two hundred miles, travelling mainly Northwest.

It was late in the evening as they rumbled along a narrow country lane and there were no signs of habitation, distant lights or other cars anywhere to be seen. The narrow road ahead was hemmed in on either side by earth-bound stone walls covered with vegetation. Had he been sitting in a tractor he might have been able to see over the top into the fields beyond, but not in the Porsche - his view was severely restricted.

Whilst the car's headlamps were extremely powerful, Jay had the impression of burrowing down a long, dark tunnel, like a fox escaping from a pack of hounds.

Then, all of a sudden, the steeply rising banks on the sides of the lane fell away and the grounds of what appeared to be a smallholding came into view. The car swept around in a broad arc as the road widened and Jay gazed curiously through a line of willow trees towards the building. Shortly afterwards Raphael pulled up outside it next to a rotten picket fence.

Through the trees, Jay saw flaking, lime-mortared walls; it was an old stone cottage. Raphael turned off the engine and killed the lights. All went abruptly dark, and Jay's eyes took several minutes to adjust to the moonlight.

*

In the same bright moonlight, somewhere over the Scottish borders, the pleasant evening breeze blew through the fields outside the ancient town of Alnwick. This far North in summer time, the night sky never gets truly dark. Even in the first silent hours of the new day, when midnight has only just passed, a pale glow fills all the northern horizon.

Wearing his rough shirt, trousers and boots, and needing only a pipe for warmth, the old man let his dog off the leash for a run across his beloved fields. The gardener, Owen McIntyre, often found solace in the open country under the stars. He worked in the grounds of Whitchester House, which was now converted into a church-run college. He didn't agree with everything they taught up there, although he recognised that they were a decent enough sort.

Ahead of him the grassy meadow sloped down towards a broad stream, and his dog had already reached it as the man climbed the style and set off across the footpath.

While taking in a fragrant mouthful of tobacco and pondering the events of the last working week at Whitchester, he happened to look upwards. The heavens were quiet as usual, though on more than one occasion in the past he'd seen the faint dot of a satellite race across the background stars.

Then -

A streak of purple lightning flashed over the horizon, focussed on a point high above his head in the still, cool atmosphere. He nearly choked on his pipe and coughed and spluttered in surprise. *Lightning on a clear, dry night like this...* he thought, astonished... *this is midsummer?*

The shimmering, crackling blaze lingered in the sky for several moments, seemingly aimed a patch of nothing but thin air. Watching it, both transfixed and bewildered, the man then witnessed the reaction of the beam: a blinding white burst of energy - similar to that of a nuclear explosion - suddenly illuminated the countryside like daylight. The deafening crash of a thunder clap followed and he sank to his knees in fear. The blaze above then died away as the shock waves reverberated through the surrounding hills.

As the scene was pitched into darkness again and his dog yelped from beside the brook, the man staggered upright and regained his footing.

Although it wasn't immediately apparent to him, the darkness indeed remained permanent for Owen this night. He'd been unfortunate enough to be looking in the wrong direction at the wrong time... He'd just been permanently blinded!

*

'This is a safe haven my friend,' Raphael informed him as they stepped out of the car. Jay shut the passenger door quietly and then paused and looked around him while the old man hauled his bag out of the boot and locked it.

All that Jay could see through the darkness of the early hours was that there were fields beyond the hedge on the other side of the road. The lane continued on past the clearing, where it narrowed again and disappeared into the night after another hundred yards. The two of them stood a short distance from the lane in the clearing, off which the ramshackle cottage stood amidst some overgrown land. The picket fence was clearly the boundary and the grounds, thick with impenetrable shrubs and undergrowth, bore no signs of having been tended for a number of years.

He could tell little of the detail of the house, but he saw that here, in the heart of the countryside away from the glare of the city, the stars shone more brightly in the canopy above them. Jay enjoyed a spot of stargazing now and then, but in the town centre there was always far too much light pollution to see things properly. Yet there was no garish orange glow out here, and he raised his eyes to see that the dark outline of this humble abode was silhouetted against a backdrop of brilliant and sparkling jewels. The hazy spread of the Milky Way stretched from one horizon to the other and, unlike the other evening in Westbury Park, everything seemed to be in order tonight.

'Shall we venture inside?' Raphael said calmly a few minutes later, as he approached Jay with his holdall slung over his shoulder. Plainly, he was not the sort of fellow who was worried what the leather straps of a heavy bag could do to an immaculate white suit - unlike Jay's mother, who had always pestered him not to sling his school bag over the shoulder of his blazer.

'Place looks deserted,' Jay remarked, slightly unimpressed by the venue.

'It is,' Raphael confirmed. 'Some squatters made it their home a few

113

months back but they've left now. The place is free and it's yours.'

'Mine?' Jay questioned, as his companion gestured him to follow though the gate and up the path. 'How can it be mine; I don't own any land or property?'

'If something is given to you, Jay, it is yours. Now, come on in.'

Jay was flummoxed by this, but he followed obediently as the old man unfastened the heavy timber door and pushed it open, dislodging numerous cobwebs and causing a loud squeak of protest from some very rusty hinges.

They stepped over the threshold into a pitch-dark void. Unwilling to venture further into the room for fear of cobwebs and other obstacles, Jay held back as the old man - who seemed to be gifted so as to see in the dark - made his way forwards purposefully. There followed the sounds of a match striking and something being turned and a dim, orange glow opened up the room before him. Jay saw an old-fashioned cottage kitchen, complete with Belfast sink and iron cooking range.

With a further adjustment of the wick, the brass oil lamp in the centre of the dusty wooden table began to burn more brightly and the old man shrugged off Jay's bag, dropped it to the floor and beckoned his companion into the room properly. Jay pushed the door shut behind him and came in.

'How do you like it?'

Jay cast his eye around the dilapidated furnishings, the cobwebs in the ceiling joists, the peeling white paint on the lime-rendered walls and the moss and grime in the windows.

'I guess,' he answered with a resigned tone, 'that if it's this old place or a cell in the basement of MI5, then it'll have to be this, won't it?'

'Don't worry about MI5, my friend; they are a small concern but nothing more,' Raphael said, kindly.

'So then, *my rescuer*,' Jay said contentiously, 'I'm supposed to lie low here for a time, am I?'

Raphael nodded, saying, 'Yes, my friend, for about two weeks I expect.'

'And just what am I supposed to do with myself for that time, and what about food; I've had nothing to eat for hours?' Jay complained.

'Why not explore the house, Jay, and let me take care of the rest, beginning with a late supper? What would you like to eat tonight?'

'Fish, chips and curry sauce,' he replied, jokingly. 'Fair enough then, I'll grab my stuff and take a look around.'

'The house has no mains electricity,' Raphael called after him as he moved cautiously through to the next room. 'You will need to light the lamps; there is a supply of oil here in the kitchen.'

How do you know? Jay thought to himself as he fumbled through the adjoining room which he guessed to be a lounge.

Had he been in other circumstances, Jay would have found an abandoned old cottage like this something quite exciting to explore, especially if it were in a reasonable state of repair, as it could then serve as a camp for him and his friends; but his friends had been abducted, and their camping territory lay many miles away.

Notwithstanding he soon discovered that there were only two serviceable bedrooms upstairs, the third, a box room, had no glass left in the window and was open to the elements.

A good deal of litter and debris was strewn in one of the others where, it appeared, the squatters - or else some vandals - had attempted to start a fire and burn the place to the ground. By the light of an oil lamp, he saw that the damp, mildew-covered wallpaper was marred by a large blackened triangle in the corner of the room and, at the seat of the fire, the floor boards had been burned through to expose the joists. The carpets also felt damp underfoot as he walked and Jay wondered whether the roof might be leaking in several places. Before the old man had turned off the car's headlights, he recalled having briefly seen a number of tiles missing.

In terms of a place to sleep, he only really had one choice; the third room had some remnants of furniture, including an overturned chair, a cabinet and a straw-filled mattress with a horrible red and orange floral pattern. The room had one small window overlooking the rear of the property. Jay came over and examined it after dumping his holdall on the mattress and righting the chair.

A heavy stone lintel bore the weight of the masonry above it, and, set in a deep reveal, a rusting steel-framed window boasted five modest square panes of glass. The sixth had not survived and appeared to have suffered a hit from an air rifle. There was a small hole punched in the middle and fractures running from it. Jay poked it carelessly with his finger and the loose shards fell out completely leaving a hole large enough for his arm to pass through. Now this room was open to the elements too!

'Ah, well,' he said, at length. His spirits then rose considerably as, most extraordinarily, he thought he smelt the smell of fish and chips cooking on the range in the kitchen. Then the savour of curry source came wafting up the stairs as well.

It struck him as quite ridiculous. How could the old fellow have fired up the range so quickly? His grandparents had one which was similar and *that* had taken about three hours to warm up enough for them to cook anything on.

Chapter 10

The Papers

The office was plain and nondescript at first glance, except that there were no windows - broken or otherwise - and no natural light at all. It could have been an underground room in the basement of MI5, MI6 or in one of any number of unknown Government buildings.

The single lamp suspended from the ceiling above the large steel desk, at which a man sat hunched over a cluster of files smoking a cigarette, recalled a certain austerity. The fact was the plans for this lower level dated back to the cold war and, for want of finances it seemed, the Executive had not bothered to have it updated to 21st Century standards even now, some thirty years later. What on earth did they tax those poor fools for?

The middle-aged man poring over the three dossiers before him looked strained, his face drawn, as though he had gone too many nights with only four hour's sleep; such was the magnitude of his problem. There were strange and unexplained things happening and his department had been quite at a loss to explain to the Minister what it meant, or, who was doing it. He ran his fingers through his thinning grey hair, flicked his cigarette into the ash tray that was already filled to the brim and picked up the topmost file.

He slipped the document out of its plastic cover and spread it over the brown, leather desk top. Beside him, a computer terminal blinked silently on standby, as its owner had resorted to reading paper files instead, in the hope of saving his tired eyes. The anti-glare screen could only delay the effects of retina damage for so long and, as this computer could contact virtually anywhere in the world in less than a second, the temptation to gawp out it for hours upon end in the hope of finding answers was very great.

The words emblazoned at the head of the file - 'TOP SECRET' - were something of a misnomer, the man reflected, considering how much of its contents was already in the public domain but, nonetheless, he had his job to do and so, quite reluctantly, he read on.

His wristwatch gave a beep and he glanced at it and then groaned irritably when he saw it was 3 o'clock in the morning. Skipping the recursive security details and introductory remarks he let his finger rest beside the bulk of the text, halfway down the watermarked page...

This same Mr Smith, we are glad to confirm, has since passed away - from natural causes - and thus we can assume that the former enthusiasm that accompanied the propagation of his message should, finally, have subsided. However, his ministry team in NZ, which comprises mainly his immediate family, together with other supporters worldwide and, worst of all, several well-placed informants, appear to be dedicated to the furtherance of the late man's aims; not only those of preaching the Christian Gospel, but also of taking some of our most cherished and sensitive information and divulging it willy-nilly to the public at large.

To illustrate the danger of this man's legacy we would draw your attention to the following extract taken from one of his books which, we understand, has sold thousands of copies in the last five years in the UK alone. We quote -

'You see, people, the nuclear issue is also one of these red herrings used to manipulate and control the population of the world with fear. The truth of the matter is that we simply cannot have a global thermo-nuclear war for the reason that nuclear weapons don't actually work the way we are

118

told they do. *Now the information I am going to show you is exact; it has been confirmed to me by people who have worked or who are working in the actual industry, so there is no doubt about it.*

'The essential point is that a nuclear bomb cannot be detonated at just any time and place. So, in that sense, there can never be a large scale 'surprise' attack. This is due to the fact that in order to achieve fission, the critical mass of uranium needs to be brought together at a particular time and place, relative to the positions of the Sun, Moon and Earth. Without the correct timing and position, a nuclear warhead will just melt, rather like the reactor at Chernobyl did, causing a considerable amount of damage but no explosion as such. The initial blast was caused by steam in the cooling system, which blew the lid of the plant and sent tons of radioactive dust into the air. Meanwhile the molten core melted through the floor and sank into the basement.

(Apparently when the engineers got bored they had a habit of allowing the core to overheat and then inserting the control rods as fast as possible at the very last minute. They were playing a game of chicken and one day they got caught out, but that's another story altogether.)

'Now, I know that your average Physics expert at college and university will tell you that I am talking rubbish, but I can assure you that this is

119

inside information that has come from the scientists employed by government to actually make and test the weapons themselves.

'So, in reality, if a terrorist cell stole a lump of uranium or plutonium and tried to blow it up, they would most likely fail to achieve anything other than to contaminate the locale with radioactivity. You see, the essential trigger to an atomic explosion is not the dynamite used to force together the masses of uranium, rather it is Gravity. Yes, people, a nuclear warhead is triggered by Gravity, which disrupts the spatial arrangement within the molten mass of uranium, and it all has to be timed to a few seconds and to within a hundred metres of a given target location.

'It is most unlikely therefore that a terrorist would have access to the necessary tables showing when and where an atomic explosion can occur on the earth's surface for a given day of the calendar. But a friend of mine in the know has calculated it for himself. He is skilled in mathematics and he is able to predict exactly when and where the nuclear powers i.e. Russia and China will carry out their next tests. To date he is 100 percent accurate. You see, there is a revolving window of opportunity which travels over the globe and, if you miss it, you may have to wait six months before you get another shot at it.

'Now this gravity trigger works in the same way

as tide raising forces that drive the tides across the oceans, it is a tangential force to gravity and causes things like water to slid sideways, and the electronic structure in things like molten uranium atoms to shear. For a more detailed description of these tidal forces please refer to the appendices at the back of this book. [Not included - see Log File xxx2177/013.]

'Now then, what is the upshot of all this information? Well, both sides in a genuine potential nuclear conflict will know exactly when and where the other side's weapons will have to be detonated, and this will render them impotent as they can then be shot down by ground-to-air missile systems which will already be primed with the necessary coordinates. Furthermore, those multiple independent warheads can never work properly, for obvious reasons.

'Notice here that I am not saying that nuclear bombs do not work, of course they do; we have all seen their effects. Take Hiroshima for example. No, what I am saying is that there can never be a sudden outbreak of global thermonuclear warfare, the true nature of the weapons renders such a scenario impossible, although there could be small scale attacks by terrorist groups. They themselves however would need to be very well informed and would undoubtedly seek help from disgruntled, out-of-work ex-Soviet nuclear technicians...

'But for us, as Christians, the important point is really this, with all this disinformation concerning the threat from atomic weapons, the population of the world are cowed into submission by fear and can, more easily, be controlled by their own governments and, in particular, by the proponents of the New World Order!' End quote -

As is abundantly clear from the disdainful way in which the late Mr Smith disseminated this most sensitive of classified information, we were forced into the position of flatly denying what we knew to be true in an effort to discredit him and his ministry. It has not been difficult to portray him as an uninformed fanatic, a religious zealot. What has been more difficult, though, has been to track down those treacherous men and women who have, for reasons known only to themselves, threatened International Peace and Security by confiding top level nuclear data with individuals such as Smith. We do indeed say Thank God he's dead (tongue in cheek). Our present efforts therefore centre primarily upon tracking down these disaffected and dangerous operatives and eliminating them from amidst our ranks.

This file is active and on-going.

The man at the desk made a grunt, shifted the papers together, and

122

returned them to the plastic wallet. Then, after straightening himself in his black, leather chair and lighting another cigarette, he unpicked the microchip seal of the second dossier.

This too had the words 'TOP SECRET' stamped on the front page, although it had come from a completely different office, Her Majesty's Patent Office in fact. It had their horrid new logo on the seal which the man had no time for; it reminded him of one of those grotty corporate makeovers.

As for HM's Patent Office itself, the general routine was as follows:- Whenever any one of the clerks stationed there came across a Patent Application that they knew - or, thought - would interest the Executive, they duly intercepted it, fed the individual applicant some cock-and-bull story about a backlog of paperwork, and forwarded the documents to the relevant department for initial appraisal.

The man's heart sank as he opened up the file and read a hand-typed manuscript by a certain Mr Leowes of Falmouth, Cornwall. It pertained to an alleged discovery of the '*Principles of Anti-Gravity by use of Gyroscopic Technology.*'

The preamble related to wide speculation that the Nazi scientists had first discovered that spinning objects could be made to float, in essence to defy gravity, some time during the Second World War.

'Yes, that's right,' he murmured.

However the application then proceeded to explain in critical and correct detail the fundamental principles underlying the discovery. The author also had the temerity to assert that he was surprised that nobody else had stumbled across it, as the maths of a gyroscope can be grasped by the average A-Level student.

'You've got a cheek,' the man grumbled, frowning at the application. 'Anyway, A-Levels are being dumbed down for the masses, didn't you realise that? We can fix this... if your drawings are viable; if not, we'll let you bask in your own self-glory.'

He took a long drag on the cigarette and continued reading the typed page. He found himself looking at photographs of a high speed drill fixed horizontally to a set of electronic scales which was reading to the nearest 0.5 of a gramme. The next photograph showed the same drill fixed vertically to the same scales, presumably revving at the same high speed and there, clear as daylight, the electronic display was reading several grammes less for no apparent reason.

The average individual would put this down to the thrust generated by the internal cooling fan of the drill but, unfortunately, this persistent individual had also mounted his Bosch dill vertically the other way around too, and, of course, the apparent loss of weight showed up again. It would not have done this if it were purely a matter of air from the fan blowing first one way and then the other.

It regrettably looked as if Mr Leowes would indeed need to be visited, but he decided to check the argument one last time in case it was flawed. The slightest error in reasoning or calculation might be enough to save him. The man slid his thumb up the schedule to the relevant block of text and read...

'We can see therefore that a disk spinning about an axis tangential to the earth's surface will continue to point to a fixed location in space, but will not show any tendency to resist gravity due to the fact that internal forces within the material take up the strain and the angular momentum of the body is conserved. However, the same cannot be said of a flat spinning disk, which is turning about an axis perpendicular to the earth's surface.

As you can clearly see from the diagram -

He turned over the leaf and studied the relevant figure: a line drawing of a flat disk with arrows representing forces and motion -

- when the disk is pulled towards the earth, every molecule of its structure is forced to undertake a longer circuit through space and, as there are no internal forces balancing this effect, the Law of conservation of angular momentum is violated. This has two obvious results 1) the rotation of the disk will slow down and 2) the disk will *resist* falling to the earth.

The outcome of this is, of course, that if one could spin a very light, flat disk very fast indeed, it would float.

The man at the desk grimaced. In making this application to the Patent Office, Mr Leowes had unwittingly sealed his own fate and, unfortunately, he was now rubbing salt into this spy-master's wounds. For, a little further on, there was an article adjoined to the application speculating upon the effect of joining hundreds of small gyros together in one compound block, miniaturizing them and powering them by microcircuit technology - which was not even cutting-edge science - and then manipulating the orientation of this massed rank of mini-gyros with electric fields. This part most certainly was cutting-edge; the folks at DERA were already doing that, the man recalled.

Mr Leowes then had the nerve to suggest that large platforms could be made to levitate if they were constructed out of these mini-gyros or, better still, if chemists could come up with some crystalline material which encompassed dipolar molecules - which are, themselves, little atomic gyroscopes - then a realistic anti-gravity plate could be designed to lift craft into Space, as some Sci-Fi writers had already postulated.

The man slammed the file back down on the desktop, stuffed it roughly back into its cover and shoved it aside. He then made a short, curt telephone call advising the relevant authority that it would be very much in the public interest if a certain Mr Leowes was detained under the Mental Health Act and carted off to have his brain wrecked at some institution.

At the close of the conversation he also advised his respondent that the administrator at the Patent Office who opened this application would, perhaps, be better served if made redundant - just to be certain.

Now in an irate mood, the man stubbed out his unfinished cigarette in the overflowing ashtray and opened up the last of the three dossiers. This one had come through numerous departments, including the Internet Monitoring Bureau and, more recently, the Anti-Terrorist Squad. He spread the papers before him and was immediately affected by the happy, smiling face of a fourteen year old Jay Robert Romero, of Brackthorpe, Northamptonshire. Though, if the data were accurate, he ought to look a little older than that these days. He made a note of the young man's birth date, listed in the particulars at the top of the page.

The next thing to catch his attention was a duplicate of the front page of a local newspaper, featuring another shot of the same young man with a great banner headline, proclaiming, '*The Miracle Kid of Northamptonshire.*' Amongst the other documents was information on a lunatic cyber-cult calling themselves '*Sacred Moose,*' along with references to a certain David Baker and Michael Murkin, and their close proximity to the subject.

'Not you *again!*' the man complained, as if bumping into an irritating colleague, or else his mother-in-law. 'What have you been up to this time? Hang on… Oh, we got a warrant out for you already - God, I'm behind the times! When was that actioned? Bloody hell I wish they'd keep me up to date.'

And with that he settled himself back in his chair and proceeded to read through the file, which was quite unlike any other he had come across.

*

Next morning, Jay awoke to the call of a bird who was hiding somewhere in the jungle beneath his bedroom window. He yawned, glanced at his watch and shifted himself on the mattress. Although damp and musty, the straw filling made for a comfortable bed. He had lain on top of it for remainder of the night hours fully dressed, having scarcely unpacked, with the intention of being able to flee the place at a moment's notice. His sleep had been remarkably sound considering the whirlwind of events that had come upon him the day before, and he put this down to the lingering satisfaction of curry and chips.

Raphael had departed after seeing Jay upstairs for the night, although it was not clear where he himself intended to sleep, and Jay wondered if he had spent the night cooped up in the car; it would have been a mighty tight fit.

Jay then rolled off the mattress and struggled to his feet, it was five past nine and the bird was still twittering in the grounds outside. He traipsed downstairs for the bathroom as, like most old cottages, there were no amenities upstairs.

The kitchen and lounge were joined end to end and the narrow staircase was enclosed behind a partition wall within the latter. It was accessed by a sliding door although this had broken away from its runner and Jay had had to lift it out of the way. The room contained two dilapidated and worn easy chairs, neither of which had cushions, a small cabinet beside the window and a wrought-iron fire place that looked unchanged from the Victorian era.

There were some newspapers and magazines lying over the floor, and one or two beer cans and glass bottles - the calling card of the previous occupants. Jay had been concerned about treading on a used syringe but, so far, he had not found any. Though now he came to think of it, the lounge did seem a little less of a tip than it had been last night. Perhaps the old man had been through and had a clear up?

Jay went to the bathroom which was essentially an outhouse on the side of the building, but decided against washing his hands and face in the sink - at least until he'd cleaned off the greenery. He then hurried through to the front and found, to his surprise, a jug of milk set upon the table, along with a packet of cornflakes and a bowl and spoon beside it. There was also a newspaper, and a copper kettle was warming on the range?

Grinning to himself he marched over to the front door opened it, and called out.

'Mr Raphael, sir, are you th— *Oh?*'

Jay stopped in his tracks, peering out into the road beyond the willow trees. He saw immediately that the sleek white Porsche was absent from the scene. So where was he? And who had prepared his breakfast?

127

Somewhat bemused, but accepting that there were so many things happening at the moment that he could not hope to explain, he merely bit his lip and wondered back inside the deserted cottage.

The kettle had duly boiled by this time and Jay found the necessary ingredients to furnish himself with a mug of tea by rummaging through the cupboards above the range.

Partially contented, he poured himself a bowl of cornflakes and casually picked up the newspaper lying on the table. It was a copy of that day's *Daily Telegraph* - his father's favourite broadsheet, although Jay himself had no particular preference. His attention was immediately gripped by the headline in bold type above a full-colour photograph of a wrecked building on the front page.

DEATH-DEFYING-

UFO crash-lands on Scottish Parliament: 100 injured but no fatalities.

Scotland's recently elected First Minister, George Drury MSP, was last night forced to declare a State of Emergency throughout the city of Edinburgh and the surrounding districts to a distance of fifty miles after catastrophe hit Holyrood. Shortly after 10 pm BST yesterday evening residents were left in terror and confusion as a fireball crash-landed on to the roof of the Holyrood Parliament building causing devastation and chaos to the surrounding area. The building - which cost the taxpayer an uncomfortable £430 Million - has been flattened by the impact and the ensuing blaze. Some people are suggesting that the object was an out-of-control satellite although this remains unconfirmed at this time. However experts we spoke to have likened the damage to that of a 1000lb World War II bomb.

Peter Hamish, an eyewitness, thought it was a comet as it plunged from the sky with, quote, 'fire and smoke streaming out behind it for miles. I thought it was the end of the world.'

Miraculously however not a single fatality has been reported so far by any of the Emergency Services, although scores of people are known to have been injured and numerous other buildings damaged or destroyed.

Today the entire city has been sealed off by the Army and Police and an exclusion zone set up around the neighbouring countryside, the great fear being (presumably) radioactive contamination leaking from the satellite's damaged reactor.

In the first few hours after the explosion there was a dearth of information coming from Government Officials both in Edinburgh and London and this, in turn, has led some to assume the worst, given the already devastating consequences arising from this incident - the Capital of Scotland will be effectively out of action until experts have cleaned up the debris and the area has been confirmed as safe.

Speculation is rife that this was an ageing ex-Soviet spy satellite, launched in the early 1980's without knowledge of Western Governments, and that it has come to grief because its uranium fuel has run out. Other more outlandish suggestions, chiefly those propagated via the internet, suggest that the US Military are testing out a new anti-missile system which is rumoured to have the capability to shoot down an incoming ICBM (Inter-Continental Ballistic Missile). *Continued on page 2 -*

Jay tossed aside the paper and returned to his breakfast. His heart was no longer racing as it had been when he'd first clapped eyes upon the headline. It seemed almost natural, he considered, that weird things ought to be happening at other places too. After all, it didn't seem remotely fair that all the trouble in the world should revolve solely around him.

At this point he was struck with a pang in his conscience, as he wondered whether his inability to keep his mouth shut about his previous affair really had triggered another temporal upheaval. He shivered slightly and continued with his tea and cornflakes in silence.

Whatever it was that was going on, whether ex-Soviet military hardware conking out and falling on their heads, or some trigger-happy Americans shooting things down for amusement, at least the papers were asking questions. Maybe they'd get to the bottom of it...?

Chapter 11

Recapitulation

There was no sign of the old man by the time Jay had finished his cereal and flicked through the remainder of the paper, so he ventured to the outhouse to attempt to clean up the toilet and sink. He had no particular wish to do so, nor yet to stay in this near derelict cottage, but as this was where Raphael had brought him, and the fact that he had apparently saved his life meant that Jay felt obliged to remain. So he set to work with a leaky bucket and a rag.

There was plenty of sun and fresh air in the bathroom, as the outside door was missing, and this allowed anybody using the room an exceptionally good view of the back garden. Jay looked around hoping to find the door, as he had a view to fixing it - albeit he had no tools, and shortly afterwards he found some tell-tale charred timbers and hinges amongst the residue of a fire in the overgrown yard.

The rotting picket fence marked out approximately an acre or so of land, broadly rectangular and surrounded on all sides by fields. It looked as though much of the ground had once been given over to the cultivation of crops. There was a small, timber garden shed in the middle of the plot, barricaded from use by a thicket of brambles, and a network of stone paths criss-crossing the site. There was no obvious lawn to speak of, except a small patch at the front, and the majority of the ground was dirt overgrown with shrubs and weeds, with the exception of a smattering of weak and unkempt self-seeding vegetables. Some of the furniture belonging to the house had also ended up 'growing' in the garden, including a broken settee that was so covered by creepers that it looked like some monstrous hybrid creation.

At the front of the cottage, things were a little less cluttered but still very much a wilderness. An untended lawn had spread into the herbaceous borders and over the path, and the grass in some places was knee high. Numerous mosses and plants were sprouting out of the stone walls surrounding the clearing, parts of which had begun to crumble as the action of the roots of the willow trees had undermined them.

The gap between the wall which bounded the road and the picket fence extended in either direction and it appeared to be some kind of track - possibly a disused railway or a medieval green lane, along which livestock would once have been driven. Jay was no archaeologist but, after a quick investigation of the track, found the unmistakeable signs of the railway - uniform grey gravel and charcoal deposits in the soil.

Indeed he spent several hours exploring the grounds and also doing a spot of tidying up. He fought his way through the brambles and into the shed where he found some rusting tools. He then cut down and burned some of the rampant greenery, including the creeper-infested settee. And, given the effort, the garden looked a good deal less desolate by the time the old man drove into the clearing in the late afternoon.

Jay ran out to meet him the moment he heard the Porsche roll up outside. Raphael stepped nimbly out of the car and grinned at him.

'Been smartening up your house then, Jay?' he remarked, casting his eyes around the scene, and then at his companion's green stained clothes and fingers.

'Where've *you* been?' Jay demanded. 'I've had nothing to eat all day long except cornflakes. Aren't you assigned to take care of me, or something like that?'

'Indeed I am,' Raphael replied. 'Why not run and get yourself freshened up and then I'll take you shopping for provisions. There is a small market town quite nearby.'

'Great idea,' Jay said, hopefully. 'Wait there a second.'

The market town of Hambury lay nestled between a number of low lying green hills, at the congruence of two broad valleys. It was a picturesque location and prime example of why so many people fall in love with Middle-England. Twenty miles away from the defunct Orpington branch line and the ramshackle smallholding that, rightly or wrongly, had now been granted to Jay, this was a well-to-do area and the last place one would look to find strange and unnatural phenomena.

And yet the majority of the townsfolk had all either read about or else heard the news relating to the freak impact up North. The 24-hour news channels had featured blanket coverage of this breaking story from dusk 'til dawn. The Internet, too, was buzzing with gossip.

And it seemed to have affected the public, because Jay noticed that everybody seemed rather subdued and quiet as he wondered through the car park of the supermarket. There was a group of youths standing idle by the recycling bins and, with the exception of one or two of their number who were taking great delight in mimicking astronomic impacts with hand gestures, most of the young were abnormally pacified, even polite - to the point of moving aside when an elderly couple approached the bottle bank with a box full of glass.

His day appeared to be passing off without incident considering how much chaos had blown up in recent days when, half an hour later, Jay, being thoroughly engrossed in reading the label of some low-salt baked beans did not notice the increasing agitation of his chaperone. Raphael was now all but constantly surveying the shoppers bustling around them, scanning up and down the aisle like a radar.

No outward appearance of a threat was visible and the nearest human being - an elderly lady loading tinned tomatoes into her trolley a few yards away - could hardly be described as intimidating. But this man Raphael was possessed of a vision that neither Jay nor anyone else in the store had. While everybody else present was oblivious to anything but groceries, he seemed equally oblivious to the mundane, and drew a surprising number of stares and muttered comments as he surveyed the scene minutely. That white suit stood out horribly. Jay even overheard one mocking voice in the next aisle to theirs compare him to 'John Lennon's granddad.'

An announcement rang out across the supermarket informing customers that all processed meat on the delicatessen counter was now reduced to half price and, without warning, a tingling sensation pricked the back of Jay's neck.

Straightening up, he dropped his purchase into the basket at his feet as the tingling became a sudden burning heat. Jay was snatched out of his relaxed posture; instantly, his adrenalin surged.

He glanced around wondering who or what might be on to him, and then he saw it...!

At the far end of the aisle a terrifying figure stood against them.

Draped in a sweeping black robe and cloak he, unlike Raphael, drew no consternation whatsoever from the crowd. It was as though they couldn't actually see him at all. But Jay most certainly could, and it shook him to the core of his being.

Looking daggers at him, this awesome dark figure, with its inanimate black eyes and oppressive shadowy form, stood head and shoulders over everyone else... and his lips were moving... He was muttering, muttering intently and ferociously beneath hearing level, his gaze fixed unwaveringly upon Jay - who'd only read about jinxes in children's story books. *They couldn't be real?*

Jay swallowed in fright and stumbled over his basket.

'Who is he?' he whispered, frantically, after regaining himself. 'Has he come to—'

Then, stopping him mid sentence, the cloaked figure raised his arm suddenly and jabbed his right, index finger at him; just like a gun.

In an instant, Raphael, with a dazzling agility and strength for such an old man, grabbed Jay by the shoulder and thrust him to the ground behind him. The old man's face flashed white as he registered the enemy's attack, apparently out of nowhere and quite undetected by the milling crowd of shoppers.

'Get down!' he cried, as Jay half ducked and was half shoved to his knees behind him, landing rather painfully on the hard floor.

Sprawling to rest on the ground, Jay whipped around just in time to see a huge dark shadow come flying down from the ceiling and race between the shelves, aiming straight at where he'd been standing just two seconds earlier.

The spirituous form collided with the food rack behind him with a shuddering crash, and Jay watched fearfully as the shelves exploded their contents in all directions. A sticky mixture of sauce and juice sprayed over his face while utter mayhem ensued in the passageways. People ran, screaming, from the area, yelling all kinds of things about terrorist bombs and earthquakes.

A number of folks were injured by the blast debris and staggered about dazedly, not so sure of where they were heading. Amidst the noise, the wrecked section of shelving collapsed moments afterwards, spilling even more tins and jars over the floor. Mess was strewn all over the place.

The old dear who'd just finished putting tins in her trolley had received a steel can in the face. It had hit her with the force of a cricket ball. Unconscious, she'd sunk over into a promotional display by the checkouts opposite Jay and his be-suited friend, falling limply to the ground with the bridge of her nose smashed in. But before her blood had even reached the ground, the fight was on again...

Gasping for his breath in shock and covered with various foodstuffs, Jay whipped his attention back to the towering dark figure, now advancing upon them from the far end of the aisle. Having missed with his first spell, he was determined to open fire again. And this weapon, whatever it was, seemed to be at the command of his fingertips.

Fleeing customers momentarily blocked his field of view, but Raphael kept Jay pinned behind him, gripping his jacket. The robed figure raised his arm again; this time he was going for Raphael himself, who was plainly getting in his way. There was without doubt no love lost between them.

Aching somewhat from his contact with the floor, Jay peered around the old man's legs, wondering whether he would live or die... or perhaps just get trampled underfoot by hysterical shoppers who were still running everywhere. Screams and cries reverberated in his ears; his heart beat jolted in his chest. Still the dark form ahead of him came on.

Another bright radiance then shone out of the old man's face and he thrust the palm of his right hand out in front of him forcefully. Simultaneously the black robed adversary was thrown backwards, as if he'd been punched in the chest by an invisible object. He was lifted completely off his feet and went careering into a large refrigerator at the top of the aisle.

In a sprawling tumble of clothing, he crashed into shelves of milk and yoghurt, making a deathful hissing sound as he fell. Then, to add to the spectacle, his black robes abruptly burst into flame sending a pall of acrid smoke billowing into the air conditioning vents. This immediately triggered the fire alarm system.

In the next instant the dark assassin's shrieks of agony, as he writhed about in blazing garments, became drowned out by redoubled screams of terror from the shoppers who were now fleeing, supermarket-wide, for their lives. In their eyes, something invisible had just crash-landed in the chiller cabinet and was blazing with fire!

As these moving images of destruction flickered past his eyes, Jay perceived what the loud jangling noise was that was starting to make his ears ache: the fire alarm bell had activated. All at once he found himself dragged to his feet again and hauled past the evacuated checkouts.

Away to his right, a frantic group of individuals were pressing to get out of the front doors of the shop while smoke wafted through the air making them choke as they tried to breathe. The public address system was vainly asking everyone not to panic and to leave their shopping where it was and head for the nearest exit without running.

Raphael frog marched Jay in the opposite direction, towards an emergency exit door that the crowds by the main entrance had failed to notice. One or two of the smaller children were nigh on trampled by the crush. Babies were crying, unattended trolleys rolled helplessly down the aisles, and all the while the smoke thickened and began to engulf everything.

Coughing in the fumes and desperately troubled by it all, Jay allowed himself to be steered through the emergency door, wiping red, tomato-flavoured gloop from his face. It opened promptly of its own accord as the old man approached it, leading his charge by the arm.

Startled yet again by this strange display of cosmic power descending all around him, Jay stumbled out of the supermarket into the clean, fresh summer air. It was an immediate relief. Outside a number of people had already assembled, panic stricken in the car park, wondering helplessly what might be happening inside. Some of them were making calls on mobile phones. Others were screaming for relatives to hurry up and get themselves out of the building.

As he hurried over the tarmac car park, Jay heard the familiar noise of sirens wailing through the town in the distance. The fire brigade must have received word already, even though barely a minute had expired since the first explosion. He wondered if they'd been forewarned by someone, or something. There was more to these events than the hand of mere mortals. Jay knew that much for certain now.

They stopped beside the white sports car and turned back to watch the chaotic scene unfolding. Two casualties were laying on the ground, covered in spare jackets and shirts that had been given up by concerned bystanders. One of them, the old dear who'd been knocked out, wasn't moving. Her face was still bloodied and some of those nearby with first aid training were checking her pulse.

A-B-C, Jay said to himself, *check the Airway, Breathing and then the Circulation; that's it.*

Whoever had tried to get him, he now realised, had also injured or upset scores of innocent members of the public. Maybe they'd even killed one; as far as he could see the old woman was showing no signs of coming to. Jay's guts churned within him as he looked from frightened face to frightened face amidst the mass of walking-wounded gathering together outside the entrance. Many seemed to feel that a bomb really had gone off.

The heightened sense of fear and anxiety prevalent amongst the general public today made them susceptible to all kinds of suggestion. Such was the climate induced by the terrifying nature of recent events; it had turned people wild with paranoia. *Then again, when invisible forces start blowing up a supermarket around you, how should a person react,* Jay wondered?

'Who...?' He stopped start, and then restarted. '*What* was that?' he asked, looking helplessly at the traumatised customers, and staff.

'One of the Enemy's witting servants,' Raphael informed him, quietly, leaning over the roof of the Porsche, also watching the troubled crowd.

In the region of fifty people had now evacuated themselves to the car park area, though none seemed particularly anxious to drive away. Perhaps they were worried about their shopping still trapped inside the smoke filled carnage. The emergency sirens grew ever louder as the fire engines approached the scene from the nearby town centre.

'He... He didn't look like one of those guys from the Secret Service,' Jay muttered, turning at last to face his guardian. 'They were all dressed up like guys from the Matrix!'

Raphael meanwhile continued to observe the people by the foyer in the distance. Jay could tell by the expression on his face that he cared deeply about all of them, but he did not dare question the old man's choice of actions just at that moment.

'No, he wasn't a Government Agent as such, a vastly more dangerous foe.'

'Who… er… What then?' Jay stuttered, and finally he caught the old man's gaze.

'In simple terms,' Raphael said, turning to him, and speaking rather more loudly because the first of three fire engines then came tearing into the car park from the junction on the main road, lights and sirens going, 'there are three sides to this, our present conflict.'

'*Three?*' Jay repeated, gawping at him. 'Whatever happened to the nice and simple good verses evil?'

At a gesture from the old man, the pair of them then climbed into the car, where they could shut out the din coming from the blaring sirens. Now that all three engines had arrived, surely they could turn them off? Yet more blue lights came flashing into the rear view mirror and Jay watched, distractedly, as the Police also turned up.

'Let me explain,' Raphael said, shortly afterwards, settling himself behind the wheel. 'You and I are both on the same side, Jay, whereas the Government, which is meant to be helping us, is generally incompetent and, more often than not, is acting on the part of the Enemy by default. You see, when an incompetent force attempts to combat evil they often end up in league with that evil before they realise what they're doing. Then, of course, there are the Enemy's witting servants, those who know full well *whose* they are and *whom* they serve.' He cleared his throat. 'Thus we have three sides to this conflict as I said: the Good, the Bad… and the just plain useless.'

'Are they all after me?' Jay whined, noticing that a smudge of ketchup had rubbed off his sleeve onto the plush fabric of the seat. He quickly tried to wipe it off but it only made the stain worse.

'No. It's just that, for the present, you happen to be one of their higher priorities. That's all.'

The old man smiled as he started the engine and fastened his seat belt.

'One of their higher priorities…?' Jay repeated faintly, doing up his own seatbelt, as the 924 surged into action and sped across the car park, dodging the aftermath of the fire.

'Do not fear,' Raphael said warmly, pulling away from the troubled scenario behind them, which disappeared rapidly into the distance after they joined the main road. 'The end result of this Temporal War is already perfectly known. The future is decreed; these troublesome times will soon be over, and then will begin the Reign of Peace.'

'I hope so,' Jay said desperately. 'Oh no! We've gone and left the food behind.'

'Not to worry,' Raphael answered, radiantly. 'Look into the boot.'

Confounded, Jay turned round in his low-slung seat and peered over the headrest. In the back he saw a plastic carrier bag, filled with provisions, slide sideways across the mat as the car took a rather fast left hand bend. Jay stared at it. Was this a miracle? He didn't know and thought it best not to ask any more questions until they arrived safely back at the cottage.

An hour later, emerging through the narrow country lane, the car pulled up in the clearing beside the wall. Jay gazed impassively through the willow trees to the fence and the cottage beyond. The weathered stone walls had stood there for the best part of two hundred years. He wondered how long he'd have to hide away here, to remain under cover, on the run and hunted by forces entirely beyond the pail of his comprehension.

The early evening breeze whistled gently up the pathway as they made towards the dilapidated old house. For the present, Jay knew this had to be his makeshift home, but for how much longer?

The cooking range in the kitchen had all but burnt itself out and so Jay hurriedly fetched a handful of split logs and kindling from the box on the hearth and re-stoked it. This he had thought to prepare as he'd laboured in the garden and now he needed something hot and wet to drink, ideally coffee, depending on what Raphael had bought.

His friend unpacked the provisions and laid them out on the dusty wooden table. The setting sun shone through the diamond latticed windows and striped his suit with the same pattern while Jay watched, quietly. The range soon warmed with the crackle of flames in the grate, and he glanced over the food on the table, wondering what he ought to do for supper.

'*Eggs*, excellent! I can do an omelette. Beans, yes, potatoes: I could chip them. Oh no, we've got no way to fry them! Never mind; is there any point asking how you came by this lot while everything else was going on?' Jay asked, without much hope of an answer.

'I am here to protect you, Jay, instruct you, and prepare you. Do not ask me questions of no importance. Our time is precious and growing shorter by the hour. Do not think that overseeing your personal safety is my only duty in the universe.'

'The universe?' Jay repeated.

'Quite. Now, why not boil up that old kettle and then we can have one final discussion? If you take the plate off the top there will be enough heat now; the fire's going well.'

'Final?' Jay blurted out. 'What d'you mean; are you leaving me?'

'Soon,' he replied, taking his seat in the corner of the antiquated room. For some reason, Jay noticed at that moment that there wasn't a trace of tomato ketchup, or, indeed, anything else - stained or spotted - on the old man's suit. But he knew that the explosion had sent food flying everywhere. Some of it remained on Jay's face and neck and over his right arm. However, there was something about this man Raphael that had caused all the debris to miss him; it was as if his being could bear no spot or blemish at all, other than the obvious signs of old age. However even that was deceptive as his reactions had been swifter than Jay's own at times.

These musings stretched Jay's ethic of humbly accepting providence to the limit. There were so many questions burning inside him. He was feeling almost mutinous as he went over to the sink, filled the kettle with water and returned to the range where he placed it over the heat.

The room was becoming unpleasantly warm and Jay pulled off his jacket, slinging it over the back of the chair. Despite his huge backlog of questions, all he managed to come up with was, 'But if you leave for good, how will I know what to do?'

Jay sat down and faced the old man, forlornly, waiting for his answer. Raphael smiled kindly at him and said, 'When the time comes for you to do something, Jay, you will know what to do. With the occasion comes the knowledge. Trust me, you have nothing to worry about. In the meantime all you have to do is survive; just stay alive.'

'*Yeah?* You looked pretty worried when that dark-robed bloke appeared out of nowhere in the supermarket. Not surprising mind you; he scared me stupid!'

'I was not scared of him,' Raphael informed him in a matter-of-fact tone. 'I was merely acting in earnest. I did not want anything to happen to *you.*'

'Hmm... It's all right for you not to be scared. But I don't have the power to blast people backwards with the flick of my hand or, say, fire a gun out of a car window with pin-point accuracy. Yeah, it's easy for *you* to say not to fear, but what about me? I've barely come of age; all my family's been taken; so have my friends; so have their families; I've got a whole host of Agents on my tail - goodness knows why - and goodness knows what I'm supposed to do!'

'Yes, Goodness *does* know, Jay. Can't you see how your life has been preserved all these years for a purpose? Why weren't the agents allowed to kill you? Why was the Occultist prevented from harming you in the supermarket today? How come you even survived the lightning strike in the first place? *Cats* are said to have nine lives, Jay, but not men.'

'I'm only seventeen,' Jay replied, little convinced, and beginning to sulk.

'You are about to fulfil a very important role, Jay; it has been determined since the foundation of the world and, what is more, only you can fulfil it.'

'Why only me?' Jay muttered, glancing up to see whether the kettle was anywhere near boiling.

The setting sun passed behind a cloud, taking the sharp edge off the daylight as it shone through the latticed kitchen window. The shadow spilled off the table and on to the flagstone floor, moving perceptibly as Jay watched.

'Jay, do you remember that lecture you attended in the Town Hall just before your birthday?'

'What?' Jay gulped. 'You weren't there... er - 'Then, considering all the amazing things he'd witnessed at the hands of the old man, he added, '- were you?'

'Yes, I was, as a matter of fact, but that is neither here nor there. I've been having to keep an eye on you for some time now, especially since the Lines crossed.'

'Lines... what lines?' Jay demanded, growing irritable and confused.

'Think, Jay, *think!*'

And then, all of a sudden, it came to him like a thunderbolt. '*World Lines!*' he exclaimed. 'They're real, you mean?'

'Yes, when you let slip details of your previous affair to your friend David, he came by knowledge that he should never have been a party to. That knowledge caused a short circuit in the temporal world; things became entangled for a while, certain connections were made and others were broken. At the time my colleagues and I were very concerned, to be honest, not foreseeing the consequences of it all, we being only finite beings ourselves.

'Notwithstanding in the infinite wisdom of the Almighty everything appears to have been set up for a spectacular triumph. However, even I might have said too much now. Goodness me, Jay, being in your presence has a strange effect upon one!'

As his young charge merely stared at him, aghast at this news, Raphael continued.

'Anyhow, that's enough details of temporal mechanics for the time being, now for the more mundane issues. Jay, I must tell you about—'

'No!' he protested. 'Tell me more about World Lines; I want to know more about *them*.' He interrupted him with a passion, his face alight. 'I'll bet you know more than old Dr Seymour. Go on... er... Oh, all right then.'

It was a stark juxtaposition; he suddenly remembered the present burden of his situation and, all of a sudden, his enthusiasm for his past love died rather, so he quickly conceded.

'Jay, I would like to tell you more about the deceit behind the mundane powers, in case you should survive on the earth after the...

after the work is done. If so, you will need to pass the information on, until the time of restitution is fully come.'

'In case I survive?' Jay repeated. 'That sounds hopeful, doesn't it?' he remarked, more aggressively. 'And what about 'in case?' I thought you said you knew it all!' There was a clear hint of mockery in his voice now.

Raphael explained, patiently, 'I have not been told of everything.'

Jay opened his mouth to protest further, but the old man shook his head gravely and he knew it was useless to argue; so he let whatever needed to be said, be said.

'Let us do a little recapitulation,' Raphael announced immediately afterwards, as they both settled over a hot mug of tea and some toast. 'Our time has almost run out and there are many things that I would have wished to discuss but, alas, we have not the time.'

'Fair enough,' Jay agreed, chomping away ravenously, 'anything you want.'

'Do you remember once telling your friends the maxim - 'things are happening which shouldn't be happening, therefore we have knowledge that we ___''

''*Should not have?*' Yeah, I remember saying that, but I didn't realise it was a maxim; I just made it up myself.'

'All the better,' Raphael commended, looking very pleased to hear it. 'My point is, friend, that I have to forewarn you what will happen without telling what will happen, to prepare you for your mission without actually spelling it out. The first reason is obvious: we do not want the Enemy to know what is about to happen, and the second is because - as you already understand - having knowledge of the future necessarily alters the future.'

'A paradox,' Jay mused, licking some butter from his fingers and taking the mug of tea.

'Not necessarily, not if we can keep the knowledge hidden. Spill the beans, let the information out and, yes, paradoxical chaos will inevitably ensue, as you have experienced first hand over the past few days and weeks. It is therefore better to avoid it.'

'Well, then, if you can't explicitly tell me what I must do, you're going to have to drop me a few big hints; that's all,' Jay replied.

'Very well,' Raphael answered, eyeing him carefully. 'You will recall your erstwhile Physics project you were given over the holidays by your teacher, Mr Roberts?'

'Yep, but I've abandoned all thought of it.'

'The works of *which* eminent scientist were you interested in?'

'Nikola Tesla,' he answered, 'but I was also intrigued by Dr Seymour too; he and I seem to share the same vision, and—'

'Forget Percy Seymour,' Raphael advised him, soberly. 'He is indeed a great man, but you must concentrate on Tesla. *Do you understand me?*'

Jay picked up the meaning behind the words, but did not quite see where it could get him. 'You're... you're not suggesting that I should try and work on my Physics project, surely not in these circum—'

'No, I didn't say that, Jay, what I said was: '*concentrate on Tesla...*' '*CONCENTRATE,*' all right?'

'Fine,' Jay said, shrugging his shoulders. It didn't make much sense.

'There is something you must do,' Raphael explained. 'Just one little thing is all it will take, and it will consign the Enemy's plan to history forever... or even to the fire, yes indeed!'

'That's not much to go on,' Jay lamented.

'No, but I have been assured that it is just enough to do the trick, Jay, just enough to prepare you, and yet leave the adversaries in the dark and, hopefully, avoid any further ruptures in the space-time continuum.'

Jay could not resist a smirk. 'Yeah, it must look pretty damaged now I've been through!'

'Some of us are good at stitches in the rift,' Raphael jested.

'You still haven't told me who this Enemy is,' Jay said, on reflection. 'In fact, I think you've left me with more questions unanswered than answered.'

He shot a questioning look at the man in the white suit who, despite having saved his very life on two occasions and maybe more for all he knew, was now becoming ever-so-slightly annoying. Yet an infinitely benevolent gaze met his own strained features and, immediately, Jay's anger dissipated like a puff of smoke.

He finished off the drink and gestured to the second mug standing on the table top in front of his companion. The man Raphael shook his head kindly as he picked it up.

'I don't really need to drink, my friend; I just do it to socialize.'

'Tell me who this Enemy is,' Jay insisted, engrossed in the man's blazing visage and not really registering his previous statement.

'Ah, yes, his name... Well, that is the ultimate question isn't it?' Upon saying this, the old man suddenly glanced upward and something about him created the impression that it might be time for him to leave.

'Do you know?'

'I do.'

'Then, tell me!' Jay urged him. 'Surely I have a right to know who it is who's trying to bump me off?'

After a long pause for thought, which tortured Jay more than anything else that had happened to him thus far, Raphael answered.

'Generically, he is known as Antichrist. Individually, however, I am not permitted to reveal a name to you; I *am* sorry.'

Almost knocking his china mug off the table on to the stone floor, Jay whispered, 'But that's just a story isn't it? A fantasy ending of the world, I'd always thought...?'

'Fantasy?' Raphael repeated, sharply. 'You think it fantasy? Have you never read the Book properly?'

'Erm - No, I haven't,' Jay admitted. 'Is the Revelation true, then?'

'As true as I sit here before you,' he replied. 'My colleagues Gabriel, Michael and Oriel could also tell you of the same, but it was I that was appointed to this task.'

'*NO WAY!*' Jay shouted, springing to his feet at once. 'You're an... an... Ang— ?'

But before he could even form the word on his lips, the shining face vanished before his eyes in an instant. The half-drunk mug of tea that had been in the old man's hand smashed on the floor as the white-suited figure disappeared in a pure white burst of light.

Jay sank backwards into the chair. He was pained, stunned and yet exhilarated all at the same time. His heart pounded within him and it felt as though his chest might actually explode. With a racing mind he tried to ascertain whether this was reality, or dream. It was hard to tell the difference these days. Was it past or present? Who had the old man really been? Could the Secret Services really hold a weapon of such power that it could make an adult man simply disappear from a rural cottage kitchen? Jay didn't think so, but this left him with only one realistic alternative.

His disappearing saviour could not have been a man at all…

Chapter 12

On the Move

The shock of the old man's sudden disappearance, right from under his very nose, left Jay in such a state of awe and wonder that he forgot all about eating supper, and retired to bed a few hours later on a virtually empty stomach. The result of this was that he found himself unable to get to sleep properly until shortly before dawn.

He rehearsed Raphael's words again and again in his mind as he lay there on his musty old mattress, the faint rustling of wind in the willows drifting in through the broken window above him. The information he'd learned had proved helpful in part, and in part bewildering. Jay was no longer sure whether he was the cause of the problem or the solution, or perhaps both. He knew perfectly well that the Law of Cause and Effect becomes reversed in temporal mechanics, a person often being able to see the consequences of what their action before having actually done it. From the point of view of the observer it appears as though the effects *precede* the cause.

And yet it was only a very simple thing that he had to do, one little thing that would finish off the Enemy - whoever he was - in one fell swoop, apparently. Then Jay made a connection. His mind immediately flew to the *Return of the King* film he had watched the day before with Mike in the cinema. What was the crux of the story? Surely, it was by the simple action of flinging the ring into the fiery chasm all the works of darkness were undone? Yes, that was it, but it did not help him with what *he* had to do, and then he recalled the gruelling journey that the hobbits had undertaken just to get to the fiery mountain in the first place, and all the death and destruction that occurred prior to the ring's demise.

Was it therefore providence that had led him to watch that film only yesterday? He sincerely doubted it because if that were the case, how come he still felt so completely in the dark? Was providence not supposed to be enlightening?

Next morning Jay emerged from the cottage with a bacon and egg sandwich in his hand, thinking to have a poke around the car, even wondering whether he ought to take a great risk and attempt to drive it himself. He knew roughly what to do, but then he remembered how much trouble he and Mike had got into when Mike had driven his mother's car down the motorway, under-age, uninsured and without permission.

Jay was seventeen now and, although his father had promised him lessons, such mundane matters had been clean swept from his mind in recent weeks. He only hoped his father was all right!

He walked down the front garden, through the creaky gate in the fence and across the disused railway track. He passed the line of willows growing beside the old stone wall and then stopped, dead, staring into the clearing. The sandwich nearly slipped out of his fingers.

The white Porsche, which was fast becoming his favourite car, had vanished - or else it had been driven away. For there was no sign of it except some curved tyre tracks in the dirt of the clearing, but they could have been made when they drove in. Jay knelt down and examined the marks for a moment and then hurried out into the lane. He looked this way and that, thinking stupidly that he might be able to catch some glimpse of the car, but, as he knew all along, it was gone; gone like its owner, no doubt in a dazzling burst of light! He turned back, thoughtfully, ate some more of his sandwich and made his way towards the house.

The morning sun shone brightly and, deciding to take in the air for a while, he climbed on to the moss-covered wall and sat there while finishing off his breakfast. The breeze blowing through the leaves above him made for a brief spell of relaxation, and he soon realised that he ought not have been surprised that the car had gone.

All he had to do, if the old man had told him right, was to stay alive and then, when the time came, do one simple thing. *Well,* he concluded, *if that's all it's going to take to save my family and friends and repair all the damage in the world, it doesn't seem such a burdensome calling after all.* And with these happier thoughts, he lay back on top of the wall and contemplated the patches of blue sky peeping through the rustling foliage. All he needed now to make it perfect was a gently flowing stream somewhere nearby.

Two weeks later, Jay's bag of provisions had almost run out. He was down to a tin of fruit salad, a toilet roll and a packet of biscuits, and he had resigned himself to the fact that he would have to survive a little longer than this stock would allow for. This, in turn, meant that he would have to venture off to the town, or anywhere else nearby to purchase food. The difficulty was that he had only the vaguest idea whereabouts he was and he hadn't brought a map.

He lay awake that night planning how best to undertake this dangerous expedition without falling into the hands of his adversaries. The railway line seemed to be the safest option. He remembered that Raphael had mentioned that Hambury, the town whose superstore they had blown up, also had a small railway station. Thus, Jay reasoned, the disused line outside the cottage must be an old branch line which, more than likely, would lead directly into the town. He could follow it without the risk of meeting too many passers-by. At home he and his friends were well used to exploring disused railway lines, which allowed one to get to places one knew, but in new and undiscovered ways. They used to spend a lot of time on these expeditions cursing a certain Dr Beeching for axing these wonderful old branch lines in the first place, which had allowed most of them to fall into ruin.

However, he also knew that Hambury lay about twenty miles away, which would entail a whole day's walk, more or less, and probably one night sleeping outdoors in the tent, which was still safely stowed in his holdall. As the return journey would require nearly two days, he would have to set off the next morning, otherwise his provisions would be exhausted, and he hated hiking on an empty stomach as it left him with no energy at all.

Having fallen into a fretful sleep, with so much on his mind, Jay dreamed a nightmarish dream. He was standing outside the front door of the cottage; it was the dead of night and pouring with rain. He had lost the key to the door and was growing increasingly cold and wet. Then he turned and, to his horror, he saw a tall, dark figure standing across the other side of the road. He was glaring at him with an intense and unflinching stare.

The individual wore a hood and, although Jay could not see into it, the individual's gaze was so powerful it seemed to pin him to the ground where he stood. It was as though Jay could not be moved even if a bomb were to go off beside him. The beam of his eyes was like two shafts, or, spears, right through Jay's chest, and they were pinning him to the front of the door like a dartboard.

Unable to escape the individual's attention; unable to hide or even move, he could only wait there in the downpour until the thing devoured him.

After a few more tortuous minutes of this stand-off however, it became apparent that the robed figure could do little more than glower. Certainly, it did not appear that he could approach any closer and the lane seemed to present an invisible barrier to him.

Suddenly Jay knew he was protected, and that his enemy could not cross over it; yet what kind of enemy *was* this that could pin a person to the ground, fifty yards away, merely by looking at them? This was a power, the magnitude of which Jay had never dreamed off, more than even Raphael had wielded... it seemed.

Nonetheless Jay could feel his opponent's fury growing, his perfect hatred, his frustration, and he squirmed to escape the hold upon him, wanting to dive out of sight and disappear into the undergrowth like a frightened rabbit. Yet still he found he could not move an inch.

The stand-off continued for another tormenting minute or so, and then the dark figure finally moved. He mimicked shooting Jay dead, imitating a gun with his fingers, and Jay instantly collapsed - falling to the ground as if really shot.

He awoke with a start, heart clamouring at a furious rate and sweat pouring off him. He sat up, wiped his brow on his shirt sleeve and turned towards the window. There was no sign of any rain and neither was it the dead of night. He could see the tell-tale glow of the coming sunrise. The dawn approached, and what a relief that was; robed figures seemed so much less terrifying in the daylight. Nonetheless it took a good few minutes for his pulse to return to normal.

At eight o'clock that morning Jay got up and, after having the tinned fruit for breakfast, gathered his things together for the journey. He piled everything beside his holdall which he would have to sling across his back like a rucksack, as it was too awkward to carry for more than a short distance. He unzipped the bag and pulled out the tent which was neatly rolled up inside its pack and then, as he searched the pockets for anything he'd missed before repacking everything as tightly as possible, his fingers collided with a large metal lump.

'Hey! *What's this?*' he said, and he grasped the cold, metal lump and drew it out of the pocket. Somewhere between wrapping his fingers around the object and drawing it out into the open, he realised, with a gasp of fright, exactly what it was - *but it couldn't be?*

A second later Jay was staring blankly at the large automatic pistol Raphael had used to deadly effect upon the Secret Servicemen. Here it was, nestling in his own jittery fingers? Somebody had stowed it away inside his bag - but who? - When?

Jay found he was coming out in a cold sweat, and he felt so weak that he could barely hold the heavy pistol steady. He sat down on the floor amidst the jumble of his belongings and stared in awe at the thing, running his finger over the laser sight. He didn't know the first thing about guns really; they were more Dave's thing. Where was the safety catch? How did the magazine open? Were there any bullets left in it?

Instinctively he put it down and rummaged again inside the pocket where the gun had been hidden, and, as if to answer his questions, he found a small piece of notepaper. He unfolded it at once and read a handwritten message that was obviously intended for him -

The safety catch is the thumb switch. The laser is activated by a slight pull on the trigger. There are four rounds left. Beware - this gun only works on mortals!

And then, turning over the scrap of paper gingerly, he read this final message -

Jay, there is ALWAYS a choice - Raphael.

'Yeah, I'm sure,' he said, through teeth bared in angst. He flicked the note aside, but, before it hit the floor, it suddenly burst into flames. Jay yelped in alarm and sprang backwards out of the way, but, by the time it hit the carpet, the paper was ashes.

When he managed to re-gather himself, Jay almost raised a grin and thought, *Well, that's what spies do isn't it; they arrange for their messages to self-destruct?*

Spurred on to accomplish his mission by the note from his guardian - albeit an unknown venture - Jay redoubled his efforts, packed up his stuff and set off ten minutes afterwards.

As he locked the front door of the cottage behind him, he had a fleeting impression that he was also saying goodbye to it, but he merely shrugged off the feeling and struck out into the warm sunshine.

At the boundary of the property Jay turned right and joined the disused railway line which ran parallel to the road for a short distance before arching away through the countryside, taking the most level route to the town. As the locomotives did not run well up hills, the railways were built along the flattest possible route between destinations, that is, unless it meant laying tracks over a marsh or some other unsuitable terrain.

This was another great reason why he and his friends loved walking the many miles of disused railways surrounding Brackthorpe; it was easy-going, provided that the path was not too overgrown with thickets and brambles. More often than not, the farmers did their bit to keep the cuttings and embankments clear wherever the line passed through their property.

In these parts, however, it seemed that the landowners were not so obliging and, before long, Jay found himself fighting his way through a veritable jungle of trees and shrubs and knee-high undergrowth, similar to what he had had to contend with for the past fortnight at the cottage.

As his progress slowed he began to get depressed and think upon more negative things. Initially his excitement had leapt at the thought that he was now carrying a weapon which could, if necessary, despatch the odd assassin or two. Though, now he came to think of it, any armed military professional could make short work of him - especially as he had the pistol buried in the bottom of his bag.

Every now and then he felt it bump into his lower back, and he finally stopped and repacked it in a tracksuit top to pad it out a bit more. It felt much more comfortable afterwards.

Armed assailants were not his only worry by any means; he knew that carrying a weapon in public was against the law, for which he could be arrested and imprisoned without trial (as a terrorist) for weeks. Furthermore, if the weapon was unlicensed or otherwise illegal then that, too, would only add to the seriousness of the offence were he to get caught.

All in all, it was a pretty miserable and tired Jay that stopped for lunch a couple of hours later. He reckoned that he had barely covered five miles, although the place he had chosen to stop was a refreshing change. After traversing numerous fences, forests and even a riverbed, where he'd had to detour because the railway bridge had been removed, he had come upon a nice spot to rest.

The broad cutting which he had been pushing through had suddenly opened out into a wide and shallow valley. Beyond the wheat fields in the distance a majestic farmhouse stood, lord of all it surveyed, within a large yard. Jay could just about make out a man walking past a couple of tractors parked side by side, and he thought he heard a dog barking somewhere as well, but could not see it for the distance.

There was a gently sloping bank of mature grass at the side of the track and he promptly un-slung the bag from his shoulders and sat down to admire the rolling view. He had a bottle of water with him, which, he now reckoned, was not going to be enough; it only held a litre and it was a hot day. Jay was wearing his shirt on top and, because of the sunshine, he decided to swap it for a T-shirt.

Half a packet of biscuits doesn't make for a very satisfying lunch, especially after an equally unsatisfactory breakfast. Nonetheless he ate and drank with gratitude, although it was difficult to keep his mind from straying to the gun hidden in his bag. More than once he considered simply throwing it away, or burying it to avoid it falling into unsafe or innocent hands.

After refreshing himself, he took out his night vision binoculars and, after detaching the infra-red scope and the night vision chip - which would have burned his eyes out - he scanned the horizon, looking for signs of a settlement in the distance. Nothing obvious came into view but he was not unduly alarmed, and he suspected that the town might lie on the other side of the railway, which, he noted, did appear to be bending ever-so-slightly to the left hand.

Jay rested for another hour and then set off again at about two o'clock.

Chapter 13

The Gypsy, the Scientist and the Lunatic

Tired and cold from his day-long trek through the country, Jay had now been following the disused railway line for over twelve hours and still had not reached the town. Either he was making much slower progress than he'd anticipated, what with all the detours he had made, or, Hambury was further away than he thought. And then, trudging along with the holdall swinging uncomfortably around his shoulders, he contemplated a rather less pleasant thought: perhaps this old branch line bypassed the town altogether and he might not come across another habitation for days?

He envisaged a school history lesson in which his teacher was telling him that the railways always took the flattest and easiest routes from where they were, to where they wanted to go. The troubling thing was that he himself had no idea where he wanted to go. Tramping over endless swathes of charcoal-stained gravel and pushing through thickets of greenery on the overgrown track side, Jay felt all but enclosed by the banks of the cutting. And as it swept around again to the left hand it seemed to be directing him somewhere with an express like purpose, but to *where* and towards what?

He wasn't sure when the twilight turned to night time. From his perspective the outlook was always pretty dark these days. It was a depressing fact of life. The natural and artificial disasters, which had shown a marked increase of late, must have left a residual dust in the atmosphere. Indeed, although he couldn't test it, he knew there was science behind it and that it was not just emotional. Were a really sizeable catastrophe to arise, that would, in all probability, block out the daylight over the whole globe - even at midday. He recalled that such a phenomenon was termed an 'Extinction Level Event.'

As his hunger began to mount, he pulled off his holdall and felt inside it. Then, remembering that he had only half a packet of biscuits to his name, he gave up and slung it back over his shoulder. His journey resumed, his worst fear realised - hiking on an empty stomach.

Not long afterwards, something travelled through the cutting on the night breeze, and it became distinctly audible above the crunching of his shoes over the blackened gravel... *voices.*

Jay stopped dead, listening hard. His breath instantly became awfully loud and distracting.

For sure, there were voices chatting away - jovially, by the sound of it - just beyond the on-coming bend in the track. At once Jay darted over to the edge of the embankment and flattened himself against it. The grass felt wet with evening dew against his cheek.

Trying to control his breathing, he grabbed the binoculars and set them to his eyes. He scanned the area up ahead and immediately saw an enhanced, green image of the artificial valley around him. It appeared to be levelling out and opening up; possibly, there was a disused siding just after the bend. A derelict, brick hut on his side of the line prevented him from seeing what lay beyond it, but, as he surveyed the edges of the solid, green structure, a hazy brightness rippled across the field of view. *Heat,* he thought, *I'll bet they've lit themselves a camp-fire.*

He waited, taking a good deal of time to decide what to do next. One thing he was certain about; turning back again was not an option. Not now, not when he'd come this far. And then it came to him, the most delicious and welcome smell in the whole, sorry world - *sausages!* Somebody was frying sausages; Jay couldn't believe it.

Feeling that the time was right and that he'd calmed down a bit, and that a couple of - presumably - homeless folk were not a significant threat to him, considering that he had night vision binoculars *and* a gun, he advanced carefully towards the talkative heat haze.

Two minutes later he acquired his target. Squatting down behind the intervening branches of a shrub and pressing the binoculars to his eyes, he examined a most unlikely scene ahead.

Three quite disparate men were sitting around a crackling fire on discarded wooden sleepers which served as make-shift benches. Their fire was set in a ring of red bricks and some sausages and other meat were frying in a pan by the heat of the flames. Despite seeing everything in an image-enhanced green, Jay still found himself all but drooling like a dog. Nonetheless he continued his surveillance for a while.

One of the reasons for the fellow's jovial conversation could have been the twenty-four pack of beer lying at their feet - half drunk. As Jay watched, the individual furthest from him finished another can and hurled it away into the bushes.

The clearing was indeed a disused railway siding and two or three lines of overgrown track were still visible, although much of it had long since been taken up and used elsewhere on the network.

And there, beyond the disused lines, was Hambury station. Jay felt mildly relieved, and such was the magnification of the binoculars that he could even make out the name of the platform although it lay several hundred yards away.

A little way ahead there was a wooden fence sealing off the defunct line from the working track, and, on either side of the camp-fire meal, a platform rose up like a low, dark wall. Many paving stones and bricks were missing from each and the only thing waiting for the non-existent train to arrive was a damaged shopping trolley, stuffed with clothes and sundry other belongings, which must have been nicked from the nearby supermarket.

Jay studied the fellows minutely, hidden in the dark some fifty paces away from them amongst the bushes. One of the men could have been his own grandfather - except for the fact that he wasn't. Approximately sixty, but with wild, black hair and slightly Turkish features, he wore a patchwork coat of gaudy colours. Jay looked up from the binoculars just to check it out, but was then startled as everything became pitch black around him. His eyes had become accustomed to the enhanced light of the viewfinder.

Returning to his binoculars, he saw that the man looked every bit what one might expect to come across in a fairground or travelling circus. His appearance was also somewhat theatrical, and Jay wondered whether he was simply dressing up.

His colleague beside him was grey-haired and wore a knitted, beige jumper. He had all the hallmarks of a middle class GP, recently out of work, who was going on a bender for the weekend with his friends, perhaps in a vain attempt to recapture his youth?

The third chap had his back to Jay, but was overweight and much quieter than his fellow revellers. He drank his beer in silence for the most part and only briefly entered the discussions. Jay saw a rather large, bald head and a blue tracksuit that was stretched a bit around the waistline.

The wind blew more definitely in his direction at that point and Jay caught another mouthful of the savour of sausages; there were frying merrily in the pan beside the fire. He lowered the binoculars and was momentarily startled again by his sudden plunge into darkness; the night vision chip made everything so much easier to see. Yet, with another great rumble from his stomach, Jay began to forget his worries and simply longed to join the party - and, more to the point, to partake of their food.

If Jay had been expecting to cause alarm, as his lone, dark shape emerged from around the corner and advanced into the clearing, he didn't. Quite the reverse occurred, in fact. For, upon noticing him a short distance off, the gypsy-faced man in the coloured jacket pointed excitedly and called, 'Oi! Yeh look jus' like me grandson, boy! Come and join the party.'

Jay almost jumped backwards in fright, and the fat man in the blue tracksuit put his beer down and turned to face him. He glared at Jay with hollow eyes and a furrowed brow. But the man in the beige jumper leapt to his feet and went immediately over to Jay and grabbed him by the wrist. Jay recoiled for a second, markedly nervous.

'James is all right. He won't hurt you, son,' the man reassured him. Jay recognized an American accent. 'Come and sit down and have some food with us.'

'T-Thanks,' Jay croaked.

He stuffed the night vision bins into his pocket, as they were rather too valuable to advertise, and followed the chap in the beige jumper over to his make-shift seat and sat down beside him. As he did so, the fat man had noticed the expensive looking item in his jittery fingers - which now also protruded from his pocket - and he seemed to have his eye upon them. Jay felt troubled by the man's listless gaze.

The man in the pullover immediately offered him a can of beer. Jay had very little taste for it, and could never drink it socially, but he accepted none the less and tried not to wince too much as he sipped a mouthful.

'Been train-spotting have you?' the fat man asked. His voice sounded hollow and monotonous and his eyes didn't move at all.

'Nope,' Jay answered, 'Just...er... just walking.'

'Now then, don't be rude, Nathan; we haven't even introduced ourselves yet,' the man in the jumper retorted. He gestured to his colleagues in turn. 'My friend here is James, James Thompson.'

'At your service, grandson,' the man with the patchwork coat growled, touching his forehead and implying a salute. Jay nodded in acknowledgement.

'My other friend here, is Mr Nathan Plevin, recently discharged—'

'*Escaped,* you mean,' James butted in.

'- recently - er - *come by his freedom* from a long convalescence.'

'Nice to meet you,' Jay replied. Though neither he nor the fat man offered one another a handshake, and neither did Jay get the impression that he was nice.

'And I'm Conner Jones. Formerly of the employ of the United States Government in the field of Atomic Research but, thankfully, no longer.'

'Ah, yeah, I couldn't mistake the American accent,' Jay responded, brightly. He seemed to have found a way to break the ice. The man in beige, however, suddenly baulked and stifled an angry frown with a little difficulty.

'That's a *Canadian* accent you mistook, young man, but who cares anyway? Tell us who you are and where you come from. Then tell us how you come to be walking into our apocalypse party.'

'Apocalypse p-party?' Jay repeated, stumbling over his words.

'Name first!' James the gypsy demanded.

'Romero, I'm Jay Romero,' he responded.

'Crikey! Yeh not me grandson, after all,' James exclaimed, apparently genuinely surprised by this news.

Jay shook his head to confirm the fact. Then he added, 'It's kind of a long story...'

All three of them then suddenly laughed - quite raucously - including the formally amiable Mr Jones.

'That's rich!' James barked.

'We've all got long stories, Jay,' Conner informed him.

'So tell us yours first, boy,' Nathan the fat man ordered, staring at him menacingly again.

The sweet smell of frying sausages grew heavy in the air, making Jay's insides yearn. But desire them as he might, he knew he'd have to play friendly with these misfits if he were going to be certain of a decent feed. And what kind of weird party was this: a veritable gypsy, a scientist and… he hated to admit it to himself, but the third man had the vacant stare of… *well… a lunatic,* Jay thought? He took another unpleasant swig of beer to calm himself and get some thinking time.

Thereafter, leaving out several critical, future-altering details, he began recounting his story hitherto as the others listened in keenly. It was quite a tale indeed.

The fire within the ring of bricks threw a dancing red glow over the faces of the four diverse figures grouped around it. All were eating perfectly burnt sausages and washing them down with copious alcohol. They also dined on pork steaks and chicken drumsticks and, as his stomach filled up and the beer went down, Jay almost began to relax, and he hardly seemed to mind as he explained to them that he had the Security Services on his tail for no apparent reason nor fault of his own.

His three companions could hardly be described as shocked by his news, and, as they themselves relived each their own peculiar and disturbing adventures of late, Jay began to see a pattern emerging.

Nathan had - as Jay had assumed - made a successful escape bid from a secure mental health unit near Cambridge and, in telling his story, became rather more lucid and communicative, forcing Jay to reappraise him. According to *his* version of events, he should never have been locked up in first place and, according to him, had the correct legal procedures been adhered to, he never would have been Sectioned at all. It all boiled down to some highly embarrassed Ministry figures and a psychiatrist on the Government payroll.

He obliged Jay by explaining that, after being cooped up with crackpots for the better part of two years and being fed drugs without his knowledge nor consent, he might well come across as brooding, unstable and insecure.

The bottom line was that, after stumbling upon some old scientific papers in the University where he lectured, which detailed what he believed to be a viable death ray, he'd approached the Ministry of Defence with a proposition to develop it along with a team of colleagues, if the Government would provide assistance and funding. He took great pains to advise the MOD that he and his fellow boffins were loyal British subjects and friends of the Crown, though it seemed to make no difference to their response.

The weapon itself involved transmitting a concentrated beam of energy over a distance with a negligible loss of power. Ordinarily electromagnetic signals - such as radio or TV - attenuate as they spread out and, after a certain distance, the signal is lost completely. This device, however, could supposedly fire the signal out like a laser beam and, because it would not be visible light, it would not suffer the same degradation as it passed through the atmosphere - giving it a much longer range than the laser with very little power loss. The projection was that it could hit targets at 4000 kilometres. For some reason, though, Nathan could not remember the name of the man who had originally designed the weapon and, as he guessed he might know it, Jay said nothing.

The upshot of Mr Plevin's application for a grant was, sadly, a wall of silence from the MOD; which was not so bad, but then Nathan inexplicably lost his job and his research contract. Then his children were taken into care by the Local Authority after he had a row with his wife, slapping her just once in anger.

Thereafter, he found himself Sectioned under the Mental Health Act, locked up and without legal representation. Thus left to defend himself in a merciless institution, he had to resort to his own near genius and, finally, he had outwitted the staff and fled the place.

Jay was struck at the empathy between them, and confounded by the similar pattern of their two stories, but what then was Mr Jones' tale?

He had been employed as test engineer at a secret US weapons plant and, when offered a promotion, thought that his life had taken a turn for the better. After all, he had a flourishing career, a nice house, a wife and children and a secure job.

During his interview with a number of very senior scientists and military figures however, he had learned something highly disturbing that caused him grave concern - he would not tell Jay what it was. After giving it some consideration he declined the job offer and, for some reason, was made redundant only a month or so later. When his house was raided the next day by armed Anti-Terrorist Police, even though he was not arrested, he realised something sinister was afoot.

Quickly the family made plans. His wife and children preferred to go into hiding with distant relatives but he himself had decided to leave the country altogether, and now only had contact with the folks back home via coded e-mails.

'My wife and I pretend to be a hooker talking to a previous client,' he informed them, 'and when e-mailing the kids I pretend to be another kid in a chat room, or else it's the youngsters sending their wish-lists to Santa Claus. You get the idea? Yes, sir, we've managed to avoid the Internet monitors for several weeks now!'

'But don't you want to go home?' Jay asked. 'I mean, will you have to stay out of the US for ever; why not go home to Canada?

'Let me tell you what's going on way up there in my home country, Jay; this may surprise you. Of course you know that in the Second World War the Nazi regime built concentration camps - and death camps - way out east in places like Poland?'

'Yeah,' he replied, wiping his mouth on his sleeve after finishing off his fourth and last barbecued sausage.

'Why d'you suppose they built them so far out there, which meant that they had to ferry Jews all the way across the country to reach them?'

Jay pondered it for a while, and then he suggested, 'To keep them out of sight, you know - 'Out of sight: out of mind?''

'Exactly,' Conner agreed. 'Jay, right now there are huge new prison complexes being built in far away northern places like Canada. They're being built for a similar purpose in our time. Have you ever heard of the phrase - 'New World Order?''

'Yes,' he replied, gravely, 'I have; conspiracy folk have been harping on about it for ages now.'

'This time the people behind it are not just after Jews, my friend; it is a much broader plan. No, they're after anybody and everybody who stands up to them, anybody who believes in National Sovereignty, Personal Identity and Freedom of Worship!'

'Who's doing it?' Jay asked.

'I don't know any particular names,' he answered, rather to his companion's disappointment. 'One thing I know, however, is that when I uncovered something terrible at work and refused that job for reasons of conscience, I think I bumped into them. Yes, sir, I am now regarded by the US Authorities with about as much favour as an international criminal. Jay, when you offend or embarrass the Government, life is not worth living, I can tell you!'

'Three of kind is what we are, isn't it?' Jay remarked.

'Here, here,' Nathan replied, passing him another can of drink; it was one of the very few remaining.

Jay refused, saying, 'No, I've already had two; thanks, but I'll be ill - trust me.'

Nathan ignored him and pressed it into his hands. 'Drink up, lad, you're one of us now.'

Gypsy James had an altogether different tale to tell, though it was not that coherent as he kept losing his balance and falling off the seat every so often, and, at other times, bursting into melancholy song. Notwithstanding he was a practitioner of folk magic, conjuring tricks and fortune telling and the like. And it came to pass one day, peddling his trade in these parts, that he'd had a frightening meeting with some formidable stranger that had, at once, convinced him that the world was about to come to an end.

And having met up with these other two souls who seemed to bear testimony to just such an event, they had happily arranged to spend what they joked might be their last few days on earth eating, drinking and making merry.

'Meh caravan's just over th' way,' he informed Jay, slurring his speech, 'it'th bin in th' family for year'th, now. Useful fer gettin' aroun' an tha'.'

'And we're his guests,' Conner said, diving forwards and catching James as he slumped sideways off the pile of railway sleepers and began snoring loudly.

Chapter 14

Magnetic Chaos

Several hours later, Jay awoke feeling cold and uncomfortable. He was lying on a concrete slab next to his bag. It was the dead of night and the orange glow of the station lights shone at him through the trees from beyond the fence. He raised his head off the slab - but that was not the only cause of his headache - and pressed the illumination button on his wristwatch: *half past one*!

Grumbling to himself about the lateness of the hour, he suddenly remembered where he was and what he'd been doing that evening. He dragged himself painfully upright and, having clambered to his feet and looked around dazedly at the cutting, he realised that all the others had gone.

The embers of the fire had subsided into a dark, grey mass with one or two spots of dull red remaining. All the beer cans had been cleared away and Jay saw that the track was deserted apart from himself and his belongings... *his belongings?*

His hand flew to his pocket. They were there, the binoculars. What a relief! At least he hadn't been robbed. He drew them out, activated the night vision chip and scanned the vicinity. True, there were no signs of life at all, although he thought he caught a glimpse of the shadowy outline of a fox slinking along the top of the bank. Soon he gave up squinting at it, as it made his headache rather worse.

Next, after he had checked that the coast was clear, he knelt down and examined the contents of his holdall. If one of them had discovered the gun, goodness knows what...! No, it was still there, wrapped up in his track suit top. Well, if they hadn't stolen that, then they hadn't stolen anything.

He did not mean to malign these people whom he had only known a couple of hours but, in light of what Raphael had told him, dare he trust anybody any more?

Feeling rather dry in the throat, a combination of nerves and the dehydrating effect of alcohol, he finished off the last few mouthfuls of water from the bottle and stopped to consider where to spend the remainder of the night. He could not lay out here in the open expanse of the railway siding all night long, and the luminous green tent would stand out a mile as soon as the sun came up. It would also be difficult to pitch it amidst all the gravel and scrub. Deciding then to search for a safer haven for the night, he struggled as he heaved the heavy bag back over his shoulder, and he made his way uneasily towards the fence dividing the disused section of the track from the working line.

As he scanned the platform opposite, lit up with bright, orange lamps, he noticed a dark shape lying ahead of him further along the siding, which veered to his right as it passed the fence to run parallel alongside the main line for several hundred yards. Although the track remained, it appeared to be discarded and was quite overrun with vegetation, and there, in the distance, was what looked like an abandoned railway coach.

If he could just slip past the station without being seen, once he set off down the disused line he ought to be able to get to the coach safely enough. It was rather too close to the main track for him not to be disturbed by passing trains, but far enough away not to be discovered, or so he thought.

He paused for a while with his foot resting on the lowest plank of the fence. Then, checking one last time for signs of life on the platform and finding none, he scrambled over and began trespassing on the railway. He made his way as swiftly as possible towards the coach in the distance and, after a minute, was out of sight of the station as the branch line ran behind a bank of trees.

Ten minutes later he came alongside the abandoned carriage and, looking around, he tried the nearest door; it opened. Acting on autopilot and fearing that his aching legs would otherwise collapse underneath him, Jay climbed inside and shut the door behind him.

It was an old coach with a corridor and separate compartments - the kind that was sadly taken out of service because people were afraid of getting raped. But for Jay this was good; the bench seats would allow him to lie out straight. Checking the interior he found the carriage to be in far better condition than he had expected. All the windows were intact, the seats were complete with cushions and it bore no obvious signs of vandalism.

He chose a compartment in the middle of the coach and shut himself in. Then, slipping on a pullover to keep warm, he barricaded the door with his holdall and lay out on the seat. It was quite a relief after lying on the ground for all that time. He feared he may only get about four hour's sleep before the first express rumbled past taking early morning commuters to London and, with that prospect to look forward to, he fell into a deep sleep.

Jay dreamed about his visit to the town hall before his birthday, about the kindred spirit of Dr Seymour - the man whom Raphael had said was great. He recalled the doctor's pet theory that he was pioneering, endeavouring to get the establishment to accept it: that of magneto-hydrodynamics. Jay loved it!

It concerned the movement of charged particles through electric fields, and their potential relation to tide raising effects. At some point in the lecture, Seymour had said that the molten rock and magma churning away in the heart of the earth acted like a gigantic dynamo, powering the whole of the Earth's magnetic field, which, in turn, protected the planet from the harmful emissions from the solar wind - the particles thrown out by the Sun. Jay had already known this much, but enjoyed having his memory refreshed now and again.

Though Seymour had also pointed out that an increasing number of geophysicists were becoming alarmed by the rate at which the Earth's magnetic field was weakening. Not through being battered twenty four hours a day by the solar wind, but because the giant dynamo within the core of the Earth was apparently winding down. Indeed, Jay and his fellow attendees had heard that there was good evidence to believe that the Earth's magnetic field had actually reversed polarity, that is, that the North and South poles had swapped over, at more than one point in geological history.

Prior to this cataclysmic event, of course, there would be a time of upheaval, of chaos and instability. Ships' compasses would go haywire, homing pigeons would get lost and navigation and survey equipment might become useless, making for mass confusion.

Possibly the most spectacular evidence of a looming magnetic reversal, however, would be the phenomenon of the Northern Lights - the Aurora Borealis - appearing over all the globe and not just at the pole. Jay imagined the shimmering, dancing rainbow formation of light filling all the sky above him. Immediately he felt entranced by it as he lay there on the seat. It was so beautiful to watch.

The random deflection and scattering of the swathes of softly coloured light became more beautiful, in his estimation, than anything else in the world, including the mountains, valleys and trees that he loved. He lay there watching it through the carriage window filling all the sky above him. He recalled a similar experience inside his computer whilst stuck in the rift three years previously.

And then a wave of dread washed over him as he lay there, and it made the shimmering light seem ghastly and out of place. This had already happened - in Westbury Park. He was *awake;* it was happening all over again!

Jay froze solid, becoming as stiff as a board on the seat, hardly daring to move a muscle. He remembered seeing the Aurora rippling down to more southerly latitudes than it should have on his birthday; he had seen it in the park. What did this mean? Now it was visible all over the country, but it shouldn't be?

Jay sat up and rested his hand upon the cold glass pane of the compartment window, squinting at the lights in the sky. 'What are you doing?' he asked the heavens in a whisper. 'Is something wrong; is someone interfering?'

He shivered, but not for the cold, and realised that the danger Dr Seymour had warned them of appeared to be coming to pass, namely, the North and South poles were on the verge of swapping over. Surely it would turn the developed countries of the world into disaster zones?

Then a huge rumbling jolt hit the carriage which lurched violently against its brakes and all the windows of the compartments rattled. Jay immediately dropped his gaze and glanced across at the station through the line of trees, expecting to see a high speed train come tearing past him at top speed at any moment. *So much for the four hour's rest,* he thought, *who wants to travel at this time of the morning anyway?*

He looked up and down the main line though, try as he might, he could not see any sign at all of a passing train; no lights; no carriages; no hissing diesel engines; no smoke… nothing. Then, after thirty seconds more of continuing noise and vibration, all went deathly quiet, except for a disgruntled bird who chirped from her nearby roost.

Jay gawped, wide-eyed, at his own image reflected in the glass.

'Earthquake,' he told himself.

'Yes,' he answered himself.

Next morning the people milling about on the platform were gossiping with more zeal than usual, and their talk involved more than just the mundane subjects, such as their ever-rising Council Tax bills with no improvement in services, and how the new supermarket was killing off many of the shops in the town centre. Jay heard more than one hushed reference to 'signs in the heavens' and 'massive earthquakes.'

He had awoken after a rather broken sleep and, after exploring some way further down the siding, he had come across a bridge which he was able to use to get across to the other side of the main line without risking trespassing it.

It was a quarter to eight and the majority of the folk at the station were commuters waiting for the next train to London and, as many of them were carrying luggage of some description or other, Jay did not stand out that much with the holdall on his back. Though, judging by some of the comments he overheard as he went into the toilets to wash and change, a number of the businessmen standing nearby thought he was merely some rambler who had simply come to take advantage of the rail operator's facilities, 'like a penny-pinching gypsy.'

Jay scowled as he went past but did not retaliate. However, after he had refreshed himself, he decided to call the man's bluff.

The same fellow who had despised him - a plump, black man in a shiny, new grey suit - had just tucked his newspaper under his arm and made towards the edge of the platform with the rest of the crowd. An Intercity 125 was pulling into the far end of the station, its diesels whistling loudly and smoke belching from its overhead exhausts.

Playing the part well, Jay marched up to him, boldly, and tapped him on the arm. The man flinched for a moment but then attempted to ignore him, pulling a disdainful face and continuing to talk to his businessman colleagues. They all tried to pretend that Jay wasn't there. However Jay persisted and, finally, he got the man's attention.

'What?' he demanded.

'Finished with the paper?' Jay asked.

'*What?*'

'Could I have the paper; can't afford my own, see? I'm a 'penny-pinching gypsy." He announced this very loudly and clearly so that everybody in the vicinity would hear it.

Aware that he was causing acute embarrassment to both the man and the group of commuters around him, he grinned defiantly at the fellow as he blustered and tried to push his way past him. However they were boxed in on all sides by this time as the crowd thronged towards the train, now drawing to a halt beside the platform, its brakes squealing painfully.

When Jay blocked the man's path for a moment longer he almost motioned to hit him; but then he gave in, thrust the newspaper into Jay's chest, and wrenched his way past him muttering obscenities under his breath.

'Thank you, sir; support your local gypsy, sir!' Jay called out merrily as he moved away through the crowd, quite unmoved by the number of bemused and disapproving faces now staring at him.

His brief altercation with the be-suited City man appeared to have caused a huge amount of consternation. Enjoying himself with the thought of it, he walked over to the café and bought something for breakfast and a takeaway cup of tea. He then made his way out of the station and into the car park where he found a bench and sat down with the newspaper.

He smiled to himself savagely, pleased that he had made a fool of the man, a man who's rudeness was surpassed only by his ignorance of the real world, Jay thought.

As he ate and drank he flicked through the paper, hoping to find a reference to the previous night's events. They could not have passed by unnoticed - unless, of course, Jay really had dreamed the whole thing, and had only thought he'd been awake.

It took him quite a while to realise that the earthquake and magnetic storm had both occurred in the early hours and, as this edition of the newspaper would have gone to press the night before, there would be no mention of them. The story would have broken after the print run, so he'd have to wait for the next day's papers or, at least, an evening edition of this one.

The smile of satisfaction he wore at the thought of humiliating the commuter lingered for a considerable time, at least until he returned to the front page and then began to read the newspaper properly. It had been a long time since the gypsy jibe had come his way, so long - in fact - that he had almost forgotten it existed.

Then, at page four, he noticed something which he had missed the first time, something which wiped the smirk off his face in an instant and caused him to tremble where he sat.

It was another warm summer's day, but a cold dread rippled up Jay's spine. There it was - a colour photograph of *him*, the same one that had appeared in the Advertiser in the aftermath of the lightning strike declaring him to be the 'Miracle Kid.' But it was not the photograph that was the problem; it was what was written beneath it. Jay read the following -

MISSING PERSON NOTICE.

This is JAY ROBERT ROMERO,

of 24 Westbury Drive, Brackthorpe, Northamptonshire.

Age 17 years. Height 5 feet 8 inches.

He is wanted in connection with the disappearance of several individuals including Robert, Carol and Alice Romero of the same address. Any sighting or other information should be reported to Thames Valley Police on the number below, or can be given anonymously to Crime Stoppers. Should you see this notice in person, Jay, Detective Beveridge assures you that you have nothing to fear from contacting him or one of his colleagues. They merely want to ask you a few questions - and hear your side of the story.

'*Codswallop!*' Jay said, feeling as though he were about to vomit up his breakfast, and wishing that he'd eaten it a little more slowly. He had gone white, white with a mixture of fear and anger; things were getting worse and worse. He read through the notice again, '*wanted in connection with the disappearance of several individuals...*' he mouthed to himself.

What on earth was Lance's dad involved for, he wondered? Did *he* really believe one of his son's closest friends had bumped off his own family...? Or was he simply being used to try to get to him... to lull Jay into a false sense of security because it was his friend's dad...?

In an instant Jay knew what it was all about; it was the work of the Secret Service again. They must have leant on the Police to put out this notice with the intention of flushing him out and bringing him into the hands of the Authorities... and once in custody, who knew where he could end up? He had heard Internet rumours that there were secret military detention centres spread all over the world that none of the human rights groups knew existed, places where people could be detained indefinitely without trial, without charges, and without hope, dark places where the Eyes of Justice could not see! There had been news stories about 'Extraordinary Rendition' - which is what the US called it - and now even Mr Jones had confirmed that this kind of thing really was going on.

Troubled greatly by this discovery of the means the Security Services would use, considering that he had done nothing wrong - as far as he knew, he glanced around the car park quickly to see if anyone had noticed him. Perhaps it was too early in the morning for most people to have got to page four of the broadsheet newspapers - they took a while to read.

After a swift reconnoitre of the vicinity he saw that nobody else paid him the slightest attention and he breathed more easily. However, now that his smiling face had been plastered all over the media, someone was bound to recognise him sooner or later - and challenge him. It would therefore be best if he could stay out of sight for a week or two until the focus of public attention had moved on. One thing encouraged him, however: if the Security Services had resorted to sticking adverts in the papers it confirmed that they were getting desperate to find him, having been unable to do so by any other means, and he felt glad for it. It was not so much that he despised the Authorities; it was more a case that he was terrified what they might do to him if they caught up with him.

After all, surviving the lightning strike had brought him under the scrutiny of the medical establishment once before... Suppose someone gave *him* a bad psychiatric report because they wanted him locked up like Mr Plevin?

He tore the picture of himself out of the page, left the paper on the bench for another passer-by, and set off for the bridge once more. Deciding he would follow the branch line to avoid meeting people, he risked purchasing a handful of sandwiches and crisps from the same café and set off at a brisk pace along the platform.

Once on the other side of the bridge and striding along behind the bank of trees, Jay managed to relax a bit, and he stopped for a moment and set light to the scrap of newspaper with his details on it. He watched until all the paper had burned away to ash, stamped on the fire to ensure it wouldn't spread and set off again. He still felt tired from his disturbed night's sleep, and the residue of the beer had left him with a mild hangover.

Nonetheless he soon passed by the section of the line that he was familiar with, where the abandoned coach was parked up on its own, and struck off into the distance.

On an impulse he checked his wallet, and found he had just under £100 to hand. *So he wasn't a poor gypsy; he was a rich gypsy.*

Chapter 15

The Dream

As the midday sun rose high above him, Jay travelled in an easterly direction, following the course of the derelict branch line. He had no problem at all navigating as it stood out all too clearly across the surrounding landscape, despite the fact that in some places the cuttings had been filled in by farmers wishing to reclaim the land for crops. He came across other abandoned rolling stock after a couple of miles or so, and, thereafter, the track had been taken up completely, leaving only overgrown shrubs and tar-stained gravel in its place. The last hint of the track was a toppling pile of rotten sleepers stacked up untidily by the bank after work to remove them had apparently ceased. It looked as though the rail gang had simply left them to decompose; after all, these old timbers were biodegradable, Jay reasoned.

Apart from a retired gentleman walking his dog, he had not met anyone else all morning and, inwardly, Jay felt relieved, having no idea what he would say or do if someone recognised him or, worse still, tried to apprehend him. He wondered what Raphael had meant by his note saying that there is always a choice. Why had he emphasised it so much? Was it another hint? Did he mean that in some circumstances - really exceptional cases - it was OK to shoot a person, even to kill them? And if he did, wouldn't that make him as bad as the Agents that he feared? What happened when there was not enough time for the normal process of justice to take place, like in split-second life or death decisions?

Jay shuddered at the thought of it all. Killing his own alter-ego had been bad enough, but what should he do if another Agent appeared on the scene? He didn't want think about it; yet Raphael had also warned him that the gun would only work on mortals - as if Jay would ever think otherwise - but did that mean that some of his adversaries were not even going to be human beings? He supposed that it had to, but if not human, then what... aliens... ghosts... demons?

Some time later in the afternoon Jay was trekking along the top of an

173

embankment enjoying the view and eating the last of the sandwiches when, up ahead, he noticed that the line passed over a riveted iron bridge. He pressed onwards and, arriving at the crossing within a few minutes, he strode out into the middle of the wrought-iron structure, taking in the view all around.

Beneath the bridge there lay a canal, and the waterway and railway crossed each other at a forty five degree slant, the canal running north-east to south-west. There was no sign of any current, being a canal, and on either side a tow-path stretched into the distance, which, Jay reckoned, dated back to the days of horse-drawn barges.

The railway bridge on which he was standing had a manufacturer's mark stamped into one of the girders: *Sheffield 1899*. If that were when the iron had been forged, then the bridge must date from about the same time, Jay thought, and yet it was also the relatively modern invention of the railway that had sounded the death knell for the age of canal barges, and so, in a way, the bridge would have brought about the demise of the waterway beneath.

The invention of the new had killed off the old; yet now the new itself had become old, and was arguably in an even more dilapidated and run-down state; at least the waterway still looked navigable, Jay thought - not that he had much experience with boats.

This was the way of things; nature was always renewing itself, Jay decided, but, in the background, there was always the irresistible, inevitable force that ages, weakens and finally kills off every living creature. Even inanimate objects like this bridge could not escape its power. Strong as it may be, Jay mused, looking over the surrounding ironwork, after another hundred years and another hundred after that, surely it would eventually cave in and fall into the waters below? The waters, which, themselves, might have become an overgrown swamp or marsh by that time, fit only for frogs and mosquitoes?

Yes, Jay thought at length, *there is no disease on earth as bad as this; nothing is so hideous and cruel as the long, slow creep of death!*

Taken by a sudden impulse to return to the past - not literally but figuratively - Jay turned around and scrambled back across the bridge and down the embankment. Moments later he emerged through some bushes beside the still waters of the canal. He stood on the left hand bank, heading north-east if it had been a road.

The tow-path was a mixture, some parts of it being bare-faced stone, other parts having grass growing over it and yet others being merely a dirt track. He turned back 'downstream' and imagined the scene with a heavy horse yoked to a brightly painted barge, drawing it slowly through the water. He had to admit it held a certain romantic appeal; not least because any promise of a quiet life seemed attractive to Jay these days. However, he would not dawdle and, feeling the distinct need to keep on moving, he struck off beside the waterway, heading north and east.

To his delight the canal served as something of a self-contained nature reserve, and Jay noticed an abundance of wildlife including waterfowl that he had not observed while journeying along the railway. He met ducks, swans and coots and caught the occasional glimpse of fish as they broke the surface of the water to swallow insects that had fallen in close to the banks. He also spotted some dragon flies which he had always found fascinating creatures ever since his youth.

He wondered whether he might meet a pleasure boat or perhaps some people spending their holiday on the canal, but he did not come across any during that afternoon. Then, as evening drew in and the air became cool, he came to a large disused wharf and a number of locked boathouses. These all appeared to have been converted from an old warehouse, and the wharf itself boasted a number of massive iron bollards and cleats, evidence of ancient moorings now encased in the surrounding stone by their own rust.

Undoubtedly, this used to be a working quay, Jay thought, but, being sure he heard voices coming from inside one of the buildings, he decided to press onwards. Perhaps this was not an ideal place to stay the night.

As it grew darker and Jay had to resort to his last packet of crisps, he stumbled upon a sight that sent his mind reeling. There, parked on the grassy bank beside the tow-path a little distance from the water, sat a beautiful, traditional Romany caravan, barge boards and canopy painted with bight multicoloured floral patterns. It looked like something Jay imagined his ancestors could have travelled around Europe in, and then he remembered that some die-hard travellers still preferred the life on the road, even going so far as building or restoring the traditional caravans.

For a few moments he could not think what on earth this old thing was doing here. How many gypsies had he come across lately who—

'James!' he exclaimed, interrupting his own thoughts. It had to be his caravan; it bore the same gaudy designs as his old patchwork coat. And now a fresh fear seemed to rise up out of the water and wash over him. He noticed that the door of the caravan was lying ajar, the shafts were resting in the mud and there was no sign of the owner or the horse. Had something happened, causing the old man to unloose the horse and take flight, something so terrifying that he would not think twice about abandoning all his worldly goods?

Jay dropped his holdall on the tow-path and ran over to the caravan. He climbed up the wooden steps that had been set by the door and went inside. There was no one in and no sign of damage or theft. As he let his eye rove over the quaint pot-belly stove with its small, copper kettle, the hand crafted cupboards and shelves, he started to think upon more hopeful lines of inquiry. Perhaps James had only just gone out for the day on horseback and forgotten that he'd left the door unlocked? Maybe he and his doomsday friends were still out partying somewhere? Perhaps someone had *meant* Jay to find this caravan and make use of it for the night?

He furrowed his brow and glanced out of the tiny square window in the rear of the box-like room. After all this was an idyllic setting and he was fairly confident the fellow wouldn't mind; surely not after owning Jay as his own grandson?

Jay stepped outside again and went over to gather up his things. The sun had already set far in the distance over his shoulder and he needed shelter for the night. Wouldn't the caravan be safer and more secure than the tent?

Given his straitened circumstances, Jay decided to presume upon the owner's generosity for the night and duly loaded his bag on board. This did not solve the mystery of where Mr Thompson had gone by any means, assuming that the vehicle was indeed his. However, if he or the owner did not show up, Jay determined to leave a quantity of cash behind after he departed, and, as he found a supply of tinned food on board and some long life milk, he reckoned that not doing so would be plain theft.

Before long he'd found evidence-a-plenty of James' interests; there were astrological charts, books on numerology, palmistry, and even a drawer full of voodoo paraphernalia that Jay quickly closed again without investigating.

Late that evening as he sat with his back against the massive wooden spokes of the rear wheel, he stared out over the calming waterside. A mallard duck was still busying herself amongst the reeds on the far bank and the absence of any detectable current meant that the canal was so quiet, it was surreal. The guilty twinge at borrowing somebody else's home without permission had long since subsided in the peaceful atmosphere, and Jay retired to the bunk some hours later.

He was so exhausted, having had a number of fretful, sleepless nights, that he dropped off easily. Indeed, he felt so overwhelmed with tiredness that he barely even cared that someone else might arrive later in the night and, if he didn't climb into the bunk on top of him, might murder him in his sleep instead.

Jay's dreams came as lucid as ever and, before long, he found himself paying a visit to a very unusual room. Though he had some vague recollection of it, he could not tell where or when he'd seen it before.

He knew it was late in the evening and he saw an old man sitting in an armchair. It looked like they were in a hotel room and he could hear the rain beginning to fall outside the window.

The old man in the seat appeared very tired this particular night and also quite cold, even though the room felt warm to Jay. The man turned slowly to gaze at the heater by the fire place; it was glowing red. Then he sighed and reclined more deeply into his leather armchair. Like him, it too showed all the hallmarks of great age. Jay remembered his thoughts concerning the 'long, slow creep of death,' and had a fleeting thought that perhaps he was seeing a glimpse of the future; perhaps this ancient and frail man was him, Jay, at eighty or ninety years of age?

Jay moved in closer and gazed into the angular and wizened features.

177

Yes, he reckoned he saw his own fresh face in there somewhere. Was this really he himself in the future? Jay recoiled, not enamoured with the prospect of becoming old, or of feeling cold when it was warm. Then, out of the blue, came a more positive impulse: if this was in fact him, at least he survived; at least he escaped the Secret Service Agents and did not die in his youth. That was a comforting thought. He stood up and surveyed the scene around them.

The hotel room was well furnished but dusty, smart but faded. Jay was in an apartment which included a small bedroom and a minute cloakroom. The old man had evidently lived here for a number of years, judging by the wealth of decaying personal possessions scattered all around, mostly buried under layers of dust.

A stained pattern on the wooden panelled door was mirrored by the grain of the cabinet on the opposite wall. Two glass panes on this multi-purpose cabinet were hatched with decorative, rosewood fretwork. The wall paper, however, seemed to have come halfway from yellow to white but got lost somewhere in between. Jay guessed the elderly resident did not have much of an eye for aesthetic niceties. Also, what should have been real hardwood finishes, if the room had been up to scratch, had begun to de-laminate in some places. This meant they were merely veneers.

Jay considered the old man again; he looked well past eighty and very tired and drawn in appearance. His face, though, still remained determined, as though deep in contemplation. All at once he tapped his scaled knuckles on the table beside the armchair. Beneath the fingers of his left hand, Jay saw a small, leather-bound black notebook.

The old man was struggling with something; Jay could see the indecision in his eyes. He pondered the notebook on the table. What was inside it? He did not dare ask, even though he was sure it was a dream... well... *fairly* sure.

Jay saw his eye alight on the decorative utility cabinet against the wall; it had a locking compartment within the small sliding drawer. Jay saw the keyhole and then, as he stared intently at it, he began to think the old man's thoughts. Is was as though his mind was no longer his... *Would it be safe in there? How can I hide it?*

And then, of all the things to test him this evening, this had to be the strangest. Incredible as it may seem, Jay seemed to change places for a moment with the fellow in the room. For a second or two, he could not remember which one of them he was. Was he old or young? Should he be standing or sitting? Truly, at that instant, he did not know who he really was... He did not recall his own name...

However, the dream was not done; Jay then drew back and became a fly on the wall, viewing the room from one corner of the ceiling. He watched, quite entranced, as the elderly man heaved himself to his feet, took up the small, black book and his walking stick, and made his way painfully over to the cabinet by the wall. He bent down, withdrew a key from his pocket, unlocked the draw and placed the book inside. Then, locking it up securely, he returned to the armchair and rested his head back with a great sigh of relief. He did not appear to breathe or make any movement after that, and Jay was filled with the sensation that the old man had just died there.

The time seemed to pass slowly with the hands of the clock on the mantelpiece, and nothing moved again and there was no sound. Jay watched and waited until, long after the rain had stopped, morning light appeared through the window.

Then, all of a sudden, three dark figures came into the room. They did not force their way in, so one of them must have had a key. These men all wore black suits and they had American accents, although Jay could not discern what they were discussing.

However, he certainly knew what they were up to: they were searching for something, searching for something in the apartment now that the old man had passed away. None of them seemed to bother paying any respect to the dead; instead, ignoring the corpse in the armchair, they swiftly rifled through his paperwork and files, opening out drawers and boxes.

Then, after a fruitless quarter of an hour, one of the men pointed to the small, lockable drawer; it would not open. One of his colleagues then volunteered to frisk the body and, sure enough, he soon found the key in the pocket of the old man's jacket. All three of them suddenly looked very excited.

The man fitted the key into the keyhole, opened the draw and extracted the little, black notebook. At last, they had struck gold - or this appeared to be the case from the way they reacted. Each one grinned and gesticulated, though quietly for fear of disturbing the neighbours - it was still very early in the morning.

Jay knew that the book contained something vitally important, something important enough for three men to steal it from the estate of someone who had only just died and barely gone cold! Jay watched as the figures tidied up the room again and then left with the stolen notebook.

Nobody else came in for another hour or so until a room attendant arrived with a breakfast tray. She promptly dropped it when she discovered the old man's corpse and ran out of the room screaming.

Chapter 16

Weapon to End all War

Jay knew that the dream meant something the moment he awoke next day; it meant something immensely important. So he purposed to spend some time recounting to himself everything that had happened since the start of the trouble and trying to see what it all pointed to. He ascertained that the owner of the caravan had not returned during the night and, with little hesitation as the scenery was so pleasant, he determined to stay put at least for the immediate future.

After taking breakfast, he made himself a pot of tea on the stove and, taking it outside to sit by the water, he began to mull over all his adventure so far.

*

The laboratory was buried deep underground in the heart of a mountain; the military planners had intended the base to be able to withstand a nuclear war, albeit not necessarily a direct hit. Though a select number of the technicians who worked at NORAD seemed remarkably confident that their facility would never be tested in such a scenario. It was as though they possessed an inner faith of some kind and their colleagues could not quite get to grips with it.

The lab in question was on one of the lowest levels of the site, those which required personnel to have the highest level of clearance and, of course, an unwavering loyalty to the System. Not even the Joint Chiefs of Staff could get in down here except by prior arrangement; certainly it was no place for doubters and subordinates.

The Command had given the men who worked here - for it was an almost exclusively male preserve - an extraordinary amount of licence. In short, the staff had permission to undertake any research and development of any technology they liked, provided they believed it could be of potential benefit and, more importantly, that they kept the Command informed of progress.

181

Specially tuned overhead lighting that was designed to mimic the daylight illuminated rows of Perspex shelves set around the walls. These shelves contained various analysis and test equipment, and there were men in anti-static overalls working at a series of benches grouped together as workstations spaced around the room.

There were usually half a dozen projects on the go at any one time, but the official who had just entered through the airlock at the far side of the room had only one device on his mind. This particular project had been under consideration for decades, but it was only in the last few months that it had appeared to be approaching a viable form.

He glanced briefly around the laboratory acknowledging a number of associates and brothers, and then made his way over to the locked steel door which led to a sealed compartment within the hub of the main laboratory. This small room was, perhaps, the most sensitive area within the whole of NORAD. There was no door handle or keyhole; instead, the man merely swiped the back of his right hand past a scanner beside the door. A sensor detected the microchip implanted beneath the skin, confirmed his ID, and the door slid open.

As it closed again behind him, he walked over to a technician standing at the one and only workstation in the room. There was a desk, a table and a bench with everything the man needed within easy reach laid out around him. He had a set of plans spread out over the table which was illuminated from beneath and was making detailed numerical corrections to the drawing. Thereafter he paused and typed up the same modifications into his computer terminal. He was very busy but looked up as the other man came in.

'The Command are pleased with our first successful test firing,' the official remarked, smiling broadly and joining his fellow at the other side of the table. The two of them then gazed down at the drawing. It was of a geostationary satellite bearing what looked like a telescopic projection on top.

'Yeah, but I bet the Russians weren't,' the technician responded with a smirk. 'The orbiting version allows us to attain distances up to three times that of the earth-bound units, maybe up to 12,000k. Only trouble is, we're having problems when the beam hits the atmosphere.'

'What's that, still getting ionisation? We heard about that difficulty; are we still getting those simultaneous mid-air explosions?'

"Fraid so, that old Soviet tub we shot down the other day was in orbit so it was no problem, but when we try targets on the earth's surface... well, that's when the trouble starts. Too much power and all we do is burn up in the air; too little and we don't reach the target... bloody paradox really. We keep trying different wavelengths but some of the guys reckon it's not gonna work whatever frequency we use. They're saying we ought to jack the whole thing in; yeah, those of us who work on this old gizmo are becoming something of a joke! 'The Antiques Roadshow' is their latest one.'

The official looked mildly alarmed at this comment, which, because of its simple honesty, struck a note of fear within him.

'What, after fifty year's work? After all the covering up there's been... misinformation... bribes... eliminations... unexplained events? To simply give it up? This man is supposed to have been one of a kind, a genius; are you sure we've applied every detail in the plans correctly? I mean, if the management decide we've gone and sunk our own economy for the sake of this damn thing... or if some jerk didn't read the book properly and it's not viable after all - '

He did not finish his sentence, however, as the technician then shook his head dismissively and patted the handle of the top draw of his desk. His expression was serene. 'Not a chance - I've read the manuscript for myself and it's all in order. I've actually got it, right here in my own desk! They let me keep it for inspiration, see?'

Upon hearing this endorsement the official became somewhat more relaxed for a moment. He gazed anew upon the working drawing lying on the table before him, almost doting over it.

'The weapon to end all war,' he breathed, more to himself than anyone else.

A ominous thrill swept through the two men standing in the room, and the technician, although he had gazed at the plans a thousand times before, understood afresh what it really was that lay on his desk.

'*Or, the weapon to end all enemies,*' he muttered quietly.

The two men exchanged fervent glances.

A duck flew past the trees and landed in the middle of the canal, making a splash and sending a small wave rippling towards the banks. Jay smiled in appreciation; he had always admired the way aquatic birds took off and landed - like miniature flying boats.

As he drained the cup of tea, he began with his attendance at the lecture in the town hall and examined every instance of the strange and unusual happenings that had followed: letting things slip to Dave; being accosted in the library by the stranger; the appearance of the Aurora; the disappearances; the Agents; Raphael and the car; earthquakes; dreams and more catastrophic events. Had he really caused all these or were they destined to happen anyway? When he had fought his image three years ago he'd only had one enemy that time and one objective in his sights. Now, however, he had no idea of the numbers of the forces ranged against him, and neither had he any idea was the objective was - except to win, but win what?

And what then should he make of this latest dream, if anything? Certainly it was not as terrifying as seeing black-robed figures in the middle of the night, but nonetheless it was pretty grim - witnessing the last few hours of some old man's life. And then he'd seen his belongings rifled by the FBI or some other group.

Then there had been that strange empathy between them. For the brief moment it had occurred, it seemed that he was no longer himself... like he was somebody else, Jay thought, and then those men had stolen the book. Whatever it was it had seemed really important to them.

The memory of Dr Seymour's words seemed to surface in his mind, like the fish in the canal that were coming up to gulp a mouthful of air every once in a while as he watched.

'So twins, particularly identical twins, will share the same World Line for nine months of their life, while together in the mother's womb. These tracks will stay closely aligned for the majority of their childhood years. In adulthood, it is likely that their World Lines will diverge completely. However, because they were so closely associated for so many years, it is plausible that a residual link survives between them.'

A residual link, Jay wondered? Was that akin to empathy? It sounded like it, but what had Seymour said next? Ah, yes, he had it memorised: 'Not only this; the potential of World Lines to explain phenomena such as telepathy and empathic feeling is very great.' Yep, that's it, Jay thought, feeling that he was making some progress.

'I propose that every living person here present has a trail through space-time streaming out behind them. This track, or plot, or World Line is a memory contained within the very fabric of the universe itself of where they have been. With all of these strings of World Lines stretching out behind us; as the world rotates about its orbit, some of them will get tangled up like wool. Grasp a handful of string and twist it in your hands; won't it get tangled up?'

'Yeah,' Jay mused, 'sure it will; maybe mine is just getting tangled up with somebody else's... but whose?'

And then the words of Raphael came to mind, 'Concentrate on—'

'*Tesla!*' Jay cried out loud with excitement and then, remembering that as much as possible ought to be kept secret, he shut his mouth again quickly and simply thought about it.

It had to be him; the old man in the dream *had* to be him! Raphael had given him the name hadn't he? And, if not, how come Jay had even found himself researching him for his summer project?

It seemed that somehow, in the ever-twisting, convoluted and labyrinthine universe of World Lines, his own trail must have bumped into Nikola Tesla's at some point. What an unbelievable privilege and twist of fate...

Slowly it began to dawn upon Jay that, perhaps, it was the little, black notebook that was even more important than the fate of the old man himself. Whereas he looked as though he'd reached the end of his natural life; perhaps it would have been better if the book had not fallen into the hands of those three men? The trouble was, what Jay had dreamed of was the past, history - it had already happened.

And, all of a sudden, Jay realised what he had to do. He sprung up from the bank and marched back hurriedly to the caravan with a definite spring in his step. He also determined not to speak a word of it to anyone.

The tow-path proved surprisingly undisturbed for the next few days, and only a passing couple on the following evening proved any sort of challenge. They had appeared to be on a twilight stroll and enjoying their honeymoon when emerging through the trees beside the waterway. Inevitably, they remarked upon the conspicuous form of the caravan parked on the grass bank. Jay had at first thought to lock the door and hide underneath the bunk when they came over to investigate but, in the end, found it much less stressful to simply talk to them and answer one or two of their more incisive questions obliquely.

The event passed off without incident and Jay was left to continue his vigil beside the waters, food running low and, all the time, wondering when the next short circuit in the continuum might occur. When it did, he would be ready for it.

It came to pass on the very next night, Jay found himself in the same dream. This time however, he became aware of things from another perspective entirely: jerked awake suddenly - although not to daylight - he found himself snatched sideways out of the bunk and catapulted out through the roof of the caravan. He then found himself soaring off into the heavens.

Somehow leaving his physical self behind and, simultaneously, finding himself wrenched a million miles through the cosmos, he could only comprehend what he experienced in momentary images. It was like taking a series of still photographs whilst watching a two-hour movie. He was being drowned in a gigantic rainbow-coloured vortex, like water draining through a vast plug hole in the bottom of an ocean. Next there came light, a myriad of shining pin-points… as innumerable as the stars. Then Jay saw that they were not pin-points, but rather holes. No, they weren't holes; they were strings, and what he perceived was their point of incidence on one plane of space.

Something was pulling him by the stomach and, glancing down, he saw that he was being hauled at what felt like light-speed through the universe by some umbilical-type cord that was stretching out in front of him. Jay could not see where it ended, if indeed it had an end.

A moment later he realised that the cord was, in fact, a tunnel. Now he was falling through it, twisting and turning like a random soap bubble being washed down pipe. He had a brief glimpse of diving head first into a universe full of white spaghetti. Everywhere Jay looked he saw only twisting and turning strands of glowing white. Every single one was moving, like a ball of wool being slowly twisted and tautened. Now and then two of the spaghetti stands would get to close, touch one another, and send sparks and flashes into the surrounding void, momentarily dazzling him.

Chapter 17

A Future Reordered

He felt so very tired this night, and it was also terribly cold. He turned slowly to gaze at the electric heater by the fire place; it made his neck hurt. The element was glowing red. He sighed and reclined more deeply into his leather armchair. Like him, it too showed all the hallmarks of great age. The long, slow creep of death was taking him; he could feel it, sense it stalking him from out of the shadows.

He examined the wizened features of his face with his wrinkled left hand. Was that a scar he felt on his right cheek? He couldn't remember ever having had such an injury; then again, he was becoming so forgetful these days...

He knew he could not evade his stalker forever. Was this really how he himself would end his days, all alone and desperately worried about the future? He recoiled, terrified with the prospect of what could happen after his death.

The hotel room about him was well furnished but dusty; smart but faded. This was his apartment in the Hotel New Yorker. It was not the best in town but was nonetheless quite adequate for his simple needs. He had lived here for a number of years, but had been unable to keep abreast of the cleaning in recent months due to failing health. And for some reason, the staff had not been in to help either. It did not make sense. Were they simply waiting for him to die? They hardly seemed to care these days, judging by the untidy mess of his possessions scattered around the place, which, he himself could hardly summon up the energy to move. Some of the items were buried under layers of dust.

The patina on the wooden panelled door was matched by the grain of the cabinet on the opposite wall. Two glass panes on this cabinet were embellished with decorative rosewood fretwork. He had chosen them many years before for that very reason, he remembered. The wall paper, however, seemed to be a strange mixture of yellow and white. Long ago he'd realised he did not have much of an eye for aesthetic colours.

He sat there, very tired and drawn, and yet deep in contemplation.

There was something important that he had to do. The safety of the world depended on it. All at once he tapped his scaled knuckles on the table beside the armchair, thinking. Beneath the fingers of his left hand there lay the small, leather-bound black notebook.

He was struggling with what to do. His eye then alighted upon the decorative utility cabinet against the wall; the small, sliding drawer was a locking compartment. Would it be safe in there? What if they discovered it; surely there would be some kind of search?

Although it turned his peace-loving countenance into a grimace, there was one sure way to keep it safe and, after all, he knew what he had to do. He had to keep the people safe. Whereas he had wanted the world to benefit from it, there were others wanted only rule, and would use whatever means they could to achieve their ends. His mind was made up and he sat there resolutely for a few minutes longer, gathering the last his diminishing strength.

A momentary loss of consciousness hit him, leaving him reeling for brief spell. For an instant he did not know who he really was... He did not recall his own name... This could mean only one thing: his time was almost up. Another lapse of reason, another loss of consciousness, and it could well be his last. Yes, he had to act, and he had to act right now for the sake of all humanity!

He hauled himself unsteadily to his feet, took up the small, black book and his walking stick, and made his way painfully over to the radiant heater standing in front of the fireplace. He bent down slowly, caught hold of the top of the heater and dragged it away from the hearth leaving the grate exposed.

He then began ripping the pages from the book with as much vengeance as his arthritic fingers could manage. He carefully piled the torn leaves of manuscript in the grate and then scrabbled amongst the ornaments on top of the marble mantelpiece.

Finding some matches, he struck one with shaking hands and dropped it into the bundle of paper in the hearth. Flames sprung up in moments and began to devour the dry pages of the book with a relish. Smoke billowed into the room as the chimney had not been swept for years and had become partially blocked, reducing the draft.

He coughed in the fumes and retreated from the blaze, feeling exhausted but immensely relieved.

Stumbling across the room in considerable pain, he returned to the armchair and, once reclined, he rested his head back and, with a great sigh of relief, he closed his eyes to rest.

The time seemed to pass in slow motion with the hands of the clock on the mantelpiece, nothing moved again and there was no sound. And, long after the rain had stopped, the first of the morning light appeared through the window.

All of a sudden three dark figures came bursting into the room. They had not forced their way in, so one of them must have had a key; perhaps it was in the collusion of some of the hotel staff? These were men in black suits. They had American accents, and were discussing something earnestly.

The men began searching the apartment. They were searching for something now that the old man had passed away. It was as if they had been waiting for him to go, and now, at last, they had their opportunity. None of them seemed remotely concerned for the dead; instead, they swiftly turned out paperwork and files, opening up drawers and boxes. Their search encompassed everything in the apartment.

Then, after about a quarter of an hour of searching and finding nothing, one of the men pointed to the locked drawer. It would not open when he tried it. One of his colleagues then volunteered to frisk the dead body and, sure enough, he soon found the key in the pocket of the old man's jacket. All three of them suddenly looked excited.

The same fellow fitted the key into the keyhole, opened the draw and thrust his hand inside the compartment. At long last, they'd struck gold! Or, maybe they hadn't...?

The man withdrew his hand despondently from the draw and turned and shrugged to his friends. It seemed to have been a red herring; there was nothing in the locked compartment after all. Next moment, one of them pointed to the electric heater that had been pulled away from the fire place and, with one accord, all three hurried over to it.

Straight away they noticed the pile of ashes in the grate. Looking aghast, one of them knelt down and felt the grate; it was still slightly warm - like the corpse - and then, with a pang of horror, the same fellow extracted the charred remains of the leather cover of the notebook. He rose to his feet and held it aloft dejectedly for his colleagues' appraisal. The book had been burnt!

After a brief discussion, during which time they seemed to realise their worst fears, the man tossed the burnt cover back into the grate sending up a small cloud of white ash. Having been frustrated once and for all, the three men then turned on their heels and marched straight out of the door, not even caring to tidy up the mess they had made in their frantic search of the place.

Nobody else came in for another hour until a room attendant arrived and discovered the old man's body sitting amidst all the overturned files and papers. She promptly screamed and ran off to raise the alarm.

Soon afterwards the Police arrived and began photographing everything with a flash light and an old black-and-white camera.

*

Jay awoke the next morning quite late. He recalled most of his experience the previous evening, including the dream and, what he reckoned to be, his traversing of the World Lines. He remembered the burning of the manuscript and the conviction that he had somehow circumvented the intentions of those evil men, albeit he did not really appreciate how.

He lay in the bunk for a time listening to the birds outside chirping a new song, and then rubbed his eyes and groaned when he saw the time was getting on for ten. He got up, washed, and made himself beans on toast for breakfast. He had determined to leave five pounds per night for the owner of the caravan when he moved on - although his finances were able to last a good while longer - and as he went outside to get some fresh air and sun that morning, he felt reasonably certain that he had achieved something useful.

Two weeks later, however, the food situation was fast becoming desperate. Tinned tomatoes, beans and sausages were all very well, but hardly constituted a proper diet and now that the bread was gone that was all Jay had left.

In the interim he had discovered a standpipe a short distance along the tow-path and assumed that the owner of the caravan had parked up on the bank for this very reason. Jay had made good use of the fresh water supply and washed his clothes and, by this lunchtime, had everything laid out on the table beside his holdall with the intention of setting off the following morning.

All he needed to decide was whether he had truly accomplished the task he had been set or not. If he had, then surely it ought to be safe for him to return home and attempt to track down the whereabouts of his family and friends. If not, then he would need to remain in hiding until some other help or direction came his way. What he would not give for another visit from Raphael today!

Jay packed everything tidily into the bag in preparation for the next day's departure and there, lying underneath his clothes was Raphael's gun. The silver barrel gleamed in the shaft of light from the small square window in the wall of the caravan. Jay stared at it: the weapon he had never used, the weapon he had never needed to use. Though, for some reason, he decided not to pack it yet. Instead, he went and made himself a rather stale black coffee.

*

Many miles away in a busy suburban street in London, a gang of builders were tearing down a garage at the top of a leafy drive that was not large enough for it owner's new car. The house, a modern, detached affair set in its own modest - albeit absurdly expensive - grounds, was owned by a couple who both worked in the City.

Outside in the street a large, yellow skip that had a notice stuck on its side indicating that it was licensed by Transport for London was rapidly being filled up with concrete blocks and broken tiles. But, as the workmen took a break for lunch, the neighbourhood decided - as they usually do - that it had suddenly become a communal amenity. Thus a number of other residents from the same road began discreetly offloading some of their own unwanted household items in it whilst the builders were out of sight.

There was nothing especially unusual about this course of events, except perhaps for the joy and levity with which the free-loaders went about their business. They all gave the impression of having had a great weight or debt removed from their lives - as though an unspeakable fear had departed the city.

Inside the skip, besides the old washing machine and sundry other goods that had arrived during luncheon, there was a pile of old newspapers. One of these was, in fact, a copy of the very same broadsheet that Jay had had the displeasure of reading only a fortnight or so previously.

Yet despite being stained with curry and cat litter and folded inside out, the main headline was completely different to that which Jay himself had read. Also, many of the subsequent articles were quite different and, on page four, there was a missing cat notice instead of a missing person notice. Jay's photograph was nowhere to be seen.

Many other papers, including the tabloids, carried no alarming stories of impending global doom, well, no more than they usually did, and the Scottish First Minister was rather more concerned about revelations concerning his private life than burning satellites crashing onto the roof of the Parliament building.

So, all in all, things were not the same and, from one commentator's point of view, even the trees looked greener, the gardens more lush, the Sun brighter and the weather more pleasant. How delightful it was to be British, he had written.

*

By evening time the air had grown cool, cool enough to send a shiver up Jay's spine as he walked back along the canal watching the mist forming above the still waters in the distance. He quickened his pace and made his way back to the clearing where the caravan was parked on the embankment.

He had received no more visitors since the honeymooning couple, there was no sign of the owner of the caravan, and Jay had decided that he simply had to move on. He could not wait there indefinitely, and the uncertainty of whether or not he had succeeded was beginning to torment him. How else could he know whether it would be safe to emerge into public life again without trying it? The alternative would be to stay put until he slowly starved to death.

His attempt at constructing a fishing rod from bits and pieces of his outdoor kit had been partially successful. That is, he had made a working rod, but sadly failed to catch a single fish with it.

As he stepped into the caravan and lit the oil lamp, he felt an ominous chill sweep through air. For a second he told himself, determinedly, that he was imagining it, but he knew better than that and could not fool himself. This was something more than the breeze.

He stared nervously at the door and then at the gun on the table. Was he now going to have to use it after all? Now, after trying his hardest to solve the riddle of what he had to do and striving to achieve it? Could he have been wrong all along?

The panic thoughts flooded over him, heralding some form of nightmarish attack. Jay was reminded forcibly of his dream in the old cottage and it felt like he was about to visit that breathtaking, robed figure again. What made him panic even more on this occasion was the fact that he was wide awake. So, if the feelings were real, that could mean only one thing... *he was actually here!*

Jay felt sick to the core; he stumbled over to the bench and sat down, clutching the edge of the table with both hands. He was trembling. He glanced again at the door; he could feel that penetrating gaze drawing ever nearer. It almost pinned him to the seat through the closed door. Jay knew he was approaching through the trees beyond the bank. It was as though the caravan had turned into glass and both he and his adversary could see each other plainly.

Sweating profusely, Jay fumbled around with the zip of his holdall, thinking desperately he ought to pack up and run for it. His eye then alighted on the gun. That was strange, he saw a scrap of paper trapped underneath it, but he hadn't put anything—

Jay dived for the note and snatched it up at once. It was in the same handwriting as before:-

Congratulations! You've done it. Have courage now it's almost over – R

'It would have been nicer if you'd appeared in person and told me that,' Jay muttered, frantically.

He dropped the paper, which did not catch fire this time, and picked up the gun. He managed to cock the weapon and switch off the safety catch. Almost immediately he put it back down again, fearing he might pull the trigger by accident as his hands were shaking so much.

There there came a heavy knock at the door. Jay retched in terror and stood bolt upright. The fear laid siege to his mind, pressing in upon all sides. A part of him wanted to snatch up the gun and fire straight through the closed door emptying the magazine into his enemy, a part of him wanted to burrow into a hole in the ground like a frightened rabbit, and yet another part of him was being driven to turn the gun on himself. He knew he could either face what was coming, or commit murder or suicide. What a choice!

He swayed on his feet, not knowing which way to turn, trapped inside a flimsy, ten-foot wooden box on wheels. Inside his head a furious battle raged...

Pick up the gun.

No!

Go on, pick it up. Raphael said you have a choice.

No.

Pick it up. Do it now! Go on, you can shoot the bullets straight through the door. Kill him now!

I don't want to.

Shoot him through the door, quick!

Although he muttered 'No' again under his breath, his trembling hand snatched up the pistol and he advanced, uncertainly, two steps towards the entrance. The visitor knocked again upon the door and Jay wondered why he hadn't just blasted it open, if he had the power; but the fellow was there, all right, standing directly behind the caravan door. He knew it.

Adrenalin was coursing through his veins, and Jay raised the gun and aimed it at where he guessed the chest might be of a man standing outside on the grass. The fatal red dot appeared and it hovered on the woodwork of the door. He knew the bullets would go through, but, just at the moment his finger tightened around the trigger, the vindictive part of his mind gave him an extra prod...

Yeah, shoot the bastard through the door. Go on!

'No,' Jay hissed through clenched teeth, and he swung around and dropped the gun on to the table behind him. He would face down his nemesis with innocent hands, whatever the cost. He was determined to live or die without shedding more blood, and if the thing wasn't human, the gun wouldn't work anyway. It was just a false hope - a useless offer of salvation.

And then an extraordinary change occurred. Even as he made the decision his fear fell off him like an unnecessary coat on a hot day. The mental siege broke and his confidence was renewed. All at once he found he no longer had any fear of death at all.

Before the visitor grew impatient enough to knock for a third time, Jay strode forwards nonchalantly and unfastened the door and pulled it wide open. The jitters only remained in his hands and fingers; the bulk of him was quite calm now.

Jay was dead right; standing there at the foot of the short flight of steps it was him. Jay came face to face with the menacing, robed figure from his dreams - and other encounters.

The individual wore a hood like a monk and stood a touch above average height. He seemed to invite a premature darkness to the scene, and stood there like a black silhouette against an otherwise picturesque twilight landscape. A presence of fear and hatred encircled him, but that had now become all but impotent against the regenerate young man.

Jay stared boldly into dark and expressionless eyes set in a veiled and pallid face. It was unclear whether or not the adversary was surprised by his nemesis' lack of terror when he spoke.

'Jay Romero?'

'Yes,' he replied, almost moved to fold his arms as he looked enquiringly upon one in front of him who was the personification of all his former nightmare and horror.

'You have interfered with my plans for long enough,' the figure

196

hissed, speaking at a barely audible level.

'What a pity,' Jay said, portraying on his face an excellently faked sympathy.

'Yes,' his enemy hissed.

And with that, he withdrew his hand from inside his robe and aimed a automatic pistol directly at Jay's head. Jay frowned slightly as - not for the first time in his life - he stared down the barrel of a loaded gun. It seemed a rather poor show for the Enemy of the whole world and, had he been in a rather different position, he might have said so.

But Jay's mind was already running on autopilot - he could scarcely avoid it - imagining a sharp impulse of excruciating pain... and then... nothing.

He had imagined being shot in the head before, but never quite in *these* circumstances.

A pause ensued and then... without another word...

'*Crack!*'

The hooded individual fired a single shot at point-blank range. Jay's head was thrown backwards and his legs collapsed under him. He crashed down the steps, sprawled onto the gassy bank below and came to rest on his back, gazing up at the heavens.

As the sound ricocheted through the trees the figure withdrew immediately and, almost before the first fresh drops of blood touched the damp soil of the turf, the long trailing robes were disappearing through the bushes in the nearby undergrowth.

The sun set below the horizon, the mist gathered over the water in the distance and, soon enough, the evening dew glistened on the skin of the lifeless body at the foot of the caravan steps.

Epilogue

The noise of talk and foot steps echoed down the corridor as the bell rang, signalling the end of another school day. It was only a week until the summer holidays began and below the surface a feverish excitement was brewing amongst everyone, except those who still had to complete the last of their end of year tests.

Although the school had ended five minutes before, a small gang of pupils had congregated outside the entrance to the G9 science lab at the foot of the stairs. Here the newly repainted magnolia walls were already suffering from the regular skirmishes with football boots, ball-point pens and chewing gum. And it looked as though another kind of skirmish was brewing in the absence of a member of staff.

A rather tired Dave Baker had just emerged late from the last lesson of the week: Friday afternoon's double Physics with the revitalised Mr Roberts. He had stepped out into the corridor, head aching and thirsty from a detailed discussion about his idea for the summer project, when he came face to face with three long-standing adversaries.

Apart from Colin Davis, who had recently turned a corner in his life and got himself off the dole, and Dean Forren, who had ceased chucking nuts and bolts around the classroom after receiving a cheeseburger in the face from Mike a year or two ago, real trouble makers were becoming rather thin on the ground. For certain there were no 'gangs' as such that were any threat to those in the sixth form.

Jay, Mike and Dave themselves represented some kind of discreet elite who, although not outwardly boastful, held an unspoken kudos over most of their peers. This necessarily led to a degree of animosity between them and other wannabes who relied more on bravado than character.

Dave reluctantly found himself up against three of these envious young men from the fifth year. Jason Drogue was a tall, dark-haired chap who was renowned for being good at maths and, looking something like Bruce Lee, was rumoured to be expert at karate - although this was unconfirmed as he had never yet been seen to fight.

He was keeping guard, watching out of the nearest window. Michael Florence, in contrast, was a short fellow with a mean face who, to make up for his stature, was rumoured to carry a blade at all times in spite of the fact it was against school rules as well as being illegal. Their leader, however, was Robert Flack; he was a burly, thickset youth with a grade one hair cut that made him look like a would-be inmate.

Dave rolled his eyes and ground to a halt, being unable to proceed out of the stairwell as they blocked his way.

'What?' he demanded, irritably, coming face to face with the leader of the gang, his associates on either side blocking the corridor.

'Where's your 'ero, Romero; ain't seen 'im for ages?' Flack remarked, making a display of cracking his knuckles.

Dave un-slung his bag just in case and answered, 'No idea, haven't seen him either, but I wouldn't tell you if I had! Now piss off I've got things to do... *Oi!*'

He made to push his way past but, Flack, who was of considerably bigger build, sidestepped and blocked his path. He was used to physical contact, being the captain of the fifth year Waynefleet House rugby team. Florence and Drogue also moved in closer, forming an effective wall against him.

Dave's temper flared and his nerves did too, to some extent. This was the last day of the week and a prime time to do mischief... but with a knife? Dave didn't think so, but who could tell? The kids were getting madder and madder these days, he thought.

'If you don't piss off and get out of my way, I'll get Roberts out here.' Then he added with a sneer, 'He enjoys putting members of the Flack Club in deten— '

'Robert's has just gone,' Drogue pointed out, carelessly. 'He left right after you did, went out the fire exit and headed straight for his car, saw him outside; hard luck!'

They exchanged grins and a sense of fear came upon Dave. He could tell they were spoiling for a fight, like a pack of maturing tigers wanting to assert their prowess within the troop and overthrow the old guard. Reason was not going to work here and, as the corridors were becoming increasingly deserted, a fight seemed to be inevitable, and it was three against one.

Dave found himself staring into three different sets of eyes, all cynical, although only one pair was really intent seeing him come to blows. Flack, it seemed, was desperate to 'do over' one of the sixth formers to increase his own standing amongst the fifth year and, if it happened to be one of Jay Romero's crew, it would be an even better result. Unfortunately for Dave, who had only stayed behind after class to discuss laser-guided bombs, he came out of the wrong door at the wrong time.

However, as the stand-off became rather protracted, and while Dave surreptitiously removed his watch - which was quite valuable - and slipped it into a pocket of his trousers for safekeeping, somebody else joined the fray.

A voice that Dave was very relieved to hear cried, 'Hey!' and, the next instant, a large, grey sports bag came flying through the air like a missile. It hit Jason Drogue on the back of his head and almost knocked him over. He staggered into the wall with a yell of pain and the other two looked around, startled.

Mike swept up to them and, breaking up the rank immediately like a ball hitting skittles, he glanced around the scene at the entrance to the lab.

'What're you hanging around with this muck for?' he demanded. 'Been looking for you everywhere. The bell went ten minutes ago!'

'I - er - ' Dave hesitated, not sure whether to explain, lest it lead to a much worse punch up. 'Nothing, we were just talking,' he concluded. He gave an unconvincing shrug as he picked up his bag.

'That hurt!' Jason spat, rubbing the back of his head and grimacing.

'Good!' Mike responded, without even looking at him. He had realised what the three of them were up to in a moment and did not believe his friend's pacifying explanation for a second.

'Go screw yourself, Murkin,' Flack muttered.

He and Mike were about the same size, give or take and inch, but his bravado had been knocked down a peg or two by this unexpected arrival, and one of his back up men was now injured. Mike turned to face him and the two of them proceeded to prove which of them could

200

crack their knuckles the loudest.

'C'mon, mate, let's go,' Dave suggested, tugging the back of his friend's shirt.

'Yeah,' said Jason, who felt very much the same way and was keen to look after himself.

Michael Florence, however, seemed more ready to do or die. 'No, let's finish this now,' he urged, apparently fingering something in the pocket of his jacket.

Mike raised a very comic eyebrow at his opposite number as if to say, *well, how about it?*

'I'm not fighting,' Dave said, more to Mike than the others.

'You can't take all three of us at once,' Flack grunted, eyeing Mike with a respectful hatred.

'Probably not,' he agreed, jovially, 'but I'll make sure I take you first!'

Their eyes met one more time in conflict and then Flack backed down, 'C'mon,' he said, and gestured his companions to leave.

They retreated silently until they were about halfway down the corridor and then Michael Florence called out, 'Everyone's gone home now, Murkin; you can toss-off your boyfriend in peace!'

Mike turned to his colleague with a hysterical expression on his face and said, 'Shall I go after him?'

Dave shook his head firmly, but yelled down the corridor, 'At least I've got a dick to play with!'

'Let's go,' Mike said, snatching up his bag and setting off for the nearest exit. Dave followed and, after buying a can of organic lemonade from the vending machine in the entrance, they walked out into the school car park.

A number of students were queuing up in the bus shelter waiting for the coaches that ferried them to the outlying villages and towns. South Fields School had proved very popular in recent years and out of a role of over a thousand, three hundred children made the daily trip to Brackthorpe from other towns and villages. Such was the reputation of the school that, for most years, it was over subscribed.

As they reached the road, Waynefleet Avenue, Mike resumed their talk. 'When did that rumour start?'

'Which rumour?' Dave asked, engrossed in plans for his upcoming Physics project.

'The 'us being gay' thing; we haven't come across it before, have we?'

'Dunno,' Dave replied. 'Saying that, there was someone I really wanted to get to know.'

'What! *Who?*' Mike demanded, suddenly alarmed.

Dave sighed, resignedly, 'That *girl* who played piano in the school jazz band up until last year; Suzie Goodfellow, I think she was called.'

'Oh, right,' Mike said, sounding a little calmer.

'I really fancied her but she was two years above us and... you know... nothing came of it,' Dave reminisced. He drained the last of his can and dropped it into the rubbish bin that had been stationed a strategic distance from the main school gates.

'You kept that one quiet, mate.'

'Yeah, well, when you're...'

'What?'

'*In love,*' Dave whispered, and he looked at his feet.

Mike laughed out loud. 'In your dreams,' he mocked.

'Maybe,' Dave conceded, 'but she's got someone now anyway, so I guess that's it!'

Mike then realised that his companion was being quite serious, and so he thought it better to cut the theatrics and said, 'D'you want to come round for tea? The folks are much more easy going now 'cause they're really chuffed with Matty's exam results.'

'Yeah, how's he doing?'

'Top of the year,' Mike replied, frowning. 'They reckon he might be heading for Oxford in a few years time, mate.'

'The university?'

'Yeah, he's set his heart on one of the colleges there that specialises in science and engineering. It seems to be his forte; he wants to work in the aerospace industry.'

'He always worked harder than any of us, especially you; you're bloody lazy,' Dave said.

'Listen,' Mike ordered, feeling rather put out. 'Next time you get cornered by Flack, Forren or one of those other morons, who would you rather came by - me, or my whiz-kid, little brother?'

'Let's go and crash out under a tree in the park,' Dave answered, 'I'm not much good in this sun.'

'Yeah,' Mike agreed, 'it'd be nice to see Jay some time, too; we haven't seen him for ages. I'd love to know what he gets up to?

Much later that evening, after several pleasant hours spent under the shade of the trees in the park, where the pair of them had taken in the view - both of things growing and of things walking past in skirts - they were making their way towards the road again.

As most people had gone home for tea by that hour, the park was all but empty and, looking around, the friends saw that their immediate vicinity was devoid of life.

And then, as they walked and talked, heading for Mike's house in Grosvenor Place...

There was an ear-splitting crack that echoed across the grounds sending blackbirds and pigeons scattering into the air from the boughs of the trees. Simultaneously, a great white swirl of light erupted in front of them. The size of a doorway, Mike recognised it as a wormhole - a portal through time and space.

Both he and Dave froze in shock, transfixed by the sight. Suddenly all the light and noise disappeared and there, standing before them, was someone they immediately recognised, although he looked very different to the young man they knew, the friend they had grown up with.

His whole body was illuminated with radiant light and his hands and face were shining like gold and, for some reason, he was dressed all in white...

'Hello, my friends!'

Dave and Mike, all but dazzled by his appearance, had to hold on to each other like drunken friends on a pub crawl just to keep from falling over.

'Y-You?' Mike hissed.

'I-Is it... r-really you?' Dave stammered, squinting because the brilliance was too intense in the evening twilight.

'It is; how are you my friends? Have you been missing me?'

As he said this, the brightness dimmed and his friends could see him plainly, without needing to shield their eyes. The three of them looked upon one another both in fellowship and in awe.

'Where have you been?' Dave asked. 'What have you been up to this time, more trouble in the continuum?'

'What's... What's with the white suit?' Mike muttered.

'The future is reordered,' he explained. 'The world has become a safer place, and the clothes... they have been given me because I've finished my course; I've run my race. Listen—'

'How did you appear out of nowhere?' Dave ventured, interrupting him.

And from that point he not only answered Dave's question, but also explained what he meant by 'finishing the course' and 'running the race.' He also had to confide in them that he would no longer be with them, at least, not on this earth. Mike and Dave were convinced - albeit they could hardly argue - after seeing him arrive out of thin air in front of their very eyes. However, his news was not good all round.

'Are you leaving us then?' Mike asked, forlornly, gazing at the familiar face before him, though now it was a face of pure innocence, radiance and joy.

Mike was fearful.

'Yes, but don't worry, in infinity we're never-ending friends. I've seen it; it's brilliant! You can travel at the speed of thought and knowledge can be seen. So you don't need to spend time learning stuff, you know it instantaneously, and wherever you want to go - you are just there, straight away!'

'Can't we come with you?' Dave pleaded. 'I want to be able to traverse time and space, too.'

Their companion shook his head. 'You still have many things to do down here. I can't take you with me yet; it wouldn't be right.'

He turned away from them, snapped his fingers and another wormhole opened up right under his hand. Flashes of light and gusts of air went surging into the vortex like sun-flecked clouds sucked into a great whirlpool in the sky.

His startled companions had once again to steady themselves lest they get sucked into it. Meanwhile he stood there serenely as his robes glistened in the light and the air roared into the portal as it would the intake of a jet engine revving at top speed.

'C'mon, mate,' Mike urged, shielding his face against the brightness once again as his friend made to leave. 'Can't you take us for a trip across the galaxy... just a *glimpse* of the next life...? You could bring us right back here, I bet... It wouldn't do any harm really, would it?'

Their friend paused for a moment as though considering the request and then, striding forwards and taking his companions each by their shoulder, he jumped into the vortex dragging them along with him. There was a sharp crack and, as quickly as it had appeared, all the noise and light ceased, and no sign of the three friends remained whatsoever.

Five minutes later an old man walking his dog came past the very spot where the nexus had occurred and the three lads had vanished thereafter.

As the dog made its way over the grass, it stopped and sniffed hopefully at the ground. However, finding a dead end to the trail, it soon gave up and, with a tug on its leash, it hurried away after its owner.

The Beginning.

A word from the Author -

The future has indeed been reordered because the multi-storey car park at Charles Cross was - until recently - in the City of Plymouth. Unfortunately since I began writing this book it has been demolished in favour of a huge, new shopping mall.

Jay's adventures are now complete, although he might appear briefly in two follow up books. Look out for them -

The Oblivion Sequence

The Privateer

Meanwhile the next book I've got planned is a tribute to Lord of the Rings -

The Apprentices

Lightning Source UK Ltd.
Milton Keynes UK
21 February 2011

167907UK00007B/98/P

9 781906 557003